Penguin Science Fiction
Fifth Planet

Sir Fred Hoyle, F.R.S., well known as an astronomer, writer,
broadcaster, and television personality, was born at Bingley,
Yorkshire, in 1915, and educated at Bingley Grammar
School and Emmanuel College, Cambridge. A Fellow of
St John's College, Cambridge, he was a university lecturer
in mathematics from 1945 to 1958, when he was appointed
to the post of Plumian Professor of Astronomy and
Experimental Philosophy (1958–73). Since 1956 he has been a
staff member at the Mount Wilson and Palomar Observatories,
where he is able to use the world's largest reflector telescopes.
He has been visiting Professor of Astrophysics at the California
Institute of Technology, and Director of the Institute of
Theoretical Astronomy, Cambridge. Since 1969 he has been
Professor of Astronomy at the Royal Institution of Great Britain.
Professor Hoyle was knighted in 1972.

His other publications include *The Nature of the Universe*
(1950; a Pelican), *A Decade of Decision* (1953), *Frontiers of
Astronomy* (1956), *Of Men and Galaxies* (1965) and *Man in the
Universe* (1966). His other novels are *The Black Cloud* (1957),
Ossian's Ride (1959), *October the First is Too Late* (1966) and
Seven Steps to the Sun (1970) which, like this book, was written
with his son, Geoffrey Hoyle. Fred Hoyle has also published a
play, *Rockets in Ursa Major* (1962), and is the joint author of
A for Andromeda (1962), a television serial. His latest publication
(also written with his son Geoffrey) is *The Molecule Men* (1971).

Born in 1942, Geoffrey Hoyle is Fred Hoyle's son. He was
educated at Bryanston, and is now working in London in the
field of modern communications and motion pictures. Not being
a scientist has given Geoffrey Hoyle time to concentrate on the
human side of this novel.

Fred Hoyle
and Geoffrey Hoyle

Fifth Planet

Penguin Books

Penguin Books Ltd, Harmondsworth,
Middlesex, England
Penguin Books Australia Ltd, Ringwood,
Victoria, Australia
Penguin Books Canada Ltd, 41 Steelcase Road West,
Markham, Ontario, Canada

First published by William Heinemann Ltd 1963
Published in Penguin Books 1965
Reprinted 1967, 1971, 1974
Copyright © F. and G. Hoyle, 1963

Made and printed in Great Britain by
Cox & Wyman Ltd,
London, Reading and Fakenham
Set in Intertype Baskerville

Preface

The very nature of the plot has forced us to set this story in the more distant future than we would otherwise have preferred. It is hardly possible to foresee the shape of society a century or more ahead of one's own time, and we have not attempted to do so. Instead we have been content to extrapolate those social trends that can plainly be seen at the moment. The story was written in August 1962. We mention this to bring out the prediction – we take a little pride in its apparent correctness – at the foot of page 22. We do not know whether to hope or fear that other predictions of the story will turn out to possess a similar validity.

The basis of the plot is to be found on pages 208 to 210. However, to avoid too much interruption of the narrative, the ideas mentioned in these pages have been shortened as far as possible. Physics regards the world as four dimensional. All moments of time exist together. The world can be thought of as a map, not only spatially, but also with respect to time. The map stretches away both into the past and into the future. There is no such thing as 'waiting' for the future. It is already there in the map.

Two problems arise out of this. The first is the so-called 'arrow of time'. Events occur in the map in definite sequences. Light emerges from a torch after you press the switch. The emphasis here is not on the word 'after' – it would be possible to turn the map round, to count time backwards, as we do in counting years B.C. Then one would say that light emerges from the torch *before* one presses the switch. This is simply a trivial inversion. What is not trivial is that light does not emerge *both* before and after the pressing of the switch.

Events do not occur symmetrically with respect to time. In the case of the torch there is an asymmetry whichever way we elect to read the map. It is this asymmetry that we refer to as the 'future' part of the map is radically different from the 'past', and this is true whichever way we turn the map.

Physics has made a good deal of progress in understanding this problem. The arrow of time may not be completely resolved, but at any rate it is being grappled with. The same cannot be said for the second problem.

What constitutes the present? Provided one considers one-self as something apart from the physical world, the answer does not seem difficult. The present can be thought of as the particular place in the map where you happen to be. It is your subjective presence at a particular spot that defines the present. But you cannot have your cake and eat it. You cannot consider your subjective presence as being outside the physical world and in the same breath consider yourself as a part of the map.

According to science, a human is an animal. He takes his place in the map along with all other physical events. In fact the events that constitute the human are confined to a four-dimensional tube, a world tube, that threads its way over a finite portion of the map. What then is the subjective present? It is certainly not the whole collection of events inside one's own personal tube, otherwise we should live the whole of our lives all at once, like playing a sonata simply by pressing the whole keyboard. Stated more precisely, the subjective present consists not of the complete collection of events but of a certain subset. How is the subset defined?

Certain clear technical issues now appear. Is the subset such that one particular member has a time-like displacement to all other members? In that case the other members could have a causal connexion to the particular member. But if so, how is the particular member of the subset chosen?

There seems to be no way of coping with issues such as these except by admitting that something else besides the four-dimensional world tube is needed. Something else outside what science would normally describe as the animal itself.

This approach need not be mystic. The required subset could be defined mathematically as the intersection of the world tube with a three-dimensional space-like surface. Thus a surface

$$\phi \left(x^1, x^2, x^3, x^4 \right) = c$$

for a particular value of c, and with $\partial\phi / \partial x^i$ $(i = 1,2,3,4)$ a time-like vector, serves to define a subset of points in the world tube. Changing c changes the subset. We could be said to live our lives through changes of c – i.e. by sweeping through a family of surfaces.

It is plausible that the subjective present has a mathematical structure of this kind. But what then are the ϕ surfaces? Could they be derived from known physical fields, for example from the electromagnetic field? That is to say, is the subjective present really controlled by normal sensory data? An obvious way of testing this possibility would be to keep the known external fields constant and to consider whether the subjective present can be considered to change.

Our impression – no more than an impression – is that changes of the subjective present do occur under conditions where the external electromagnetic field, for example, is essentially unchanged. As a rather imprecise example of what we mean, suppose two visits separated by many years are made to a particular place – say, to a mountain – and suppose the weather and the lighting conditions are generally similar on the two occasions. Exact identity of condition is of course impossible, but we find it difficult to believe that major differences of the subjective present, such as might be felt by an individual, are determined by slight, and perhaps even unnoticed, changes in the external conditions – e.g. by the slight shift in the disposition of grass and boulders on a mountainside.

The ϕ surfaces we feel must have the property of not being closely reproducible in the sense of this example. The fantasy of the present story lies in the properties we have ascribed to these surfaces, in fact to the functional behaviour of ϕ.

6 April 1963

F. H.
G. H.

Contents

Chapter One

Night Thoughts

Hugh Conway shifted uneasily. An hour before his wife had
come to him with such fervour that he knew she must have
been unfaithful again. He could hear her soft breathing, a
more regular rhythm than his own. It wasn't surprising, not
with Cathy's beauty, the completely flawless beauty that
you couldn't take your eyes off; the sort of beauty that you
had to see, that couldn't be described, photographed, or
painted. They had been married for ten years, and still
Conway couldn't keep his eyes off her even though he knew
it annoyed her. Even other women, women who might spend
hours in front of a mirror, acknowledged it. For compensa-
tion they shook their heads and said sharply it was a pity
Cathy had not been equally blessed with brains.

For ten years Conway had been on the hook. For ten
years they had staggered from one domestic crisis to another,
from one social absurdity to another. Things had seemed to
be going better during the last few months, but now this new
affair had started. The odd thing was that in the abstract
he valued intelligence more than beauty. In the last few
years there had been half a dozen other women that he'd
liked, that he could talk sensibly to, and that he'd have been
happy with. More than once he'd made up his mind to put
an end to the inane, futile life with Cathy. But then, in some
unguarded moment, he'd be riveted again; the old chemistry would start up in his blood, and that would be it. He
wondered why Cathy herself didn't break it up. She only
despised him for his weakness. Probably she regarded him
as a convenient base from which to conduct her operations.

Literary types had always written their own variations on

the theme of 'Love and War'. But only a hundred years ago they'd been talking about there being two cultures. Now the old literary culture was dead, and the scientific culture, if by that you meant physics, wasn't in much better shape. Their places had been taken by a new culture.

What a tiger he'd have been if he'd lived in the middle of the last century, and known what he knew now. Conway allowed his thoughts to play with the prospects. It was, he decided, the confusion of the present that was the devil. Being a good scientist didn't help. It only made you more keenly aware of the uncertainties of the future. The 1960s was the time when they'd first thought of going to the moon. He could have told them exactly what they'd find when they got there. There'd been quite a bit of argument about whether they'd find dust or lava. As it turned out they'd found both. Funny to think now that that first trip to the moon has set the whole world alight. It had been the touchstone of national prestige. Now it was just a pinpoint in the past. Today the world was alight again. Everybody said it was the biggest thing ever; and for once, Conway thought, everybody was right. Funny too to think that in 1960 they hadn't had the slightest suspicion about it

Even as recently as a hundred years ago the astronomers had known almost nothing about the proper motions of the stars. The line of sight motions were, of course, known from the Doppler shift. But the transverse motions, even of quite near-by stars, only caused them to change their directions by a few tenths of a second of an arc each year. It hadn't been until the coming of high-quality satellite telescopes that angles as small as this could be measured in any particular year, although over twenty or thirty years it would have been possible to measure the cumulative effect from the ground. But nobody had been willing to start a programme that wouldn't pay off results for thirty years. So, not until the nineties of the last century did the proper motions begin to be really well known. Not until then was it possible to decide just how each individual star was moving in space.

The same sort of measurements, parallax measurements, had given accurate distances to the stars – at any rate, for distances up to a thousand light years. And with the distances and motions fully known, it was possible to build a model of how all the stars were moving in the neighbourhood of the Sun. With the solar system at the centre, you could imagine each star represented by a little dot. Attached to each dot was an arrow, the direction of the arrow showing where the star was moving, and the length of the arrow showing how fast the star was moving. That was the first stage. Then you had to make a correction. If you wanted a model of the stars as they are now at the present moment you had to allow for the fact that we do not see the direction of the stars as they are, but only as they were at the moment when the light started out on its journey to us. If you want the model as it is now you have to move each star a bit along the direction of its arrow. The amount you have to move a particular star depends on two things – its speed of motion and its distance. The distance, because there has been more delay in the light from a distant star than from a near-by one. And the speed for the obvious reason that a star moves more out of its position every year the faster it is moving.

Suppose that all this has been done and that you have a model showing the positions and motions of the stars as they are now. Then by following each star in turn along its appropriate arrow you can find out where they will all be a year from now. Or ten years from now. Or a hundred years from now. In fact, you can find out whether any two arrows will meet each other. If any two arrows do meet each other you know that some time in the future those two particular stars will come near to each other. Of course they can hardly be expected to collide, for stars are very tiny things compared to the distances between them. A direct collision is vastly improbable, but a close approach is quite another matter.

Conway began to figure the probabilities. Assume an approach within twenty astronomical units, the distance of the planet Uranus from the Sun. That gives a target area of ten to the minus eight square parsecs. Taking thirty kilometres per second as the average speed of the stars relative to any particular star, and taking the mean density of the stars as one per cubic parsec, the chance of an approach to any special star was just ten to the minus eight for every thirty thousand years. So over three billion years the chance was one in a thousand. In the lifetime of the solar system there had been one chance in a thousand of just such an approach of another star, and this really wasn't very long odds. Taking all stars together, there had been more than a hundred million approaches between pairs of them during the whole history of the Galaxy.

All this the men of the twentieth century would have followed. And they wouldn't have been particularly surprised to learn that the Sun was going to be one of these hundred million cases. The unexpected thing was that this particular moment – the late twenty-first century – was the time of the encounter. It wasn't a billion years ago, and it was unlikely to be a billion years hence. It would be now, the year 2087.

A special name had to be found for the approaching star. At an early stage, helium lines were detected in the spectrum, so it had seemed obvious to use the Greek name for the Sun, Helios. This was towards the end of the twentieth century, before the last remnants of a classical culture were lost.

Of course, it wasn't clear to begin with just how close Helios would approach the Sun. The target area was very small, so that small errors of measurement led to big errors in the answers. The first estimates gave a distance of closest approach that exceeded ten thousand astronomical units, that is, about three hundred times the distance of the farthest planet, Pluto. Then a half century of unremitting effort showed that the approach was to be a good deal nearer than this. By the year 2025 the best estimate was a thousand astronomical units, 961 to be more precise.

The mounting interest of the public had helped to maintain the popularity of the physical sciences at a time when nuclear physics and the study of elementary particles were steeply in decline – the latter because it had become too difficult. Fundamental astronomy was once more in vogue. As Helios came closer it became easier to make accurate measurements. During the sixties, excitement mounted furiously as it became more and more clear that Helios would actually move inside the orbits of the outer planets. By 2070, a definitive value was obtained. At its closest, Helios would be a mere twenty astronomical units from the Sun. It would be 15,000 times brighter than the full moon, although at that distance it would still have only a fortieth of the brightness of the Sun itself.

The orbit of the Earth would be disturbed, but not enormously so. After Helios had receded away again the Earth's path around the Sun would be more elliptical than it was before. This would be the main effect. The result would be an accentuation, not enormous, but certainly perceptible, of the seasons of the year. And the year itself would certainly be changed from the immemorial $365\frac{1}{4}$ days. But nobody knew yet exactly what the changes would be.

If the effects on the Earth's motion were to be comparatively slight, this was manifestly not the case for the outer planets of the solar system. Helios would exert as big an influence on these as the Sun did. Indeed there was a likelihood that the three outer planets, Uranus, Neptune, and Pluto, would be stripped away entirely from our system.

Because Helios was to penetrate our system it was clear that we should penetrate the planets of Helios itself, if the incoming star had any planets. Astronomical theories showed that this was a marginal issue. The larger mass of Helios was a point against the existence of a planetary system. But it was quickly pointed out that Helios was spinning around only very slowly, like the Sun, and this scarcely seemed credible unless a system of planets had indeed developed. In the event, just at the turn of the century, two planets were in fact detected observationally. They were large fellows, like Jupiter in our own system. Their American discoverers named them Hera and Semele.

This was before the development of quantitative social studies had changed our cultural and intellectual standards, before those philosophers of the nineteenth and twentieth centuries who had inquired into the nature of man's thinking had attained a popular distinction exceeding Newton and Einstein. The new fashion was to have its opportunities, however. For when, forty years later, two further planets were detected, of about the size of our own Uranus, they were named Hegel and Kierkegaard.

And now a fifth planet had been found only a few months ago, by Conway himself. It was much smaller than the others and had therefore been difficult to pick up against the background glare of Helios. It was much more like the earth in size. Apart from this simple fact, little so far was known about it. Conway's mind ranged over plans for the future. There was a tradition that whoever discovered a new planet had the honour of naming it, like the rule that had operated a century or more ago in the naming of the chemical elements. Conway smiled to himself in the darkness. Because he was British and because the British, according to the rest of the world, were still immersed in the twentieth century, he had refused widespread international pressure to adopt the name Spinoza. Instead he had called it – Achilles.

Chapter Two

Tight Little Island

Hugh Conway scraped a fragment of butter over a piece of hard half-burnt toast. Cathy made a pretence of reading *The Times*. The financial page too, Hugh noticed, as he cocked an eye over the top of the paper. He studied the flawless complexion and the pile of dark, soft chestnut curls, thinking, for perhaps the millionth time, that he was an ass. She put down the paper and looked at him squarely with deep-blue killer eyes.

'Well?' she said.

'We're having another conference. I'll probably be away about five days. And I was wondering if you'd like to make a trip up to Town.'

That was the last thing she'd been expecting. With a wary flash she came back at him, 'How much? How much can I spend?'

Hugh knew that a few days in London, spent in the intimate company of some new boy-friend, was exactly what Cathy had been scheming towards. By offering her the trip on a plate he'd forced her back on to her final line of defence -- money. He smiled wryly.

'I'm overdrawn at the bank. And I'm not paid till the end of June. If you look up at the top of the paper you'll see that it is still only the middle of May.'

'Bob Shaw doesn't have any difficulty about money,' returned Cathy with the merest twitch of her nose, 'and he's only a rag-bag of a fellow, as you always say.'

Hugh snorted, 'Property development. Property development in Slough.'

'Well, why not?'

'I'm not putting my slender resources into any development in Slough, even if the Americans are taking to the place.'

Elbow on table, Cathy cupped her chin in her right hand, 'You could do something better, couldn't you?'

Hugh smiled now. 'It is my job to do something better.'

He paused for a moment. Then shot it straight out, 'Well, who is it this time?'

She looked blankly across the table, the soul of innocence. 'What do you mean?'

'You know damned well what I mean. Who is it?'

Cathy giggled, 'I thought it was a mouse. It turned out to be a tiger.'

'Stop being absurd.'

'I'm not being absurd.'

Hugh put his second boiled egg into the cup and absently began to crack the top.

Cathy now had the bit between her teeth. 'I don't ask you who you sleep with when you're away.' She smiled broadly, and Hugh felt the old, but still sharp, pangs of jealousy.

'I don't sleep with anybody,' he exploded.

'Don't you, darling? Well if you did I wouldn't want to know about it.'

Cathy leant back in her chair so that her hair fell backwards, as if to suggest that the subject was closed.

'You know perfectly well we're not talking about me.'

'No? If I should sleep with another man, what does it matter to you, so long as you don't know about it.'

'Of course it matters.'

'Why?'

'Because it affects both of us.'

Cathy pondered this for a moment. Then wrinkling her face to show that she was making a serious effort she said, 'If you don't know about it, it can't affect you, can it? If it was to affect me, then it would be wrong. But I don't allow it to affect me, do I?'

With a vicious stab of his spoon, Hugh sliced the top off the egg. It was hard-boiled.

'It's hard-boiled,' he yapped.

Cathy looked down at the egg as if she had never seen one before. 'You're always making a fuss about things that don't matter.'

'But the first one,' he nittered, pointing to the bits of shell on his plate, 'the first one was soft-boiled. It was so soft-boiled that if I'd held it up the whole egg would have run out.'

Cathy stretched herself lazily, 'Just like the two of us, dear. You hard-boiled, me soft-boiled.'

Fuming helplessly, Hugh jumped up from the table. He stalked from the breakfast-room to his study, stuffed a pile of papers which he had been reading the previous evening into his brief-case, walked back to the kitchen, and shouted, 'Those eggs are substandard.' Then he stormed out of the house, thinking that, in an age of female emancipation, the arguments of patriarchy were no match for those of matriarchy.

When he had gone, Cathy took on an air of set purpose. She went to the telephone, dialled, and got a wrong number. Deciding that she was using the wrong code, she consulted a small red notebook. Very deliberately, reading the numbers as if they were some strange hieroglyphs, she tried again. A voice answered.

'Will you put me through to Mike Fawsett, please?'

There were two ways of going between the Conways' house in the sleepy village of Alderbourne and the Helios Project Centre at Harwell, the site of which had been a nuclear research establishment in the dim distant days. There was the super-S highway, or the winding, tree-shaded lane that had not changed much since the eighteenth century. In fact, the whole English countryside had not altered much since the eighteenth century. In the last hundred years the population of the British Isles had risen from fifty to seventy millions, but the increase in building had been almost entirely in the cities. In spite of their growth, the cities hadn't managed to achieve quite the same sprawling, amorphous character as had their American counterparts; Los Angeles had now stretched out as far as Albuquerque, which perhaps explained why Americans were favourably disposed towards a property development in Slough.

Hugh decided that he was too furious to risk driving along the highway and took the country road. The may hedges were in blossom, and it was all quietly beautiful as he followed the ridge of the Downs. By this route he came into the Helios Centre from above. On impulse he parked the car and got out to stretch his legs. Then, squatting on the grass, he gazed down on the Centre, the Centre where the decisions affecting man's greatest adventure would be made. He sighed softly as he contrasted the grandeur of the world of ideas with his own petty domestic squabblings. The buildings below shone brightly in the sun, reflecting gold mixed with opalescent blues.

Ten minutes more brought him to the parking-lot, the one sordid spot in the Centre. Five minutes' walk, and he entered a long, curving, strip-like building, made of glass and metal. The staircase had the sweep and magnificence of an eighteenth-century manor house. His feet made no sound as he walked up the steps. A light ahead beckoned him as he strolled, silently, down a long, curving corridor. Turning off the corridor, he went into a room that almost defies description. It was not small, but neither was it very large. It was not barely furnished or decorated, but it would be difficult to say just what materials had been used in order to set it out. It was entirely silent to the tread, as had been the corridor and the staircase, but it was not entirely silent. There was a faint hum of electric motors. There was a magnificent old table in the centre. But the dignified effect was spoilt by a dozen or more absurd pads of white paper spaced at regular intervals around it. This was the Committee Room.

By this time all important decisions affecting the structure of human society were taken in committee. Everybody knew that the system was wrong, but by now no one had the power to stop it. No committee was willing to vote to destroy itself. In the early days a few men had found themselves, more or less by chance, to be possessors of the power to persuade their colleagues – they were natural intellectual salesmen. And like good salesmen, who can dispose of anything under the sun, they could get their way on any matter, however absurd. What had begun as a purely amateur sport had gradually developed into stark professionalism. Nowadays one one did not become a good committee man by chance. One became a good committee man by sheer unremitting effort in which every working moment was spent in planning and scheming how to operate. But not all committee men were good. There had to be some who were bad, simply because some members had to possess an adequate knowledge of the essential facts. It was by now quite impossible both to be a good committee man and to know anything. The trouble, of course, was that those who knew what they were talking about never got their own way, although supporters of the system claimed that this was a good thing.

Hugh was one of the first to arrive. He busied himself in a futile, unprofessional way with his papers. Even though there was something he wanted from this particular meeting, his mind wandered from the business in hand. He jerked his thoughts back from Cathy. He must try to remember that only one other member of the Committee would be British. He must try to remember the motives and opinions of the other members, to put himself inside their skins. Above all, he must try to make use of the complex of emotions that had led to the Helios Centre being built in Britain.

The common man of the twentieth century would have been surprised to have learnt just how far the trends of his own day had been carried through into the twenty-first century, just how far the logic of ideas had been pressed. The development of the deterrent is, of course, an outstanding example. To our innocent ancestors, civil defence meant exactly what it said, defence to protect the civil population, to protect the man in the street. To us now, this is an outrageously archaic notion. In fact, two-thirds of the way through the twentieth century, a few perceptive pioneers had already realized that civil defence was to become the outstanding weapon of aggression. With ruthlessly effective civil defence a nation could afford nuclear war – almost. And if the other side couldn't afford it at all, you could bully him just as much as you pleased. So what started as the sole concern of the individual became a matter of major national policy, in America, in Europe, in Russia, and China. Refusal to take part in effective civil defence programmes became a treasonable crime. It seems laughable now to think that at one time civil defence consisted merely of building a shelter in one's own garden. As we all know, effective defence lies in evacuating whole cities at a moment's notice, in fact at the very worst and most inconvenient moments. And, of course, one cannot be said to be prepared to do this unless one actually does it. Remorselessly. This means that the times of evacuation cannot be announced beforehand, it is the essence of the matter that people must not be prepared. The warning comes in the middle of a wedding, a funeral, a confinement. It causes the restaurants of the Champs-Elysées to disgorge their diners into the street, gourmets with their napkins still tucked into their collars. All this in the interests of *l'honneur*.

Through a series of accidents the British had escaped all this. In the sixties of the last century their politicians had at last realized that power had become a shadow. A little genuine power could be won, however, by joining in a United Europe. This they earnestly strove to do, but their efforts were thwarted through a series of mischances, an intransigent French president, the conservatism of their own people at home, and the lack of conservatism of the people abroad. At all events, the British were kept outside, and power vanished for ever from Whitehall. Gone was the need for expensive military budgets or for the remorseless logic of the deterrent. The British slept in their beds, the forgotten men of the twenty-first century.

Or not quite forgotten. For to the harassed American, the ulcerous Russian, the thought of a few weeks' holiday in London became indescribably precious. New York became almost entirely automatized, Paris became the city with thoughts only for the glorious future, in Moscow puritanism lay like a dead hand on the people. Only in London could one dine in peace. Only in London could one follow dinner with a little play that didn't matter at all.

Because of its enormous attraction for tourists Britain was extremely prosperous. Other parts of the world, Africa in particular, split themselves asunder in their rivalries, in their attempts each to become the workshop of the world. Small financial crises triggered each other across the globe like falling rows of skittles. And throughout all this the British lent money here and there on profitable terms, as the Swiss had done a century earlier.

The Swiss at last abandoned their neutral position and threw in their lot with Europe. Communication through radio and the aeroplane, prosperity and power, achieved what invading armies could not do. It was the enormously rising prestige of Europe that did it. The Swiss gained status by joining, it was like marrying the daughter of a noble house. One effect was that the various small international organizations that had made Switzerland their home felt obliged to seek new quarters. Britain by now had become the obvious place. After all, what was Britain except a raft afloat in the sea, a raft exposed to the wind and weather, populated by a calm people who went about their business without ever realizing that the world was a serious place to live in? It was just the place for bored international secretariats to move to.

The decision to build the Helios Centre in Britain was a more serious affair, however. This was not a small matter. Its ramifications affected every major nation in the world. And just for this reason it could not be placed in any one of those major nations. Quite obviously the Russo-Chinese bloc would not permit the Centre to be sited in the territory of the Euro-American bloc. And, of course, vice versa. Africa was too hot, dusty, and industrial. South America was a serious possibility, but the fact that most interested parties were in the Northern Hemisphere, the attractions of London, and the precedence established by other International Agencies, swayed the day. So the Helios Project came to be established at Harwell.

Around the year 2040, the British Government made an attempt to get itself back into the power complex in a small feeble way. The belt of power spreads in an ominous girdle across the northern latitudes of the Earth. The two division points, one in the Bering Strait, the other to the east of Germany, unified during the short period of Western ascendancy in the 1990s. The West is the West, America and Europe, and the East is the East, Russia and China. The leaders of neither group want war, for war would put an effective end to the exercise of their power. But neither do they want a cessation of tension, for this also would produce an important down-grading of their functions. Besides, it had been proved mathematically by the social scientists, now dominant and rampant, that a world without tension would be a world in decline. The problem is to live with tension without allowing it ever to break loose. Our main safety factor lies in our ability to predict, again with mathematical precision, just what the other side will do in a given set of circumstances. Unpredictable behaviour by either side would soon lead to disaster.

All this was first recognized, long, long ago by the scientists of the Rand Corporation, a decade or so before that organization took over the effective control of American policy from the Pentagon. To begin with, the fly in the ointment was that one side didn't quite know the basis on which the other side made its calculations. Without this knowledge things could go wrong – they could become unstable, as the mathematicians said. Nobody at first had the impudence to suggest the obvious solution. But little by little steps were taken towards it. A hundred years ago the most closely guarded secrets were those that concerned methods of calculation, military logistics as it was then called. Then secrecy was gradually relaxed. Papers on the subject began to be published quite openly. Finally, after a series of seventeen summit meetings, the answer was reached, the answer that an intelligent child might have arrived at after five minutes' study. The military planners of both sides should get together to discuss their suppositions and hypotheses. So it came about that biannual meetings between the planners and mathematicians of both sides were arranged. The meetings would allow them not only to make sure they understood each other but to arrive at a common basis for future developments. The seminar was the answer. But the question immediately arose where the meetings should be held. It was here that the British Government made its bid. The meetings should obviously be held in Britain, that raft in the middle of the ocean, beholden to neither side. But, of course, this was not to be. It was decided that the meetings be held alternately, first on the one side, then on the other. That is why they were arranged biannually, and have been so ever since.

'Gentlemen, the meeting is integrated,' boomed the voice of the Chairman, 'the time is half past nine.'

Conway wrenched his mind back to Helios and today's meeting. He thought to himself, not for the first time, how screamingly boring it all was. How boring compared with the world of ideas!

Chapter Three

First Preparations

Conway had known that this would be a critical meeting. He had never before had to sit in on anything quite like it. Very difficult decisions had to be taken, and lives would depend upon them. And the meeting wasn't properly constituted; it didn't have the right technical knowledge, it was too high-level for that. There were still higher levels, of course, but it was unlikely that anyone would have the energy or determination to change what this committee decided.

The first part of the meeting, up to coffee-time at eleven o'clock, was taken up mainly by four speakers. There was Dr Hoddas, a Hungarian. Conway, as he drank his coffee, would have been in some difficulty to remember a single word that Dr Hoddas had said. For Conway had long since learnt the art of not listening. If you listened to everything that was said you became utterly exhausted and were unable to take effective part when the really important issues came up for discussion. In fact, the exhausting of a meeting with pretentious inconsequential nonsense was a part of the technique of a good committee man. It was also part of Dr Hoddas's technique to speak in a guttural French. He was equipped with a large dictionary in which he insisted on looking up words and phrases.

Professor Bombas from Tanganyika had urged that, whatever decisions were taken, the small nations should not be left out. Conway wondered just what he meant by this. Perhaps that the metal coils be made in Togoland, the graphite chambers in Colombia, the computer in Greenland, and the whole thing assembled by a friendly consortium of Americans and Russians. If so, God help the crew.

26

Doctor Leyburn, the economist, wanted decisions to be taken as soon as possible, so that exactly what was involved financially could become known to the respective governments. Conway also wanted the decisions to be taken, but for a different reason, because Helios and its retinue of planets was approaching them by seventy kilometres in every second, and the later they started the harder would everything become. Irichenko wanted parity. Whatever the West was going to do, the East would do and, of course, vice versa. He emphasized this critical observation with an enormous blow on the table, and was on the point of raising his fist for a second time when he remembered that emphasis was regarded as bad form in the West.

The after-coffee-pre-lunch session was worse. They spent it discussing whether they would go for a landing, instead of simply sweeping in orbit around the planets of the Helios system. They decided they would go for a landing. Conway had known that would be the decision. It was so inevitable that it could have been decided in thirty seconds.

The next question, which they closed in on after lunch, a lunch of five courses and four wines, was – which planet? There was of course only one possibility, Achilles. But nobody was going to admit this. Long reports on the four big fellows, Hera, Semele, and the two philosophical planets, were read out. It was just as impossible to make a landing on them as it was to make a landing on Jupiter or Saturn. So it all came back to Achilles. The point of course was that Conway, as the discoverer of Achilles, had to have his position devalued. It was a basic rule that no technical expert should be allowed to get on top of a committee. It was time for him to speak up: 'Mr Chairman, there is an important point that I'd like to draw the Committee's attention to,' he began. 'Really we know very little about the surface of Achilles. It may be just as hostile as the surfaces of the other four.'

There was a staccato burst of Russian from Irichenko. It was translated to Conway as, 'Why don't we know?'

'Because it's a small planet, and it's still very far away.'
Conway allowed a silence to fall. He knew they must come
back to him. The Chairman writhed in his seat, squirmed
his neck, and said, 'Well, Professor Conway?'

'My point, sir, is that the whole question is so uncertain
that it might be better if we contented ourselves with a
purely orbital flight.'

There was a shocked silence. Heads turned in his direction.

'But, Professor Conway,' said the Chairman in an unnaturally soft voice, 'we've already decided that. We've
already decided that we're going to go for a landing.' He
spoke as if to an idiot child. Everybody felt superior to him.
Within ten more minutes they'd decided to make a landing
on Achilles.

That was as far as they got the first day. As they walked
out of the room, mumbling as they went, it didn't seem to
occur to them that perhaps the most momentous decision
in the history of mankind had just been taken. For quite
certainly the decision had now been taken, irrevocably
taken. In theory the decision could be revoked by higher
authorities, but it wouldn't be. In theory all decisions were
in the hands of a few men, but those few couldn't possibly be
familiar with the details of every problem. They were
obliged to take advice from below. Provided a committee
was properly constituted, provided all relevant matters were
fully discussed, advice was never refused. Society had
worked itself into a position where it was as much as the
top men could do to rubberstamp the decisions of those
below them.

If Conway had been a good committee man, he would
have gone with the rest of them to the hotel, he would have
dined with a few selected colleagues, and he would have
tried to lobby them on the matters he knew must come up
for discussion the following day. But because he was not a
good committee man he decided to go home, to see whether
Cathy had taken up his suggestion of a visit to town. To his

intense chagrin he found that she had. Furious, he poured himself a stiff drink and bit savagely into his lonely sandwich.

Cathy paid off the taxi-cab. She allowed it to drive away before making sure that the man had brought her to the right place. The lighting outside the restaurant was subdued rather than bright. She could just make out the name, La Riviera. It was the right place, it had never occurred to her that it mightn't be.

Mike was waiting for her. He was a big powerful fellow, with shortish hair, handsome rather than good-looking. In his official dossier he was described as well coordinated, and the figures given for his reaction times were very good indeed.

He grinned affectionately. 'Hello there, Cat. How about a drink?'

If Conway had seen them move together to the bar he'd have grinned wryly and thought that Cathy always chose them that way, so as to give him a sense of inferiority. But perhaps she worked things the other way round too, perhaps she used his brains to give the Fawsetts of this world a sense of inferiority.

Conway, grimly chewing his supper, thought about the sacredness of the committee system as he did so. 'Why do I feel it's my duty to be there again tomorrow morning?' he demanded of himself. All they would do would be to spend three hours deciding that they'd gone as far as they could go, and that the next stages lay with the technical committees. And after a lot of talk the technical committees would decide that the next stages lay with certain individuals. And at last, when the work lay with individuals, something would get done. What will it matter in forty years' time if I don't go to that meeting tomorrow morning, he thought to himself. I'll probably be dead then anyway. Better to do something that's really important to me, to go straight up to London and bring Cathy back by the scruff of the neck. The decision taken, his mind began to race: how was he to find one person in a city of ten million people?

He felt rather ashamed of himself as he went through the papers in Cathy's desk. But he had to find some sort of a clue as to where she might be. There wasn't much to go on, bills from London stores, cheque stubs – Cathy was astonishingly careful about money – and, surprisingly, a batch of newspaper cuttings. They were all about space expeditions and activities. The news of his own discovery of Achilles was there amongst them.

It took him barely an hour to reach the outskirts of London. When he stopped for petrol he noticed a small café, with the usual mechanical and electronic amusements, where he managed to find change for the phone. Driving along he had been turning over in his mind how best to find Cathy. It would be useless trying to comb endless restaurants and night-clubs, so he dismissed that possible line of inquiry. His original thought of telephoning some of Cathy's favourite dives didn't seem such a good idea either. Why should she go to any of the places they'd been to together? What's the use? he thought to himself, feeling rather ashamed of hunting his wife. Why should he worry? – but he did worry.

He came back to reality just in time to avoid a taxi. He found he had crossed to the south side of the river and was driving aimlessly through Lambeth, heading for Greenwich. He parked by the bridge and spent half an hour staring moodily over the water. Up river, London glowed like a monstrous aurora. He wondered idly about information theory, about exactly how one would formulate his present predicament in a mathematical way. One tiny piece of information, that was all he needed, and he'd be able to find Cathy within half an hour. Without that bit of information he had to go about things in a tortuous elephantine way. Even the police could do no better. There was something terrifyingly anonymous about a really big city.

Still, when you considered that it seemed to be the aim of

society these days to reduce every individual to the status of a punched card, perhaps it wasn't altogether a bad thing. He began to speculate on a future where every place, London even, was controlled by a gigantic computer. It would be obligatory wherever you went, every shop, restaurant, or hotel, even when you walked along the street, to put your own identification card into an electronic scanner. It would be a crime not to do this every quarter of an hour or so. Then the computer would know where everybody was at all times. And you could ask it questions: where is Cathy Conway right now? A small tug hooted as it swirled under the bridge at his feet. Conway shivered as he walked back to his parked car; he had a terrible feeling that he'd just had a vision of the future. It would be easy to justify such a system in the interests of defence and security. The way it would start would be with a few selected individuals, individuals of special importance, who would be flattered by the constant interest in their movements, who would for the most part fall in with the system. Then it would work its way down through the social ladder. People would feel it gave them status. Come to think of it, royal families had lived under the system for centuries.

Conway crossed the river by the Greenwich Bridge. As he wandered along the bank he heard the sound of upbeat music coming from a small dockland pub. He stepped up to the solid oak door, which silently opened.

The dense smoke fumes made his eyes water as he tried to focus on the milieu. A band was playing 'Undecided', a jazz tune from the early twentieth century.

At the bar stood a large blueblood. A red scar ran from his left eye to the corner of his mouth. Leaning against the far end of the bar was a sultry but attractive girl.

Conway threaded his way through empty plastic beer mugs to where the girl was sitting.

'Two Scotches,' he said to the barman. 'Make 'em doubles.'

The girl smiled. The strong liquor began to make him feel

more human. She turned and faced him. He could now see that she was slight but well covered, with warm brown eyes which looked at him sympathetically.

'Hey, what's the trouble,' she said, pulling her stool nearer.

'A slight case of jealousy,' replied Conway. 'Two more whiskies, please.'

Conway's troubles began to disappear as he relaxed. He forgot about his mission and concentrated on the girl in hand. She didn't seem very interested to hear his theory on following people's movements.

At the fourth whisky Conway came into his own. He started to talk flippantly about committees and how ridiculous they were.

The girl looked up suddenly and put her finger to his lips. 'Not here, people might get the wrong idea about you.'

'What wrong idea?' Conway said savagely.

'Oh, forget it, would you like to dance?'

As he stood up he felt the pub rocking gently. Somehow he was manoeuvred to the dance floor, where he sagged into the girl's arms.

'Come on, Conway, we can't have this,' he grinned happily to himself.

He felt soft hair brushing against his cheek, like Cathy's. He floated off with the memories of Cathy and himself. Now when she danced like this it was a cover-up for something.

'Ouch, mind my feet.'

'Sorry, I was dreaming.'

'I know,' she smiled resignedly.

'*La Jalousie.*'

He felt himself being taken back to the bar.

Seated again, he felt more secure and bent solemnly towards her. 'What do you do? I am a physicist.'

'I help people,' came the tart reply.

Conway chuckled, 'That's amazing. I'm glad there are people who still help each other.'

Conway's chuckle echoed as though he were in a large auditorium.

'It's not closing time, is it?' he said to the girl, but she'd gone.

The silence was broken by the scar-faced tough, who was standing over the pianist.

'I said, I don't like it.'

The man at the piano took no notice.

The control in the big man's voice snapped.

'I don't like it,' he screamed.

Conway rose slowly.

'I don't like you or the tune, so why don't – '

The impact on the floor was terrific as Conway hit it. He started to laugh, but stopped suddenly as a boot caught him on the thigh.

Pulling himself up on to the bar-stool, he saw the girl standing by the door with his jacket. Infuriated by the kick, he swung the bar-stool into the crowd gathering next to him. Thud. Silence. Then all hell broke loose.

It was some time before Conway realized that it was not himself but the band who were being attacked. Smiling he slowly unscrewed the pump-handle from the bar and started hitting heads in all directions.

They blurred in front of him. The floor and the ceiling contracted and expanded like a concertina until a grey light seemed to fill the room.

The girl tried to pull this windmill out of the confusion. Finally she succeeded. Outside she heard the first wail of the airborne police.

Conway was still flailing his pump-handle as she pushed him into her car.

She drove quickly through the silent streets, listening for the sirens.

The car stopped. Conway stumbled out and saw a plate-glass window. He tried to hit himself.

The girl took him firmly up to her apartment, where he collapsed into a chair.

Conway woke with a furious hang-over. Vaguely he

remembered getting himself into a tough spot, and he remembered something about a girl. Involuntarily he looked to the other side of the bed. With a faint sense of relief he saw it was empty. Struggling upright he found his clothes thrown carelessly over a couple of chairs. There were various feminine items about the place. So his memories weren't far wrong. Gingerly he dressed himself, thrust his face close to a mirror, put out his tongue and said, 'God, I look awful.'

He tried to keep his head still as he walked out of the bedroom.

'How do you feel?' she asked.

'Terrible.'

She handed him a couple of pills with a cup of coffee. His unsteady hand shook the liquid in the cup round and round, making him feel giddy.

'Any better?' the girl asked sympathetically as he finally managed to sit down.

'I feel like a bloody goldfish in a revolving bowl,' replied Conway.

The girl grinned and went out, leaving him alone with his aches and pains. His mind fought its way through the mercifully thinning alcoholic haze. Does doing the job one is best suited for also apply to being a good prostitute? he wondered.

Of course, one had to draw the line somewhere. The question was where. Didn't that depend when you lived and where? You drew the line one place today and another place tomorrow. Conway decided it was all a hypocritical conspiracy.

Somewhere a shrill persistent ring bore in on his brain.

'God, must that telephone always ring,' he moaned to the girl as she came back into the room.

'Oh, belt up,' she said angrily, 'that telephone call was to tell me to get out of this flat.'

'Why,' asked Conway, rather startled by the outburst.

'Because of the little fracas you had last night. May I

remind you?' She handed him the pump-handle. Conway looked at it in surprise, remembering nothing.

'Now, if I don't leave the district they will have me beaten up like the band last night,' she explained rather coldly.

'You could go to the police; they would straighten the matter out.'

'Like hell they would! What do you think I'm running here – a Sunday school?'

Conway was beginning to focus more clearly. Suddenly he dug up what he'd been trying to remember – the sound of an Australian voice, a voice offering him a flat, not far from here on the other side of the river. One of the rocket engineers, Henry Emling, was going off to Cape Canaveral for a year. He'd been too busy to take much notice of the offer. But then he really couldn't . . .

Conway stopped in mid-thought; there was no let-out in that direction – Emling was a wild fellow, who gave not a damn for status, form or respectability. He'd hardly be more than amused if he knew that the girl had got the flat.

'There's a flat on the south side of the river that I might be able to get for you,' said Conway, to save himself from being a hypocrite.

Later that morning Conway stood outside the dress shop where Cathy bought most of her clothes, thinking up an excuse for going in.

He didn't learn very much except that she was with a friend, a man called Mike.

To satisfy his curiosity he went round to the bureau of information. His hunch was right. The man was obviously Mike Fawsett.

Conway took a second taxi back to his own car, which he had left near Regent's Park. He was in a grim mood as he drove out of London to the west. He knew now why Cathy had the pile of newspaper cuttings, dealing with the exploits of astronauts. With a sinking feeling he knew that this was not just a casual affair.

Chapter Four

The Rocket

It was blowing hard and beginning to rain by the time Conway reached home. He loaded a large pile of wood into a big wicker basket and began to light a fire. The smoke was rising in the grate when the telephone rang.

'Is that Hugh, this is Alex. How did things go today?' Alex Cadogan was one of the foremost rocket engineers at the Centre. Much would depend on him in the months to come.

'I'm afraid I didn't get to the meeting today. I woke with a lousy headache.' Absolutely true, thought Conway. There was a short shocked silence. Cadogan could hardly believe that anyone would fail to attend a Higher Committee Meeting, even if he did wake with a lousy headache. Conway had more than a suspicion that Cadogan would dearly have liked to attend Higher Committee Meetings himself, good engineer that he was. Funny the way that people who could do a job superlatively well always wanted to be doing something else. 'Why don't you come over for a drink tonight,' went on Conway. 'Oh yes, I'm feeling all right now. By the time you get over here I'll have found out what happened today.'

After Cadogan had rung off, Conway put through a call to his secretary, Edith O'Malan.

'Oh, Professor Conway, what happened?' she asked.

'I had a bad head all day I'm afraid,' he answered.

'But we've been ringing your number all day.'

Ye gods, thought Conway, they can't leave you alone even when you are ill. He wondered whether there was anybody, anywhere, today, who could count his life his own.

Only a couple of centuries earlier there were fox-hunting, fire-eating squires in plenty who would have gobbled up on sight whole handfuls of these committee-sitting wallahs. But nowadays not a single fire-eating squire was to be found. The nineteenth century was almost as far back in time as – well, as the time of Achilles.

'I've been having a few of these turns lately,' he excused himself lamely. 'So I really thought that I ought to go up to town to see my doctor.'

This seemed to satisfy her. It had come to a pretty pass when one had to satisfy one's secretary.

'I hope it's all right,' her voice faltered.

'Probably a tumour or something,' he said.

'Oh no, Professor Conway, it's not as bad as that.'

Conway wondered if it was as bad as that. 'What happened today? Did the Chairman send any word through to the office?'

'They decided to refer things to the technical committees. I think there was quite a discussion about it.'

Of course there had been quite a discussion about it. So they had decided to refer things to the technicians after all – perhaps some day they'd really do something for themselves.

Alexander Cadogan arrived about half an hour later. He was a slow-spoken, heavily-built chap, born thirty-five years ago in the State of California, just about a hundred years after California became the rocket-building centre of the world. His head for alcohol was prodigious.

'I'd like you to meet an old friend, Chuck Lamos – Hugh Conway.'

'Glad to meet you. Have you eaten?' asked Hugh.

'Not yet, but a sandwich will do us fine.'

'A sandwich is all you'll get, Cathy's away.'

'Off on a trip?'

'A few days in London. Help yourselves to a drink, boys. I'll see what I can dig out.'

'Aren't you going to tell us what happened?'

'Oh, they decided to refer things to you chaps after all – amazing, isn't it?'

'Which doesn't surprise me.'

'How soon will we get the green light?'

'You know it will have to go right up to the top before you can get that,' answered Hugh. 'You might as well assume you've got to go ahead and carry on right now from there.'

'I reckon that's right, they're not likely to start wiring up the motors themselves,' grinned Lamos.

When Conway came back with the sandwiches he found Cadogan pacing up and down with heavy steps in front of the fire, 'Hugh, it's going to be one hell of a job,' he said.

'The century's understatement,' grunted Lamos. 'It's the double requirement that's the very devil. Big momentum change and rapid momentum change. I suppose there isn't any chance you've got your speeds wrong?' he asked.

'Come off it,' grinned Hugh. 'You know we've got things nailed down to within a few per cent – except for the precise velocity of escape from Achilles. But it's probably not much different from the Earth, give or take a few kilometres a second.'

'Say ten down and ten up, with the necessary safety factor about thirty kilometres a second under high-thrust conditions. How much under low-thrust?' asked Lamos.

'About two hundred,' growled Cadogan, as he bit into his sandwich. 'Not a very nice prospect, is it?'

'As Alex says, it's going to be one hell of a job.'

The problem was a far more formidable one than anything that had been attempted before. At first the two engineers were reluctant to accept the fact that there was a basically new situation here. But as the hours passed Conway's arguments gradually convinced them. It wouldn't do to use the normal techniques, it wouldn't do to make the normal sort of trip, like the one to Uranus. Normally it was possible to arrive in the outer parts of the solar system with a practically zero velocity. But if they did this, the Helios system would sweep past them at about seventy kilometres a second. It would be like running to a railway track only to see the express train thunder by. Somehow they had to get aboard. And since there was no stopping this particular train it would be necessary for their rocket to develop the same speed. It would be rather like driving a car alongside a train and attempting to jump across from the car to the train the moment the car had exactly the right speed.

And, of course, when they wanted to come back home, it would be necessary to do the whole exercise in reverse. Otherwise the landing party would simply be swept away with Helios on its journey through space. All in all, they figured out that a total momentum drive of at least two hundred kilometres per second would be necessary for the whole trip. This was ten times greater than was necessary for a trip to the Moon. Reckoning on a final returning pay-load of ten tons, the all-up weight would exceed 10,000 tons, even if they could manage an exhaust speed as great as twenty kilometres per second. Moreover the trip could not last for more than a few months. So this meant that they couldn't use an electro-magnetic ion rocket. They'd have to use a free-floating nuclear engine, free-floating in a magnetic field. And, as Cadogan said, those things were real buggers. Especially if you had to have a big thrust, such as they would need to land on Achilles.

'We'll just have to have two of 'em,' said Lamos, 'one inside the other.'

'It's damn well going back a century,' grunted Cadogan. 'I want to be sure there's no way of avoiding such a bastard.'

But they decided there wasn't. There was also the problem of getting started. Somehow they would have to get their machine into orbit around the Earth to begin with.

'That means the best part of a 100,000 tons of lousy chemical fuel,' mused Lamos. 'We can do it, but it isn't going to be a picnic.'

'That's your worry, not the Committee's,' grinned Conway, as he squirted soda into a glass.

'Damn all committees, and their mothers, and their grandmothers,' muttered Cadogan. 'They wouldn't be so free with their decisions if they had to do the work.'

'When we've got her in orbit,' went on Lamos, 'We'll have to strip all the rubbish off her.'

'I see,' said Conway, 'so the crew will be able to start with a nice clean ship.'

'That's right, and I can tell you one thing – they'll take it for granted.'

'At least we'll give 'em some work to do after they've landed,' Cadogan's lips twisted as the thought struck him as mildly amusing. 'They'll have to get rid of the bigger reactor, and that won't be a nice job,' he added.

The plan was to have a two-stage nuclear device, the first stage to get as far as Achilles, and to make the landing. The need for the big thrust wouldn't do the delicately suspended reactor much good. So the idea was to get rid of it and of all the outer fuel tanks before starting on the homeward trip. Effectively the crew would then have a new rocket unencumbered by excess weight. But the job would be a tough one, even if the atmosphere of Achilles should turn out to be more or less normal. And even if there wasn't anything to hinder the work – or anybody !

Who might there be? This question was outside the terms of reference of Conway's committee. Otherwise he would have been more interested in attending their meetings. But he knew that the general view was that there would be no trouble from an alien intelligence. And any bacteria or viruses there might be were likely to be so different from their terrestrial varieties that there would be little or no interaction. No radio signals were coming from Achilles. This was already known. This meant, according to the military, that there was no highly intelligent life on the planet. It was just possible that there might be a civilization like that of ancient Rome, not quite sufficiently developed to have discovered the advantages of radio communication, but certainly advanced enough to overwhelm the landing party by sheer weight of numbers. However, the sociologists estimated that the chances against this were about a million to one. It was known, they said, that civilizations such as those of Greece and Rome were transitory, lasting for no more than a few thousand years. Even if developments on Achilles were similar to those on the Earth, it was most unlikely that the present moment would just happen to coincide with the brief existence of such a civilization. The arguments looked good. Even so, Conway thought, it would hardly be pleasant to have dinosaurs breathing down your neck while you were trying to do the delicate technical job of stripping your rocket.

It was to be many months before Cadogan would be able to show Conway the fruits of their conversations that night. But a day was to come the following April when Alex would show him through the gigantic hangars where the Achilles rocket was being assembled. He would see the vast tubes with their thick graphite walls, surrounded by super-cooled magnetic coils. These gave an enormous pinch to the magnetic field at two points on the axis of the rocket. They were necessary to prevent the reactor from simply drifting away into space, or from drifting the other way towards the inner guts of the rocket. The reactor, in fact, was held captive between the two pinched points. Laterally it was held captive by a weaker field. This was maintained by an outer solenoid. The field could be weaker towards the graphite walls simply because there was no way through it. In contrast there had to be small openings of the field along the axis. The hot plasma surrounding the reactor had to be reflected as it approached the openings, and this of course meant a strong pinch.

The problem was to prevent the walls from being burnt up, and this was solved by the injection of liquid inert fuel over the whole wall. The rate of injection was controlled by feedback devices which adjusted the flow in accordance with the energy output of the reactor. The greater the output, the faster the flow. What happened was that radiation, intense radiation, from the reactor first vaporized and then ionized the inert fuel, which then streamed outwards along the wall and ultimately formed the jet of the rocket.

As regards the inert fuel, what they wanted was a low molecular weight, not too low a boiling point, and a high density. Unfortunately the spending of hundreds of thousands of millions of pounds over the years had not succeeded in changing the laws of chemistry, whatever priorities the committees put on their projects. So the best inert fuels were exactly those that could have been deduced from chemical handbooks a century earlier. Ordinary ammonia was as good as anything, with its three atoms of hydrogen to one of nitrogen. After ionization it gave a molecular weight only a little above two. Hydrogen itself would have given a much better molecular weight, but the density was hopelessly low, and it was also difficult to keep vast quantities of hydrogen in a liquid state.

Successful rocket design had proceeded by increasing the temperature of the sheet of gas close to the walls as it sped on its journey into space. Operating temperatures were now in the neighbourhood of a hundred thousand degrees, which gave the best exhaust speed of about twenty kilometres per second. With such a high operating temperature the walls had to be shielded to prevent evaporation of the graphite, and this meant that they had to be protected by the outflowing gases themselves. If the sheet of gas should become too thin, the walls, and eventually the controls of the motor itself, simply burnt up. If the rapidly-flowing sheet of gas was too thick, more than sufficient to protect the walls, then the inert fuel was used uneconomically. There had to be a fine balance, and this was why the feed-back devices that controlled the flow were so crucial. The reactor itself, suspended in its magnetic field, was of course of the gaseous variety, controlled in its operations only through the magnetic field.

A further complication had been added to the Achilles ship. To avoid carrying unnecessary weight, storage tanks had to be jettisoned as the inert fuel was used up. The problem was one of geometry. The motors had to be at the rear of the rocket. How does one jettison the fuel storage tanks without jettisoning the motor itself? The problem could not be solved with the motors in a fixed position, they had to be moved steadily backwards as the rear part of the rocket was stripped away. This was done by mounting the whole reactor system on a central shaft, the shaft being screwed backwards as the flight proceeded. Towards the front, but buried deep inside the gigantic structure, was a second smaller, but otherwise identical, rocket. It weighed perhaps a thousand tons. This would be used for the homeward flight. Inside it were the crew's quarters. There was no question of any observations through port-holes. This was quite unnecessary, for at the front in the extreme outer skin of the rocket was a host of electronic devices, arranged to transmit their information to the crew inside – radio aerials, television cameras, ultra-violet and X-ray 'eyes', and three telescopes, one of eighty inches aperture.

When, many months later, Conway was shown over this vast conglomeration of electronic and nucleonic devices, it seemed almost impossibly complicated. It seemed almost impossible that it should all work correctly. Yet on paper it had looked very straightforward. But Conway knew himself to be one of those strange people to whom calculations on paper appear a lot simpler than the real thing. It always amazed him how complicated a simple electric plug could be made. If he stopped really to think about it, the coils that produced the pinch effect, so critical to the correct operation of the whole affair, were just an application of elementary electricity. Yet, with their cooling equipment, their voltage controls and other feed-back devices, they seemed strange, menacing, and enigmatic.

Although he could hardly believe it, Conway realized that to most people things were the other way round. It was usually the calculations on paper that seemed obscure. To most people calculations only acquired a meaning when they were translated into material terms. It was a question of the way you saw the world. Conway saw it in terms of the abstractions of the mind, not in terms of concrete everyday things.

120175

Chapter Five

Personnel

Mike Fawsett looked himself over carefully in the bathroom mirror as he shaved. He was trying to decide whether Cathy could properly be described as demanding. He decided that she could. He heard a disturbance in the bedroom, a waiter was bringing breakfast. He showered quickly, rubbed himself down, slipped on his dressing-gown and pushed open the door.

'Coffee's almost cold, darling.'

Cathy was sitting up, her back to the bedhead, a large cup cradled in her hands. She smiled, not because she was amused, or because she was welcoming Mike, but because she was utterly at ease. She looked him over, smiled again and, without realizing it, stretched herself slightly.

'I don't mind it cold,' he said.

'The one thing they never seem able to do is to get the coffee hot. The best hotels are the worst.'

These self-contradictory remarks were somehow typical of Cathy. He wondered if he should broach the subject on his mind. He knew that his name was on the list of possible candidates for the flight to Achilles. But the list was certain to be a long one, and four men would be chosen. He also knew that every candidate would have a completely first-class record, not only of expeditions into space, but also in their medical and psychological histories. He knew that a straw would decide between those who were chosen and those who were not. A single dissentient voice would be sufficient to rule a man out. This was bound to be the case when someone equally good was available to replace him. One possible, and even likely, voice was that of Cathy's

45

husband. He wondered if Conway was a vindictive man. After all, he wouldn't need to be particularly vindictive. It would only be ordinary human nature. He wondered for a moment whether perhaps Conway might not find out; then, looking down at Cathy as she buttered a roll, he dismissed the thought. Nobody he had ever met was more open than Cathy. You took her or you left her. She didn't care.

'Jam or honey?' she asked.

He ignored the question. 'Cathy, you know I'm up for the big trip?'

'I know. I saw the list among Hugh's papers.'

'You don't think he might do something to stop me?'

'He won't. I'll see to that. He'll do as I say.'

Cathy leant forward and pushed away the breakfast trolley. She put her hand round Mike's head and pulled him towards her.

Tom Fiske was brought up without any difficulties on the sand lots of Scranton, Pa. His parents were entirely unknown, apparently having decided at an early stage in young Tom's career to part company from him. After spending eleven of his first twelve years in an orphanage, Tom decided to chance his luck as a free-lance operator. He worked in the evening and attended high school by day. So unwilling nowadays are the inhabitants of the highly prosperous countries to engage in any form of physical activity that Tom found very little difficulty in eking out a bare living. In summer there was any amount of gardening to be done. Winter was more difficult, but there were the mails around Christmas time, there was the snow to be cleared in front of people's homes, and after a couple of years of experience he found that doing leg-work for professional debt collectors could be tolerably profitable. He had a good nose for sniffing out information, he was not regarded with a suspicious eye, his skin was thick perforce, and his legs were fast.

As he grew older, as he became interested in the other

sex, he came to realize that these activities were not very profitable, nor did they carry status. He thought hard about being a professional ball-player, and if the big-time clubs had given him a fair try-out it is possible that he would have made it.

At the age of eighteen he had a serious discussion with himself. Candour compelled him to admit that he was getting nowhere. It was true he was eating, but only in hamburger joints, reeking of evaporated fats. There seemed no hope at all of making the sort of moolah that would enable him to buy a house on one of the hills to the west of the town, where he might raise a family in peace, and in contemplation of the American scene. Actually this was not entirely true. Tom's real enemy was not the under-privilege of birth but a genuine ignorance of what to do. He was handicapped neither by physical shortcomings, nor by low intelligence, but by sheer lack of know-what. There had never been a time since about the year 1950 when a 'young man who knew' could not make himself a million dollars by the time he was twenty. Luck made no difference, but know-what certainly did.

So it came about that the U.S. Army found itself with a raw recruit on its hands. Tom enlisted, and so avoided the draft, shortly before his nineteenth birthday. At that age he was a rather gangly youngster, just about six feet tall, with a close-cropped head that would have grown a shock of red hair if it had been given time to do so. His face was mildly freckled, and his ears stuck out sufficiently to give him a slightly aggressive look, without being really noticeable. The psychological tests he was given were really a waste of time, for the readiness of his smile in the face of past experience manifestly showed that he had the right temperament. At that time there was a gap in his front teeth – one of them had been knocked out in a gang fight about five years earlier.

But they did give him tests, physical as well as psychological. Although the results, especially the physical results, were abnormally good, nobody took very much notice of that. His whole background was too amorphous for him to be taken seriously at that stage. He was first sent on a tour of duty in Bolivia. This did little to help his future career, except perhaps to give him a catholic outlook on things in general. Then he was hauled back to the U.S. and given an eight-months' training as an electronics maintenance engineer. He survived the course and got the first break of his life by being sent to winter at the Mount Erebus station in Antarctica. After three summer months he volunteered to see the winter through at this remote spot, according to some the nearest in its inhospitality to the satellites of Jupiter. On the way back to base camp the following spring he and three other colleagues were overtaken by a series of furious storms. These would not have mattered but for a series of freakish mishaps to their equipment. Even in this day and age it is possible to run close to disaster on the Antarctic Plateau. They managed to make base, but only after a desperate struggle. The doctor who examined Tom was first astonished and then suspicious. His condition when compared with that of the other three men appeared to be too good. At first it seemed to indicate that Tom had somehow managed to avoid pulling his weight. When further investigation proved this to be by no means true a thorough report on Tom was made to Washington. The report rated an electronic check-over. This meant that the whole of Tom's past history, so far as it was known to the Army, that is to say so far as it had been committed to punched cards, was fed into an electronic computer. The computer delivered its report; Tom was well within the range of physical and mental characteristics required for a candidate to space school. He was accordingly sent to the Department of Space Medicine at Santa Barbara, California.

The normal physical tests, endurance and reaction times, showed up nothing particularly unusual, nothing much different from hundreds of other well-coordinated cadets. But the results were sufficiently satisfactory for him to proceed to more advanced training. This meant acceleration tests. It was then that something really unusual began to emerge. It wasn't that Tom liked being accelerated at x times gravity any more than anyone else, but his recovery time was quite abnormally quick. After prolonged acceleration he could return to coordinated physical and mental activity long before the normal recruit. From the emergence of this freak ability it was only a question of time before Tom got his first trip into space. It was a routine flight to the Moon, in which he performed well enough to graduate as an astronaut.

Now it was a question of the long haul. Lots of young fellows had started equally as well as Tom, but it was another matter as the flights became more numerous and longer in duration. Tom simply took it all in his stride. A gap in performance slowly opened out between him and the average man. The longer time went on, the wider the gap became.

It seems whatever the human race sets itself to do there will always be a few rare individuals who manage to perform almost unnaturally well, as if they were not members of the species at all. So far as space flight was concerned, Tom was one of these. He was a natural, his name a cert for the trip to Achilles. He wouldn't be the leader, he didn't have the right educational or social background, but if anyone stood the course it would be Tom Fiske. And if he needed any further recommendation, he now had a girl, 36-25-36, five feet six and a half inches, green eyes, fine hair dyed blonde, the secretary of a big noise in the top organization, the Rand Corporation. This was judged by the psychiatrists to give him additional stability.

During the months that followed Cathy Conway had several assignations with Mike Fawsett. Inevitably serious rows with Conway followed in the wake of these arrangements. For his part, and for his own sake, Fawsett kept the affair as much throttled down as he could. He knew that the moment of decision was not far away.

Hugh Conway had no intention of raising the matter of the choice of the Achilles crew with Cathy. He intended that she should raise it herself. All he had to do was to leave the relevant committee papers lying around in his study. She would be sure to find them.

It worked out as he planned. She did raise the subject, but in a manner that simply took his breath away. Late one evening, when they were going to bed, Cathy turned to him, entirely naked, candidly and boldly, and said, 'You're going to make sure that Mike gets in, aren't you?' Strangely, it shattered his confidence. He himself might be a clever fellow, but surely his wife was unique. Had any woman ever before had the sheer gall to look seductive simply to demand – yes, demand – that her husband should do a favour to her lover. Conway doubted it.

'I'm not going to lift a finger to help that Fawsett stumble-bum, if that's what you're getting at.'

'You know what it means, Hugh. It means we're finished if you don't. I'm not going to go on living with a mean-minded man.'

'You think it's mean-minded to refuse to help a man who's seduced my wife, do you?'

'He didn't seduce me,' began Cathy indignantly. Then her voice trailed away as she realized that she had fallen into a small trap.

'You're quite shameless. Look at you now,' went on Conway.

'If I can't undress in front of my husband, who can I undress in front of?' It was the usual story. In any matter sexual Cathy had the perfect defence, on anything else she was worse than hopeless. 'But you're quite right,' she went on, 'the way you stare at me it isn't decent. After ten years it's abnormal. There must be something wrong with you.' Acting up the part she grabbed a dressing-gown and slipped it around her shoulders.

'How can you expect things to go on working if you're always sleeping around with some nuke or other?' he asked.

Cathy's face reddened slightly, 'I don't sleep around with nukes.' And of course she didn't. 'If you're going to be nasty, I'll tell you this. If you'd sleep around a bit we would get along a lot better. You ought to see a psychiatrist. It ain't natural the way you are always looking at me. Anyway, how can you know I'm so good if you never go out with anybody else?'

Conway didn't know whether to get mad or to laugh.

'And you know what I'm like. You've known right from the beginning. You can't make a leopard change its spots.'

There was justice in this. He had known. Before he married Cathy various people had told him in measured asides that she was classified in her psychological record as a pseudonympho. He'd never really known the technical meaning of this term – by now he'd simply come to associate it with someone like Cathy. He'd known perfectly well what she was like and he'd made the masculine error of supposing that he could change her. In this he had really been unfair. It was perhaps because he could think so that their marriage had lasted for so long, three times as long as the average. Many of his friends would also have subscribed to the view that he was abnormal.

'Don't you realize that I couldn't get Fawsett into the party even if I wanted to. I'm not choosing the crew.'

'Rubbish!'

'I mean it. You know perfectly well that these things are only settled at the top.'

Cathy pondered this for a moment, and then said, 'But you could do your best.'

'All I can do is to promise not to do my worst.'

She sat on the edge of the bed looking down for a moment and shook the mop of brown curls. When she looked up at him her eyes were ablaze with indignation, 'But it's *your* planet,' she burst out.

Instantly the shadow of Mike Fawsett vanished like a puff of smoke. Cathy's lips were as compulsive as they had ever been. Afterwards, she fell almost instantly asleep. Conway was left with his brain racing.

There was nothing for it but to go back to his study again. He moved the light blanket gently around Cathy's shoulders and tiptoed from the room, pausing for a moment to listen to her breathing as he always did. It was as steady and regular as that of a child. With a clear perception he realized that Cathy was abnormal in the sense that she lived more in the present than a normal person. The past had some meaning for her but not a great deal, while the future was still dim and inconsequential. Once Fawsett was on his way across space she would forget all about him. But of course the trouble would arise again with increased emphasis on his return, if he returned. Conway would have found this analysis ironic if he had known just what was going to happen to Cathy.

Down in the study he rummaged among his papers. Because his private estimate was that the crew of the Achilles ship had no more than a fifty per cent chance of survival, let alone success, his inner wish had been to recommend Fawsett strongly for a place in the crew. But he had been tormented inside himself by the story of David and Uriah, except of course that things weren't quite the same way round in this case. After all, Fawsett wanted to go. But this had hardly seemed sufficient. It seemed somehow wrong to send a man to what might be his death when you yourself stood to profit from that death. So until tonight he had been balanced in his mind as to what he should do. But now he was decided. Cathy had settled the matter for him. He was damned if he was going to lose his wife because of a scruple, for he knew that she would surely leave him if he should black-ball Fawsett.

Conway's doubts were based on many arguments, none of them very conclusive, but adding together to a solid amount of evidence. Now he had one more thread, a thread as yet unknown to anyone else. He had a crucial new result from his observations. If it had been almost anyone else, the news would already have flashed around the world. Since about the year 1960 scientists had announced their discoveries almost before they had made them. Not that Conway was close, but he believed in having a little time to digest his own work before it was mauled over in public. He knew what the newspapers would do with this one. Shuffling his notes he came to what he wanted. To the inexpert eye it was just a pen tracing, a thin line that rose and fell in a complicated and apparently unpredictable way as it moved down the length of a long strip of paper. It was the spectrum of Achilles. Most of the complicated behaviour of the line towards the right-hand end of the strip was due to the presence of water vapour in the atmosphere of Achilles. What Conway had been looking for were slight modifications of this water vapour pattern. His finger found the relevant place. There really couldn't be any doubt about it. They were the bands of chlorophyll.

Chapter Six

The Russian Ship

Conway's discovery caused a major stir, as he had anticipated it would. It meant that there must be some sort of plant life on Achilles. Previously they had only had the very green colour of the planet to go by, strongly suggesting the presence of plant life, although there was just the bare possibility that it might come from a green inorganic salt.

Speculations on the possibilities of there also being animal life were now rife. The lack of radio signals was of course again given prominence, but it was pointed out that weak signals could not be detected because of the masking effect of Helios itself. The angular separation of Achilles from the star, as seen from the Earth, was only about three degrees. Radio waves emitted by the star, random noise without any coherent signal, slopped into even the biggest radio dishes, producing a completely effective jamming of any weak signal from Achilles. So there was this possibility, but it wasn't taken very seriously. After all, a terrestrial television transmitting station could easily have been detected, if it had been sited on the approaching planet.

But although the public wasn't much worried, military planners took matters more seriously. It was inevitable that they should do so, for it is the nature of military planning that one must take all possibilities seriously, however absurd they may be.

The argument was: if there was someone on Achilles who was planning an invasion of the Earth, then that someone might have deliberately damped down all forms of radio emission. They might not wish to give their presence away.

When it was pointed out that the Earth itself had given its presence away, for instance by more than a hundred television channels in Europe and the United States alone, the psychologists pointed out that this was an outcome of terrestrial tension. A more developed society, with less tension, might well have stayed its hand. It might have waited to see if it could pick up any signals from the other fellow before making any signals of its own. There were no radio astronomers among the military planners or psychologists, otherwise they would have pointed out that that was precisely what they themselves had been trying to do for over a century.

It was therefore inevitable that plans should be drawn up to meet a potential invasion from space. The Achilles project was not only exploratory, it took over the functions of an advanced patrol. And the crew would be briefed accordingly.

A beneficial result of all this was that some genuine co-operation between East and West was plainly desirable. In fact, it is well known from psychological studies that adjustments in human society take place in such a way as to maintain a state of constant tension. In plain terms, if for some reason current problems disappear then new ones must quickly be invented. Similarly, if troubles mount up, the new ones proceed to devalue the old ones. Knowing all this could be demonstrated by strict mathematics, everybody at the top suspected that the danger of a space invasion would be over-emphasized. The top generals felt that the mathematical psychologists were taking them for a ride, and the psychologists themselves thought that this was probably so, although they couldn't be sure. This is not as absurd as it may sound. Mathematical psychology is of course based on what used to be known as the theory of games. And it is essential to the theory of games that there should be at least two sides. This assumption runs through the whole mathematical structure. The trouble in the present case was that no one knew whether there was another side or not. Nobody quite knew how the mathematics went, strictly speaking, if there was complete uncertainty about the existence of an opponent. The result was a state of confusion. Everybody suspected that they were being taken for a trip, but no one was quite sure how.

It was inevitable that there should be summit meetings. For many, many years these had been disguised as intimate family gatherings. The Russian President, at the moment Vladimir Kaluga, would depart from Moscow for New York or for Paris accompanied by his two sons and three daughters, the daughters being accompanied by their husbands and their children, and their servants, interpreters, general hangers-on and advisers. They would be met at the airport by the Euro-American President and his wife, in this case Lee and Martha Kipling. It was an interesting difference of culture that the Russian President was always a widower and the Euro-American President always a married man. In their respective territories these qualities were regarded as a sign of vigour.

The party would be moved safely, to Nantucket Island perhaps, or to some château on the Loire. There they would get down to business, their families forgotten. It was the only way to achieve a comparatively sane interchange of ideas. At an official summit meeting, held in the full glare of international publicity, all previous positions must necessarily be maintained. All official contacts were reduced to the state of intellectual trench warfare. Only when they were ostensibly in the bosoms of their families could the leaders of either side deviate by a hair's breadth from the implacably straight paths along which they were set by their respective communities. Even if you lost your shirt you must still preserve your face, as one highly-paid political commentator put it.

Even so, world publicity would do what it could to impede their every movement. Wherever they were situated, whether in the fastness of a Rhineland castle, or on a farm near the banks of the Shenandoah, newsmen would swarm into the district, and helicopters would plant television cameras on every available vantage point. A small child, at the age of innocence, would not be allowed to pick a bunch of flowers without its picture being instantly transmitted to the waiting multitudes in the pulsating world outside. In spite of the modern newfangled devices it was all very much as it had been in medieval times. Except that monarchs were then described in a flowing language of some magnificence; they were not referred to boldly as Lee, Vlad, and Marty.

It was at one of these homey, fireside parties that the West first divulged its list of astronauts for the Achilles expedition – Fiske, Fawsett, Larson, and Reinbach. Larson was to be the leader, with Fawsett as his second in command. Kaluga carried the news back to Moscow.

It is not known who was responsible for the Russian stroke of imagination, almost of genius. But it is pleasant to think that somewhere behind a dull grey wall of concrete somewhere in Moscow, and behind the flinty exterior of some close-cropped Russian committee man there lurks a touch of romance. The Russo-Chinese list for their expedition was announced about a month later. It was: Alexander Pitoyan, Nuri Bakovsky, Ivan Kratov and Tara Ilyana.

The United States fell slap-bang into the propaganda trap that had been prepared for the West. Once Americans had digested the incredible news that a woman was to be sent on the Russian expedition it was quickly pointed out that the performances of Russian women athletes closely approached those of men. It was broadly hinted that Miss Ilyana would turn out to be practically a man in all her essential qualities. Visions of rough, tough, Russian women breaking stones along the road to Archangel were conjured up. The remnants of the once-powerful Hearst Press even went so far as to publish the headline COMMIES TO BLAST THREE-HUNDRED-POUND WOMAN INTO SPACE. The editor in question was allowed twelve hours of self-congratulation before the trap was sprung. Ilyana turned out to be a curvaceous blonde with a high I.Q.

Somewhat more than a touch of inspiration had gone into Ilyana's selection, however. Without the work of Nicolai Popkin, a young mathematician from Rostov, a proposal to include a woman would have been regarded as an amusing and welcome joke by the higher committees, but it would not have been taken seriously. Inevitably sex was always a difficulty where long space voyages were concerned. Young men cooped up in a space-ship for months on end naturally found themselves turning lightly to thoughts of love. The strange result proved by Popkin, subsequently to become famous as Popkin's Theorem was, that there would be far less talk and thought about sex if a woman were included in the party. A few laymen had doubts about this result but their views were brushed aside, for mathematical rigour could not be gainsaid. Rigour there seemed to be – at least the mathematicians said so. Three Academicians, consulted as referees, found Popkin's argument both elegant and satisfying. It was said that the shock-haired young man had used a particularly subtle lemma.

Once decided on their course the committees proceeded with ruthless efficiency. It was immediately clear that a major propaganda victory could be scored. The thing to do was quite obviously to choose a girl who in her appearance might have been taken as an ideal representation of American womanhood. So the hunt was on. The search was of course confined to members of the Young Communists Party. It was also restricted by the requirement of an excellent educational background. But after that, the Russian authorities were only interested in vital statistics, and in those qualities that were literally superficial.

Thousands of dossiers, in the form of neat packets of punched-cards, were sent from the provinces to Moscow, where they were analysed with the aid of a computer. The computer was of course supplied with a programme of selection, the gate of which was very narrow. Almost fifty girls managed to pass through the gate, Ilyana being one of them. There is no telling how she was chosen out of this short list but Tara Ilyana was certainly a pleasant young woman with a well-integrated personality.

It would have been hard for anyone from the twentieth century to understand the shattering effect of Ilyana's inclusion on American public opinion. Everywhere one heard the gloomy prognostication that now 'they' were finished. The social temperature had continued to rise in an unbroken steep curve ever since the middle of the twentieth century. By 2087 everybody lived in the way that film stars used to live a century ago. Marriages lasted on average about a year.

It was the discovery of how to prevent children in broken homes from becoming insecure, made about seventy years ago, that really produced the difference. It was one of the few really genuine social advances, to stop the furious fighting that used to take place in the law courts over the custody of children. No wonder they felt insecure when such things were going on. Now this was all altered. The old tribal structure had come back with the young being thought of as members of the tribe, rather than as belonging to a particular person. But woe betide the child who didn't belong to the tribe – who didn't belong to the right social bracket, like young Tom Fiske. Then things were really tough, but no worse than they used to be. Anyway, with the kids getting married at thirteen or fourteen – entering the sexual parabola as the psychiatrists call it – there wasn't much childhood to worry about.

It is of course well known that astronauts are a great success with women. The pattern has been with us for more than a hundred years, ever since the absurd early idea of sending married men on the first trips into space was abandoned. By a like token it was clear that Ilyana was going to be a great success with men, even before she ever set her well-shaped foot into the Achilles ship.

The second most interesting member of the Russian team

was Alex Pitoyan. A slim dark young man, he was the only Muscovite in the team. Seven years earlier he had graduated from Moscow University with excellent marks in Physics and Mathematics. Different from other able young men of his time, he showed no taste for mathematico-psychological studies, but became interested in complex orbital calculations. The field was not a particularly difficult one, since the use of computers had largely obviated the tricky analytical work of previous centuries. Within five years Pitoyan had become a master of the subject and of the use of computers in general. Now it was perfectly clear that the orbits of the Achilles ships could not be pre-set. They would have to pass through very complex gravitational fields, and no one could say exactly what initial orbit was the correct one. The available data were not good enough for that, and were most unlikely to become good enough, even though observational measurement was becoming more and more accurate as the Helios system approached our own. Inevitably the orbit would have to be altered while the ship was in flight. The crew would have to play it by ear and make appropriate corrections as the need arose. One possibility was to send all available information back to Earth for the terrestrial laboratories to make the necessary calculations, and for the appropriate corrections to be sent back to the ship. This was precisely the Euro-American plan. The Russians on the other hand decided for safety's sake to include a computer in the ship. They also decided to send a genuine scientist, not someone with a merely superficial training. Pitoyan was a good effective choice; medical reports showed that while he was not in the class of the normal astronaut, he could be expected to survive the rigours of take-off and landing, and from a mental point of view it was quite likely that he would more than hold his own.

Soon after the announcement of the composition of the party he decided that it would be nice to make Ilyana's acquaintance on a rather more informal basis than had been possible on the occasion of their meeting at the House of Astronauts. The affair prospered for a little while but was then brought to an abrupt halt by the authorities, who warned him very sternly that if this behaviour were to continue he was out. The behaviour was sharply terminated. Alone in his tiny flat, fifty yards off Tchaikovsky Street, he shrugged and grinned to himself. It would be simpler after take-off.

It is an old idea that there might be somebody in the world exactly and precisely like oneself. Add a sinister touch to the situation in which you happen to meet that person, and what do you do? According to tradition you are supposed to crack up. Actually nature is very prolific. Essentially the same individuals are constantly being born, often simultaneously, and often in widely different parts of the earth. The circumstances of birth and the different conventions of the societies in which they are brought up proceed to clothe these individuals with a façade that hides their basic similarity, but like is apt to ally itself with like if they are brought together under basically the same circumstances. No one could tell exactly where the ancestors of Tom Fiske had come from, judging from his appearance probably from Norway or Denmark via the south of England. The ancestors of Ivan Kratov and of Nuri Bakovsky had probably moved into Russia from the direction of the Pripet marshes about fifteen hundred years ago. Whether their forebears at a still earlier date were ever associated together must of necessity be a matter of doubt and speculation, but certain it is that all three were basically the same individual. Laid over one of them were the doubts, miseries, and uncertainties of a free society. Laid over the other two were the inflexible certainty, the pride, and the boredom of a culture that thinks it knows exactly where it is going.

An observer from entirely outside the human race would indeed have discovered much about their respective cultures, their behaviour would have allowed him to measure the merits and demerits of the societies that had raised them.

To the Westerner who claims that the case of Tom Fiske was not a fair one, that Tom Fiske was not a fair representative of their culture, it must be said that if Fiske had been brought up as the Westerner imagines in theory that all children should be brought up, then he never would have made the grade, he would never have got within the remotest sighting distance of the Western party to Achilles. The comparison is of necessity a fair one. And the conclusions our imaginary observer might reach are not clear. Which system they would favour is quite uncertain.

Suffice it then to say that Kratov and Bakovsky were basically courageous tough men. Where Fiske had been dragged up, not brought up, they had received the most careful of graduated trainings. They had both started life at a crèche. They had been told that Russia was the greatest nation on earth, and because the people who told them this provided food, warmth, and shelter, they saw no reason to disbelieve it. They were not intelligent enough to think outside the carefully organized social structure in which they were embedded. They saw no reason to behave in any way differently from the other boys around them. In all respects they were exactly the same as the others, except in their ability to survive physical discomfort without appreciable mental strain. So that, at the time they were chosen for the Achilles expedition, they were undistinguished individuals, their characters essentially unformed, precisely because they were not unique and because their education had been designed to suppress, not to bring out, all small differences between one person and another. Once again, if they had not been chosen, those who were would not have differed in any sensible respect. They were the products of a system, a system that had erected a tiny gate through which only men of a very restricted type could pass. On the voyage itself their qualities might begin to mark them out as real people, not as packets of punch-cards to be fed to a computer.

There was an ironic similarity in the design of the Russian rocket. Just as the men were essentially the same men, so the rocket was essentially the same rocket. And just as the men were overlaid by superficial differences, of no real consequence at all, so the rocket looked different to the casual eye. When mounted in its outer container, the container of the chemical fuel that was to get it into orbit around the Earth, it measured a hundred feet across the base and was five hundred feet in height. The American rocket on the other hand measured only sixty feet across the base but was a thousand feet in height. The Russian looked squat and ugly, compared to the pencilled elegance of the American machine. But basically they were exactly the same job. They were powered in the same way, and the logic of their construction was the same. It had cost the best part of a hundred thousand million pounds to produce the superficial differences. It was however, exactly these differences that everybody was proud of. They said that they were 'essentially' Russian or 'all' American as the case might be.

130175

Chapter Seven

The Launching

Mike Fawsett marched up and down the brightly lit hall as he waited for the Atlantic shuttle, which was already an hour late. The timing of really big flights was absolutely precise, to the second. Funny that they couldn't run a three-thousand-mile hop efficiently.

Mike himself was equally at home on either side of the Atlantic. His mother was American, his father British. His early education had been in England, but he'd come over to the States for graduate training, and had spent most of his life there since. To get himself into space school he had taken out American citizenship, and by now the difference between him and a native-born American was mainly that the law still prevented him from ever becoming President. But this scarcely worried him, for with his inclusion in the Achilles crew he had achieved the ambition of a lifetime, of more than a lifetime. He was marching up and down now not because he was nervous or impatient at the delay but because of an over-abundance of physical energy. This constant desire to be moving, to be flexing his muscles, had always been a difficulty on flights into space. It was a bit odd he thought to himself that they chose physical types for these jobs, when an armchair man might find things a lot easier.

He hadn't seen Cathy for three months. It had been absolutely essential to stick unswervingly to his training. The new ship was quite a bit different to anything he had ever been in before. Now that they were getting near take-off they'd been given the green light – to make the best of their last week-end. The more he saw of Cathy the better the authorities would be pleased. They'd know about it of course, they'd have her dossier. The main point was that he was in the clear.

The speaker announced that the Atlantic ferry was in. The waiting crowd moved closer to the exit gate. Then he saw Cathy coming, one of the first out – she must have simply floated through all formalities. He kissed her, 'Cat, darling, you're late.'

'Oh, am I? I can never get the time right when it changes.'

'I've got everything fixed.'

She looked up at him, thinking that she too had got everything fixed. Hugh had gone down to the south of Florida for the big launching. This left her quite free to spend the last few days with Mike.

They took the monorail into Manhattan. They passed high above the Triborough Bridge and above the East River. It was really much more impressive than actually flying. It was nearly 4.30 on a November afternoon, and the lights of New York were just coming on. The whole sight of it delighted Cathy. It wasn't that she was unsophisticated, or that she hadn't seen it before, but that her memories of the past – of her last visit to New York two years earlier – were now dim and vague. Mike's arm around her shoulder was the reality.

Their section of the car branched off the main line at Fifty-second Street. Within thirty seconds they were standing on the pavement of Fifth Avenue. Mike carried her bag along one of the cross streets and they were almost instantly inside a block of expensively furnished apartments.

'I didn't know you'd got a place in New York, Mike.'

'I don't have, but I've got a friend.'

'Look what I've brought for you.' Cathy was already beginning to spread her things over the bedroom. She opened up a package, and there was a large soft toy. It was a donkey with big black hoofs, a black top, and a white patch for its mouth and nose. The ears were long and sagged down the back like a lion's mane. The eyes had a quizzical look. 'It's a mascot. You can't keep your pyjamas inside it.'

He looked at the absurd toy with an embarrassed grin, wondering where he could get rid of it quietly.

After the past months he had a great desire for Cathy, but when he tried to kiss her she pushed him away quite firmly. Of course, it could be the journey that had tired her, but Mike had more than a suspicion that she was levelling the score for his neglect of her during the last few weeks.

With the coming of night the people who thronged the streets of Manhattan during the day mostly retired to their homes, down the Jersey coast or far up the valley of the Hudson, or into Westchester and beyond to Connecticut. Those who provided services and entertainment stayed behind, apart from the very few who actually lived in the city. It had changed a good deal over the last century. Nowadays there is no land on Manhattan, not even the smallest patch, that is available for cheap living. The whole island, from the Battery in the south to its northernmost tip, is now solid with office premises. The only exceptions are the eating-houses, the theatres of Broadway, hotels, and a very few private apartments grouped around Central Park. Looking backwards over the whole history of the development of New York one notices a consistent pattern. The amount of the island developed for business administration simply depended on the state of the economy of the Union. In the very early days only the southernmost regions were used. The rest of the island was available at small cost to anyone who wished to live there. By the middle of the twentieth century, the movement to the north had reached almost to Sixtieth Street. Beyond were about thirty more streets of prosperous residences and hotels. Then came Harlem, and the cheap tenements of the Puerto Ricans. All this has long since gone. Everywhere, north to south, east to west, stand the office blocks, medium sized by New York standards. It would be easy to erect buildings of the size of the old skyscrapers, but the removal of such edifices is unduly costly.

Strangely enough the stresses to which the modern New

Yorker is subject in his daily life are probably less than they were a hundred years ago. For nowadays nobody living there conceives that life could be in any way different from what it is. To the great mass of commuters it seems entirely natural that one should spend the whole of one's life in commuting. The very first memories almost are of the daily routine of making the school bus. The alarm bell at seven o'clock, the hurried shower and breakfast, the short walk to the end of the street to join the others. This was now the universal pattern. Nowhere was a child to be found who ambled along alone, happy in a world of his own imagination, content to arrive late at school and not thinking it important. The psychologists said it was a good thing that there were no such children, for they would have lived unhappy lives themselves and produced tensions and unrest in others.

Fifteen hundred miles away to the south, Conway was standing looking out over sandy land-locked pools towards the sea. He was dressed in shirt and slacks, the shirt open at the neck, the November night pleasantly warm with a slight wind blowing from the sea. The count-down was on. If everything went well the first of the two gigantic rockets would take off in two hours' time. There had to be two of them, one for an emergency. Both would be put in orbit around the Earth, engineers would strip away the outer covering – the sardine tin as they called it – and both would be given thorough final tests. If both passed these tests then he supposed that some committee or other would spend a half-day deciding which was to be used for the actual flight. Both would not be used, for one must be kept in reserve in case of a disaster. He had driven out from the launching area to get away from the rising tension. It was an amazing phenomenon, some ten thousand men – engineers, electricians, electronics experts, service personnel, scientists and mathematicians – all of them gripped by one single complex of thoughts, the launching. Not a single one of

them could think outside that pattern. Not even to save
their lives. If danger was to threaten, men would risk their
lives without even knowing that they were doing so. Conway decided that it must have been a bit like this in the old
battles. It was a common thought process that simply took
charge and directed a man towards an end that was not his
own personal one. Conway shivered as he wondered whether
it would ever be possible to control in a pre-directed way
these cooperative thought structures. They grew only by
chance now, by trial, sometimes they developed, like this
launching business, and sometimes they didn't – but suppose you could control whether they developed or not. Then
you really would have an ant-heap. He turned round and
looked towards the aura of light where the work was now
going on. Was there any real difference between an ant-
heap and what was going on over there?

Conway drove back to the control area. Up to a certain
point the lights ahead of him seemed to brighten, but after
a certain stage, through some physiological quirk, they
appeared to reach a constant level, even though he was
drawing nearer to them all the time. He could now see the
lights glinting on the thousand-foot-high metallic outer
casing of the first rocket. He glanced briefly at his watch.
Within little more than an hour this great flashing needle
would be streaming upwards on the first stage of its
journey into space. He braked the car to a standstill by
the roadside and got out for a moment to stare across at
the thing.

Could one doubt that this was a magnificent achievement? It was a question that Conway had often asked himself before. He had never been able to give a satisfactory
reply, and now as he looked across at the shining streak of
light, still three miles away, he found himself as far away as
ever from an answer.

When you came down to the bare bones of it there was no
denying that here was a magnificent expression of the
abilities of the human race. It wasn't just the ideas, it was

the organization too. Then why somewhere deep in himself did he revolt against it? Perhaps he himself had a malfunction. He knew that that was what the psychologists thought about him. He knew that in the files he was said to be badly adjusted and unstable, he knew that no one at the top would take the slightest notice of any sociological pronouncements he might make. They would listen to him on technical issues, but that figured. It was well known that a brain suffering from abnormality was more likely than the normal to show streaks of brilliance. In fact it was well known that thorough analysis of the lives of all those whom Conway himself would have placed as great men showed them up as socially sick men. Perhaps they were right and perhaps they were not. Perhaps it was an attempt of little men of small consequence to devalue their betters.

This in a way was the root of the matter. It was really the contrast between the frenzied importance that was attached to this rocket here, and the systematic devaluation of achievements of comparable magnificence when they happened to come from one or two people. For the great achievement by an individual was always harder to understand and conceive of and to appreciate, whereas this rocket business was obvious to everybody. It was really the mentality of the society that had produced the thing, rather than the thing itself, to which he objected. It was because they did it all so seriously. The decision to go to Achilles had been taken as a matter of policy, not of adventure. Policy should never have been allowed to cross the threshold into the world of ideas.

Somehow it was all there in the things that were around him now. The millions of kilowatts that were being burned in the launching-field away to the west, the glint of metal in the distance, the smell of gasoline from the road, the beer cans that also glinted near his feet, and the star Helios that was now rising to the east. Soon it would dim the lights of the launching-field.

The guard checked very carefully through Conway's

papers – he couldn't understand why anyone with Conway's priority status wouldn't be already on the field.

'You're kinda late, aren't you, sir?' he asked.

'It's not due up for another hour or more, is it?'

The guard shrugged and allowed him to go on. Conway wondered how in the middle of all this hysteria they managed to get the damned thing off the ground at all.

He parked and walked very deliberately towards the spot where he knew the senior engineers would be assembled. When he found Cadogan he saw that the burly Californian was in one hell of a temper. Conway would have given heavy odds that Cadogan was suffering from a bad headache. He couldn't understand why, for the development engineers had long since been out of the active side of the job. First it was the turn of the development engineers, then of the production team, and now, at the actual launching itself, of the operational engineers. Cadogan wasn't allowed even the slightest of decisions at this stage. Perhaps that was what was making him mad.

Conway turned away lest they should see him grinning in the grey light that now suffused the whole area. The pattern was consistent, the way every profession despised the others. The theoreticians, the chaps who worked with mathematics on paper, despised them all. The observers and experimentalists despised the engineers, and the development engineers despised every other form of engineer, and so on along the whole chain. Yet society couldn't get along for five minutes without the whole bunch of them. It was really that they were all like children, perplexed and apprehensive of what they didn't understand.

'How about a drink?' he asked Cadogan.

'Best idea we've heard around here.'

'What'll it be?'

'Straight Scotch.'

It took Conway ten minutes to find the bar, and he had to assure the bartender that the drinks were not for anyone on ops. He carried them back across the compound in a small hand refrigerator. He glanced at his watch. Cathy would be in New York by now, probably dining somewhere about West Forty-seventh Street. He wished he had doubled the size and strength of his drink.

In place of the electronic signals coming over the loud-speakers a human voice began to count off the last seconds. A flicker of light developing instantly into a ring of fire appeared at the base of the rocket. As always, Conway had the sickening feeling that it was never going to move. It seemed to stand there for an eternity. When he had almost given up hope it began to move very slowly upwards. Suddenly it accelerated away from them leaving a patch of yellow flame in the sky. It seemed a miracle that such an enormous thing could be moved without toppling over.

The roar lessened to a less painful level. They waited without moving, dreading that the speakers might announce some malfunction. But when the announcement came it was to say that the ship was already in orbit; it was in the right orbit, and within an hour the team of five hundred engineers would be stripping away the now obsolete outer casing. Conway looked once again towards Helios, but only for a flash. For although Helios was not overly bright, he knew that if he looked at that fiercely blue point of light for too long it would burn out a spot on his retina.

None of them had eaten, so they made their way to the restaurant. They began by ordering a long row of ice-cold double Martinis.

'God, how I hate that old-fashioned chemical stuff,' said Cadogan. 'I was all goose-pimples as it went up.'

'It's a pity one of the old-timers couldn't have seen it,' someone said.

'That's right. They didn't know what they were starting.'

By morning the whole world knew that both the first rocket and the second reserve were safely in their parking orbits. Fawsett and Cathy heard it over breakfast.

'How long does that mean we've got?' she asked.

'Another day, Baby.' He saw Cathy wince and realized that his transatlantic switch was a mistake.

'I don't know exactly when we shall be taking off, but certainly within three or four days after that.'

'But why can't they tell you when you'll be taking off?'

This was the sort of question that Cathy was always asking. It defied an answer, it was the way that things were done.

'They'll be giving us our final briefing.'

'But they've been briefing you, or whatever it is they do to you, for months now, haven't they?'

Mike sighed, 'Well, something unexpected might have turned up.'

'But it hasn't. I don't see why you shouldn't go straight to the place. I do if I want to go anywhere.'

Fawsett really couldn't see either, but he knew he wasn't going to start breaking new ground now. Besides, he was doubtful if he could stand up to another three days with Cathy. He found himself wondering how Conway managed it.

'Well, we'd better make the best use of the time we've got,' she said.

By now he was coming to realize that Cathy was using him, not the other way round. It had never happened to him before. He began to wonder how it came about that her marriage to Conway seemed to go on and on for ever without breaking up.

'We could always have stayed in bed,' he said.

'You said there wasn't any breakfast service. So we had to get up,' answered Cathy, taking a long drink of orange juice. He noticed that whereas she had an aversion to fattening foods she always managed to maintain a hearty appetite. This seemed typical of her.

'I'm ready now.'

He felt it would be unmanly and unmasculine not to lead the way back to the bed. But when they got there it was she who pulled him down on to her. With her arms round his neck she whispered, 'We must get the most out of every single minute, darling.'

The light was greying dawn. During the night there had been an early snowfall. For the most part the flakes had simply melted as they reached the ground, except that there were two inches of wet brownish slush everywhere along the side of the pavements. Mike slowly dressed himself. He had about two hours before he must report. And he had a head-ache, not the thick fuzzy headache of a hang-over either. Cathy was still sleeping peacefully. He moved about the room making more noise than he need have done. Still she slept on, almost without moving. God, he thought, does she do nothing but eat, sleep, and fornicate.

If Cathy had been awake and if she could have read his thoughts, she would have told him that if one wanted to be vulgar there were words that one could use more tastefully. And she might have added, if she had managed to formulate the thought, that in a man's world what else was there for a woman to do.

Eventually he shook her by the shoulders. When she opened her eyes they were quite blank for a moment. Then they seemed to focus, she put her arms around him and said, 'Oh, Mike.'

'No, no, not now, Sugar.'

This made her let him go.

'I've got to move very soon. I wanted to say good-bye.'

The thought that Mike really had to go rushed in upon Cathy. She jumped quickly out of bed and cried, 'I'll have my clothes on in a moment.'

Again he took her by the shoulders, 'No, for God's sake, no. I hate that sort of good-bye. Let's make it now, here.'

Cathy's face was alive with emotion, 'Promise me Mike, promise me that you'll come back safely.'

As if he could promise anything of the sort, as if he wouldn't do his damnedest to come back. 'It's all going to be very simple. You know I've been out there scores of times before.'

'But this isn't really the same, is it Mike?'

'It isn't exactly the same, but it's the same sort of thing. It's going to be maraschino cherry,' he added.

She clung to him at the door, and there were tears in her eyes as he waved across to her from inside the elevator. On the way down he knew that Cathy had not been acting a part. It was just that she was – well, he'd better face it – a bit physical. It was a cold, raw morning outside. A lousy morning to be beginning such an adventure, and he still had the headache.

Cathy sat for perhaps an hour after he had gone, staring vacantly in front of her. Then she went to her bag and found to her relief that she hadn't forgotten her little red address book. She found the number and began one of her usual battles with the telephone company. It worked out all right in the end; eventually she was put through to Hugh, 'Can you meet me if I come down today?' she asked.

Conway used every ounce of influence he could muster to find a good place near Miami. His luck was in, a friend turned out to be a friend of the President of Reactors Incorporated, who had a bungalow on a private strip of beach. The key to it was sent down to the rocket base by helicopter. It was mid-afternoon when he met Cathy at the Miami airport. As usual she kissed him as if absolutely nothing had happened. In the car she moved across the seat towards him. It seemed incredible but she really behaved as if she had forgotten the whole business. When they reached the bungalow he took a shower and then busied himself mixing drinks. He found Cathy outside, changed into slacks and a shirt, sitting in a deckchair looking down at the slope of the beach towards the sea. 'It's nice to be here,' she said, 'it was horribly cold and wet in New York.'

They kept them waiting around for the best part of two days. There was absolutely nothing for them to do at the assembly sector, except to drink endlessly, and to talk about the girls they'd spent the last two days with. Reinbach had spent them with an actress in her cabin on Malibu Beach. She'd been hot stuff, but not quite so hot as she thought she was. Still, he hadn't had a bad time, not when he reckoned what they were in for, except that he'd had to go into some big surf to pull out a young kid and had got himself a belly full of salt water, which he could still taste in his mouth. Larson had spent his leave with a couple of sisters and made a big point of the need for recovery. The first day he slept for fifteen hours, the second day he did three sessions in the gymnasium. Fiske and Fawsett were more reticent. Fiske had been with his girl from the Rand Corporation. She had tried to pressure him into marriage, having a shrewd suspicion that he was an easier proposition now than he would be on his return. When he pointed out that there was a rule against married men she said they could get married secretly. But Fiske wasn't falling for that one at this stage of the game. He wasn't going to risk losing at the last round. Mike listened to the chatter about girls, said as little as he could, and thought that they didn't know what they were talking about.

After the fourth Scotch, the night before take-off, he suddenly had a big idea. It would be worth millions if he could exploit it – just his luck to be off into space at this moment. For he'd discovered the secret of sex appeal. When you considered what girls were willing to pay to cosmetic manufacturers, mere pedlars of daubs and rose-water, what would they be prepared to pay for the real thing? The trouble was that the real answer was too simple, once you saw it it was obvious. He realized it from thinking about Cathy. What was it that made it for her? Her looks – yes, partly. But even without her looks she'd still have been dynamite. It was this that gave him the answer. Sex appeal wasn't a mysterious quality, a subtle alchemical conjuring trick, it came just from being interested in sex, as simple as that, genuinely interested in sex. A pretence, however cunningly disguised, could never compete with the real thing. This cleared up a point that had always puzzled him.

He'd often wondered why so many of his friends with the marriages that worked best were married to quite plain girls. He saw it now. The plain girls had discovered the same answer.

The space shuttle had them out in orbit in half an hour. Several hours' manoeuvring followed as they made small corrections to their orbit. The idea was to bring them alongside the ship that was to carry them into the depths of space. It is strange to recall how the first orbits of the Earth, around the year 1960, were greeted with world-wide excitement. For now not one of the four astronauts deigned even to look outside. Larson, the leader, was concerned with a mass of official papers, Reinbach and Fawsett read paper-backed novels, while Fiske concerned himself with the sporting press. Yet when they were brought alongside, all four crowded to the viewing tube.

'Boy, what a beaut,' muttered Fiske. And a beaut she was, sleek and powerful, ready at a touch to hurl them on their journey towards the unknown planet.

The Russians waited until it was known that the four astronauts were safely transferred to the big ship before announcing that their own ship had already been in flight towards Helios for two days. The West groaned, and earnest commentators on the television networks assured viewers that the East had scored yet another propaganda victory; they were always ahead.

Actually the Russians had had their difficulties. The inclusion of Ilyana in the party was all very well at the stage when everything was on paper. It was a useful goad for pricking the capitalist warmongers of the West. But as the project took shape and neared completion it was gradually borne in on the Russian planners that they really were committed to sending a woman into space – and on the most difficult and hazardous journey that had yet been attempted. The mathematicians demonstrated very plainly that any withdrawal would lose more ground than had been gained by the original trick. So Ilyana had to go. When the matter was referred to the engineers they made light of it. After all, it would be possible to take the girl out to orbit under quite low acceleration. This could easily be done in a specially designed transit vehicle. It wouldn't be a bad idea to take Pitoyan that way too for he wasn't a professional either. The accelerations of the main ship as it moved away from its parking orbit around the Earth would in any case be quite gentle. The only dicey part would be the actual landing on Achilles, and Ilyana would simply have to take her chance. Nobody in Moscow would have dreamt that Ilyana was to come out of that particular episode rather better than the others.

A small, but not negligible, advantage was to be had from leaving the parking orbit quite quickly, at a moment when the direction in the orbit was parallel to the Earth's motion around the Sun. This meant that a fairly powerful acceleration had to be used, in fact as powerful as the reactor motors could reasonably stand without risks being taken. Both Pitoyan and Ilyana had had a rather bad passage during this phase. When it was over, but while they were still feeling groggy, Pitoyan was rather annoyed by the excessive attention that Kratov and Bakovsky were giving to their female colleague. He consoled himself with the thought that, once recovered, he should have little difficulty in cutting out such a pair of corn-growers.

Bakovsky set the ship on a slowly ascending climb out of the plane of the planetary orbits. Helios was not moving in that plane, so it was essential to move upwards at about 45° in order to make the interception at the right point, at the right point if they were ever to be able to return safely, that is to say. Pitoyan quickly recovered his self-respect by checking that the course had been correctly set. This was his line of business, and the others acknowledged it.

Ilyana had been thrilled by the sight of the Earth as they had moved up to their parking orbit. She had made a tape recording, in pleasant flowing terms, describing it all. The tape was returned to Moscow where tens of thousands of copies were made. These were sent out, throughout the length and breadth of the Russo-Chinese Union. They were played in schools to earnest-faced children, children who spent the summer herding goats in Uzbekistan, to slant-eyed children on the river Lena, and to girls with pigtails in Odessa. Ilyana was very proud.

The Earth had looked very beautiful as it receded away from them, now it was a rather small distant disc. Ilyana spent many hours at the viewer, entranced by the beauties of the colours and by the ever-changing patterns. She watched a storm developing in the Atlantic and wondered whether the effects would reach as far as Moscow. On the dark side of the Earth she could see the lights of cities, and this sent shivers down her back. It was improper to think it, but she couldn't help thinking it – of all the things that were going on in those cities, of how important the Earth seemed to the people down there, and of how little it looked in the tele-scope – no bigger than a firefly. She thought it was rather like being a god to look down on it, and then despised her-self for such bourgeois thoughts.

She liked it when the region of her birth around Kiev came into view, and was exasperated that the picture was not a great deal clearer. Pitoyan told her that it was the refracting effect of the Earth's own atmosphere, and this of course was correct. She knew she would have a bit of trouble with Pitoyan. Not that that would have mattered very much in itself, but it would upset the other two, whom she thought of as being very nice and sweet and rather harmless.

It was also fascinating to look at Mars and Venus, and Jupiter and Saturn. It was true that she had seen them just as well in books, but somehow it seemed infinitely more exciting actually to see the planets. Everywhere it was black except that the stars shone as beautiful points of light. Along the Milky Way there was an endless carpet of star-dust. It reminded her of childhood stories, of the diamonds in the

Tsar's palace. But the Sun seemed alive, she could see things wriggling on its surface like snakes. She saw the lances of the corona as they streamed out many millions of miles into space and felt an overwhelming fear of the relentless tongues of flame.

Pitoyan found that things were not as easy as he had expected. He had thought that there would be lots of times when Kratov and Bakovsky would both be thoroughly and soundly asleep. But the way it turned out the lights were always on, and there always seemed to be someone thoroughly awake. The situation was impossible, the opportunities nil. What Pitoyan had not reckoned on was Popkin's Theorem. All this had been taken account of in the calculations. And Popkin was perfectly right, the amount of talk on sex in the Russian rocket was absolutely nil in contrast to that in the American rocket, now two and a half days behind.

They were travelling at this time at about thirty kilometres per second. This meant a distance of about two million miles a day, so that the Russians were some five million miles ahead. But there was still a very long way to go. It was like winning the first couple of matches in the baseball season. It meant little or nothing.

To both rockets there was a constant flow of information and of questions from Earth. The time for a message to get through was still only about a couple of minutes. Later on, when the time would widen to about eight hours, they would have far more privacy. Only genuinely important information would then be sent.

140175

Chapter Eight

150175

The Voyage

For the most part the messages were concerned with technical data, but there were also more personal messages – what was the crew eating, how were they sleeping, how did they manage to occupy the time. It had all been gone into a score of times before, but the public wanted to know about it again, especially since for the first time a woman was in space. The bulletins concerning Ilyana swept the headlines. When it turned out that her pulse counts, her electrocardiogram, and so on were entirely normal, there was an outcry from women's organizations all over the globe, particularly from the United States. They asked why a woman had not been sent into space before. Governments disdained to answer this question, for there really was no answer to it.

The public maintained its interest for as long as the public is capable of maintaining interest in anything at all, that is to say, about ten days. Interest waned and withered and was replaced by the remarkable story of a gorilla living with a harem of human women in the Massif Central of France. Investigation failed to reveal any gorilla, but it did reveal the existence of three good restaurants, the proprietor of which was a very smart businessman from Paris.

The four professionals in the Western rocket spent no time gazing at the star-dust along the Milky Way. They went about their business with a slow unhurried precision. They too set their ship on an inclined path up from the plane of the solar system. Just as the basic design of both was the same, so they moved along nearly parallel paths. It was true that the slight divergence might carry them a few tens of millions of miles apart, but this was only a small fraction of the total length of their journey, which was to be measured in thousands of millions of miles.

Life in the ships was almost indescribably inactive. There was of course the routine checking of instruments, the preparation of the messages to be sent back to Earth and the reception and interpretation of incoming messages, the careful checking of themselves – heartbeats and the like – but this took only a small fraction of the twenty-four hours of each day. By the standards of the first space-craft they were luxuriously housed, but by any terrestrial standard they were packed like peas in a pod. It was here that one of the two essential qualities of the long-trip man showed itself. The first necessity was the obvious one, of being able to take big accelerations, of being able to take a physical beating, and still react quickly at the end of it. The second was in some ways more difficult, simply to lie there for weeks on end, in this case for months on end, doing nothing. It was even worse than being a prisoner of war in the old days, for there was no compound to trot round for a bit of exercise. For the most part a man didn't talk to his companions but just lay there reading, thinking, sleeping, or resting with a vacant mind. The ability to keep quiet was an absolute must for any long-distance astronaut. One chatterer in a ship and you'd had it, either you throttled him and chucked him out into space, or in a couple of months you were all prime for the nut-house. You spoke either in monosyllables or else tersely in highly-developed space slang. Exceptionally, Larson and his crew did in fact do a certain amount of talking from time to time, their subject being the inevitable one, the presence of Ilyana in the Russian rocket. Their visions of what must be happening there were lurid in the extreme. They cursed their own authorities at some length for not having the same idea. It was the best idea since the old chemical fuels went out.

Actually the situation in the Russian rocket was becoming more tense. Gradually the tiny container became the whole world, became the whole universe. The combine-harvesters sweeping across the landscape of his native steppes now seemed much less real to Kratov; the great crowds in Red Square began to evaporate in the mind of Nuri Bakovsky. The effect of the pounding and kneading that their personalities had received almost from birth was perceptibly weakening. They began to cast covert glances at Ilyana. At first they felt guilty about it. Nothing such as the Americans were imagining was taking place, but the tension was building up. Popkin, if he could have been there as an unseen observer, would have had less confidence in his Theorem.

The rockets had been on their outward journey for about a month when the first slightly disturbing incident took place. A burst of radio waves was detected from the Helios system. There was a major scare on Earth.

It was generated in the following way. The radio waves were first detected at the European Radio Astronomy Centre in the Aosta Valley north of Milan. The science correspondent of the Parisian newspaper *Le Figaro* happened to be there at the time and heard about it over lunch. Within an hour he was in Milan phoning through to his friends in all the major capitals. Radiating from the capitals, telephone lines were set tingling to a score of internationally-famous scientists, some of whom made the mistake of answering the phone. They were told that a burst of radio waves had been picked up from Achilles. What did they think of that?

The news was so shattering that most of them answered the question instead of slamming the receiver down. Conway said it was bad and that he didn't like it at all; others expressed much the same opinion. Within a couple of hours it was on the news-stands everywhere throughout the world. Conway had just time to see his name in large type before he received a call from officialdom. An angry voice told him that the radio burst wasn't from Achilles at all, it was from the star Helios. But it was a good scare whilst it lasted.

Conway kicked himself for being so foolish as to fall into

such a silly trap. Over the hundred years during which Helios had been intensively observed there had been three comparatively short periods, of a year or two each, during which the star had become a strong emitter of radio waves. It started with the emission of a few isolated bursts, but then the bursts became more frequent until they overlapped each other. At this stage there was a continuous roar of radio noise from Helios that had proved a most serious nuisance to radio astronomy. Then after a while the bursts became less frequent, they no longer overlapped each other, and gradually the whole thing died away. It was obvious that Helios was running into another of these episodes.

Over the last hundred years more information had been accumulated about Helios than was available for any star, except of course the Sun. The mass was fifty-two per cent greater than that of the Sun and the brightness was almost ten times greater – Helios being not only more massive but more evolved, as the astronomers said. This meant that, whereas the Sun had a future of about eight billion years in front of it, the future of Helios was limited to about one billion years. But long before that time was over, perhaps after only another five hundred million years, any animal life that existed on Achilles would be fried to a crisp. It had occurred to Conway, as well as to the military planners, that any such animal life – if it was in a position to do so – might consider that a switch of planets would be advantageous. But does one bother about what is going to happen a few hundred million years hence?

Because it was more evolved Helios was not quite as blue in colour as it would otherwise have been. The effective temperature at its surface was about 6,500°, which meant that the maximum of its spectrum fell in the green region, not in the yellow as with the Sun. Helios was a blue-green star and Achilles was a green planet. The distance of Achilles from its star had of course to be considerably greater than the distance of the Earth from the Sun, otherwise everything on Achilles would already have been fried to a crisp anyway. The much greater brightness of Helios would have seen to that. In fact the whole system was just a little bigger than the solar system in every respect. Its planets were just that bit more spread out. It was as if the scale of our own system was rather more than doubled, as if the orbit of the Earth were moved somewhere out beyond Mars. It wasn't at all a big change, our own system could easily have been like it. But then the Earth would have been much too cold. The oceans would have been permanently frozen and, instead of plant growth covering the rocks, the land masses would have been grey, black, and brown. That is at the present stage of course. Eventually the Sun would evolve; it would get hotter; and a time would come when even a more distant Earth would warm up until the waters melted and life might begin in the resulting slime.

But if the burst of radio waves from Helios had not signalled the presence of little men with antennae, it did create a difficult problem indeed. The West had gambled, apparently unjustifiably, on a more or less constant interval of thirty years between these seizures of the star. The last one had been nineteen years earlier. So it had looked as though the next wouldn't happen until Helios had swept on its way past the solar system. Yet here it was, beginning again after only nineteen years, and this was extremely awkward. The noise emissions would jam the messages from the spaceships back to Earth. There was no problem to begin with, there was still a large angle between the directions of the ships and the direction of Helios, but later on the angles would become much less – not much more than 3°. The difficulty arose in the transmission from the ships to the Earth, not the other way round. This could be serious because, unless the ships could signal through their precise positions, speeds, and directions of motion, the appropriate orbits could not be worked out by the terrestrial computers. Then it was more than doubtful whether they would be able to navigate themselves through the tricky gravitational fields.

The authorities did their best to keep these issues hidden. But in the West secrecy can only be kept if a very large number of people are willing to keep it. Except where dire punishment can be enforced, a large number of people are never willing to keep a secret, not with enterprise the key-note of success. There was an almighty hoo-ha when at last somebody blew it.

Nobody of course could be blamed for the behaviour of Helios. But the Western administration could be blamed for not showing the same foresight as the Russians in sending a scientist on the voyage. There was more than a chance that, whereas the Western rocket would go astray or be forced to return empty-handed, Pitoyan would be able to work himself through the difficulties. People fumed to think that the Russians had done it again. It was clear that Lee and Marty Kipling would not win the next election.

At first sight one might wonder why any jamming at all should occur. After all, the big dishes, the ten-thousand-foot dish in the Aosta valley, for instance, would be pointed towards the ship, not towards the star. There should be 3° or more between the directions of the ship and the star, so why any jamming? This was the question that the committees wanted a clear answer to.

They got an answer, but to them at least it wasn't clear – sidelobes. Nobody could quite understand this. It was pointed out that if a telescope was pointed at an object, one simply did not see things that were three degrees away. The scientists said this was perfectly right, but that radio waves weren't the same as seeing things. The answer came back that committee members had always thought light and radio waves to be really aspects of the same thing. Were the technicians trying now to say that this was not so? The technicians said that it was so, but that the frequency of radio waves was not the same as for light and this made all the difference. Indeed the same phenomenon did exist for ordinary light but normally it was too small to be noticed. There was a big difference due to the frequency and of

course due to a profusion of star-spots on Helios. It was all a
question of sidelobes. The word became bandied about the
corridors of power – after all, an election depended on the
darned things, whatever they were – these sidelobes.

The big question was what were they going to do about
it. The problem of the sidelobes had simply got to be licked.
The cost was irrelevant. The committees became irritated
and appalled by the dunderheads of scientists who claimed
that the problem just couldn't be solved. It didn't matter
what you were willing to pay – it still couldn't be solved.
That seemed incredible.

Then at last it all boiled down to there being one slight
loophole. A dish of thirty thousand feet would be about ten
times better than the present ten-thousand-footer in the
Vale of Aosta. This might help, although the engineers
pointed out that unless a bigger dish could be made with
the same precision as the present ones as much would be
lost as would be gained. This also seemed incredible but
there it was. Orders were given for the instant construction
of a super-S dish. Cost was immaterial. Conway nattered
and raved about it. 'Can't the fools see they can't win this
way,' he stormed. 'A gain of ten will be useless. The blasted
star is bound to win out. They'd need a million-footer to
beat it.'

Nothing was said to Larson and his crew. There was no
point in upsetting them – sufficient unto the day is the evil
thereof. So the flight went inexorably on. For every second
that the committee men talked, for every second that the
constructional engineers worked at the monstrous new project, the ships moved another thirty miles towards their
destination.

The situation was tense indeed in the Russian rocket. It
was being temporarily stabilized by Pitoyan, who had to
switch from his former tactics and play the part of the dis-
interested party man. He let the other fellows see that he
disapproved of their glances at the girl's legs. He studiously

looked the other way whenever she undressed. His unspoken chiding served to return Kratov and Bakovsky to within the perimeter of their training. Such feedback effects among the psychological currents had been correctly foreseen by Popkin.

George Larson and Uli Reinbach were on a sleeping jag. It sometimes happened on a long trip that the sheer void in your own mind caught up on you. Then you would sleep maybe for a week at a time. In fact you'd quite likely just go on sleeping and sleeping unless there was someone there to waken you. They'd all have gone to sleep endlessly if it hadn't been for the small sounds that were artificially generated in their cabin. The utter silence of space did that for you. Before the effect of the silence, and of the long wait, became well known, there had been cases of whole crews drifting into a hypnotic sleep. There had been bad tragedies, failures to correct orbits at the right moment and of ships passing for ever out of the solar system, ships that would continue to hurtle through the void for as long as the Galaxy itself should last. That was why Mike Fawsett and Tom Fiske remained awake while the two others slept. There always had to be two of you awake, just in case one should go to sleep. It was a danger that they knew all about and, being professionals, they knew how to deal with it.

Mike Fawsett was filling the latest details on micrometeorites into the log-book. There were instruments on the outside of the rocket that detected an occasional impact of these very tiny solid particles. They were still to be found around them, even though they were well up from the plane of the solar system. One good feature of being up here was that it cut out the risk of being hit by a great chunk of rock. This was always a worry when you were down in the plane, on a run past Jupiter, especially when in the asteroidal belt, which consisted of chunks of rock resulting from the original break-up of asteroids. The particles that they were getting now came, very likely, from comets which moved as much out of the plane as they did in it. Mike wasn't thinking very much about it all, however. He was thinking what an idiot he'd been not to make absolutely the most of his week-end with Cathy. He remembered something in Shakespeare but he couldn't quite recall the exact words – it was something about being cloyed with a surfeit of sweetness. Well, he could do with a bit of sweetness now. Tom Fiske was thinking much the same thoughts as he read through the latest message from Earth. But then the message caught his attention.

'Scan this,' he said to Fawsett.

The message read: 'Return if difficulties encountered. Stop, repeat stop. Correct orbit uncertain. Return, repeat return at your discretion.'

Mike read it through twice and he still couldn't understand it. For the past two or three weeks they'd been getting messages that were all a bit off-centre. It was as though nobody down there was taking any notice of what they said, as if they weren't receiving transmissions from the ship.

Mike made a series of checks on their bearings. It wasn't very difficult out here on any of a thousand of the distant stars that stared unwinkingly from the black depths. It seemed as if they were trying to read into the innermost corners of the mind. After being brought up on the Earth, after looking at stars that twinkled in a friendly way, this steady glare was disconcerting. It was rather like eyes without lids. One never got used to it.

The stellar bearings checked with those of the gyros. There was nothing the matter with their course. Mike had had the idea that perhaps they'd somehow got themselves exactly on to the line joining Helios to the Earth. Then it wouldn't have been surprising if the terrestrial receivers had been unable to pick them up against the background of the star. But everything was perfectly O.K. They were a good two and a half degrees outside that line.

He decided to do something they should have done weeks ago, to turn the aerials round towards Helios instead of towards the Earth. Of course they had kept a close watch out for all forms of flare activity and of the emission of streams of particles, but it had never occurred to any of them to worry about radio emission, not while they were receiving Earth. They hadn't bothered to do this before because they expected only meaningless noise.

The receiver saturated instantly. There was no gain setting low enough to stop it overloading. So Mike quickly turned the aerials off the star. This was the source of the trouble, although like the committees he couldn't see why. They woke Larson and Reinbach. Once he'd washed down a couple of pills with a glass of water and once he'd understood what it was all about, Larson began to swear steadily.

'It means we blueblooded well can't make it,' he ended.

'We could try,' said Fiske.

They all sat silently for quite a while. Each man knew what a 'try' would mean. It would mean they'd lose momentum, and in correcting their mistakes they'd waste fuel. The margin of safety was small enough as it was. If they wasted twenty per cent of their momentum drive they couldn't get back to Earth.

'There's two things to be done,' began Larson at last. 'We try for it, and maybe we lose twenty kilometres a second. All right, then we can just park around the job instead of going down on to it. That'll save us what we lose. Or we can go right ahead and down and make land. Then we don't get back. But we can get back far enough for our fellows to find us, once this scintillator has gotten itself out of the way.'

They thought about it for a while. That was the way it would be on a normal trip. But one of the things that had been hammered into them during the months of training was the danger of judging by past experience. The difficulty was that the gravitational fields changed faster than you moved. What looked like the right orbit now would turn out to be the wrong one by the time you got there. None of them was very clear as to why this was so, but they'd been put through tests of exactly this sort, tests in which they were asked to guess orbits in advance and in which they'd been completely fooled. In their hearts they knew that it would be easy to lose, not just twenty kilometres of momentum, but the whole of their fuel supply. It would be dead easy to find themselves attached to Helios instead of to the Sun at the end of it all and for them to be swept out of the solar system altogether.

An odd idea was forming in Mike's head.

'We could always contact the Russes,' he began. 'They've got a boff and a computer in their job. Why couldn't they compute our orbit for us?'

'Jesus, we'd never hear the last of it,' said Reinbach wiping his face. 'They'd radio straight through to Earth and we'd be for the plank when we got back. It would be better to turn back right now.'

'They can't radio back to Earth,' answered Fawsett. 'They'll have the same trouble as we have.'

'That's true too,' acknowledged Larson. 'They couldn't say anything until afterwards, and I reckon afterwards will be too late.'

They pondered this for a while. There was a lot in it. Face-saving and face-losing is a game in which correct timing is absolutely essential. The master stroke of today looks old hat by tomorrow.

'They could always give us the wrong orbit,' grunted Larson.

'That's a problem we can come to when we reach it. We haven't got the orbit yet.'

'And I'd say there wasn't much chance of them giving us it.'

'Well, we can't do any harm by trying. What do you say?'

They decided after talking it out to try to raise Earth once more. If that failed then they'd make their appeal to the Russians.

Pitoyan had some difficulty in deciphering the message from the Americans.

The appeal for help didn't surprise him at all because they had already had information from Earth that communications were not being received. The very frankness of the Russians on this point can be regarded in the light of self-congratulation, emphasizing that no matter how far the unexpected might arise they would still be masters of the situation.

Pitoyan's prestige had of course risen enormously. Without him the rocket could not reach its destination. Previously he had merely represented a measure of safety, of insurance, but now everything turned on his knowledge and skill in calculating the orbit ahead of them. And now the Euro-American capitalists had been obliged to turn to him for help. This impressed and overwhelmed Kratov and Bakovsky more than anything else could do. To them, as to all ordinary Russians, the West was a fairyland, steeped in delicious vice. To keep up their self-respect Kratov and Bakovsky still continued to send back their diurnal messages towards Earth. To Pitoyan this was futile and ridiculous, and he felt himself now to be the effective leader of the expedition.

Pitoyan felt like ten men when he awoke. He awoke because Ilyana's hair was tickling his nose. He dressed quickly in order not to excite the suspicions of Kratov and Bakovsky. Then he turned to his work with a zest. It was just because of this that two days later an orbit was sent out from the Russian ship and was received some two minutes later by Tom Fiske.

There was really nothing that the Euro-Americans could do but accept the orbit as it was given to them. They set their ship on the prescribed course and determined to keep the strictest possible check on future developments. It had surprised them a little to be given the complete orbit. They'd expected the Russians to give them only the starting speed and direction. This way they'd have a better chance of checking that the Russos weren't up to any tricks. It didn't occur to them that as far as tricks were concerned they were thinking along quite the wrong lines.

By now they were about equidistant between Helios and the Sun. When Conway had gazed at the star across the gasoline-tainted pavements of Florida it had seemed a small, distant, blue-grey disc. But now it was clear which star was really the monarch of the skies. The Sun was a dull faint orange disc. One of the most frightening things about these long distance trips was the way in which the Sun faded into comparative insignificance. In comparison, Helios was a brilliant object projected against a black sky. It is a matter of some difficulty to know what colour one should call it. One might say that the Sun is white and Helios a white steely-blue, but the human eye is a most primitive colour-measuring device. In fact Helios shone out a magnificent turquoise blue.

The weeks continued to pass, and the distant glittering disc imperceptibly grew larger and larger. Comparing one day with the next there seemed to be no change but gradually a new splendour emerged, of brilliance and light, of sparkle and of awe. As they moved into the Helios system the blazing ball in front of them was growing rapidly bigger, dramatically bigger. It was approaching the Sun's normal size but was apparently incomparably brighter. It is true that scientific instruments revealed the cold fact that it was only ten times brighter, but it didn't seem so to the now almost silent crews of the approaching ships. Its surface detail was almost indescribably complex. There were the crimson-red tongues of flame, prominences similar to those of the Sun but on a larger scale. These could be seen only at the limb where they lifted themselves hundreds of thousands and sometimes millions of miles above the surface of the star. The darker areas of the surface glowed orange almost like the surface of the Sun. These areas were quite small patches lying embedded in brilliant blue seas. For once they felt lucky to be cut off from communication with home, for they knew their words would be totally inadequate to describe what they saw. It was better to take films which would show things as they really were.

The accelerations of their ships were surprisingly gentle. There was none of the sound and fury of a take-off from Earth. They had to change speed by fifty kilometres per second, but since they had at least a couple of weeks to do this in they did not feel the gentle push that was bringing their motion into consonance with that of the Helios system. Below their feet the suspended reactors pulsed at a low level. The inert fuel was injected steadily along the cylinder walls, where it was heated into a sheet of rapidly streaming gas.

So far they had paid little attention to Achilles itself for it was still only a point of light. For a long time the outstanding planets were Hera and Semele. But now there came an inversion. Achilles was growing brighter than its rivals. This could mean only one thing. They were closing the distance. It was only at this stage that Larson and his crew became sure that they had not been sold down the river. It had always been possible that the orbit they were following was a false one. It had been hell waiting to know whether they were in the right orbit or in an orbit that would throw them back where they had just come from, in one that would leave them permanently attached to Helios, or in an orbit that would take them entirely out into space away from both stars. But now they knew that the Russians had played it square.

These days they were to be found more and more at the telescopic viewer. Achilles filled a good-sized television screen, and the image was reasonably clean. There were two overridingly dominant colours, orange and green. The strange thing was that although the picture was good they could still see no details. It wasn't that the atmosphere of Achilles was blocking their vision, as is the case for instance for the planet Venus, it was just as if there didn't seem to be any details. There were large green areas, and there were large orange areas. Occasionally they picked up a flash, however, and this they knew to be the reflection of sunlight in a liquid, almost certainly in water. Simple measurements now confirmed what was suspected about the mass and size of the planet. In conformity with the general pattern of the Helios system everything was just that bit bigger than in the solar system. The mass was one and a quarter times that of the Earth, and the radius was also a trifle larger. Gravity would be a bit greater than on Earth, but only slightly so, certainly not enough to be of the slightest worry to them.

The composition of the atmosphere they already knew pretty well. Almost twice the oxygen density of the Earth, a little less nitrogen, water vapour and carbon dioxide. And they said to themselves, they'd seen it all before. To men who had stood on the surface of the Moon and on Mars, it looked pretty good. As Reinbach said, 'If the Earth was like that it would just about be perfect.'

Larson moved over to the controls. Any fool could manage it now. He set the dials, checked them, pressed the re-set and, with gentle pressure from the main control lever, started the ship down towards its parking orbit.

Chapter Nine

The Landing

A difficulty about making a landing on any planet, which was not realized in early days of space flight, when everybody was only too keen to make a landing at all, was that you only get one bite at the cherry. If you put down at what turned out later to be the wrong place – well, then you'd had it. You couldn't simply blast off again and make a second try. It cost too much fuel. And an ordinary simple aeroplane, if you were to take the trouble to carry one with you, suffered in the same way – it needed too much fuel. But they did have very fine mobility machines. Machines that walked on eight great padded legs. They had been found enormously more serviceable on broken ground than caterpillar tractors. The first time down on a planet, or at a particular spot on a planet, was always a tricky matter. You never knew whether you were going to find yourself on steep mountain slopes or on hundreds of miles of soft quicksand. A combination of the two was the worst – quicksands lying on top of large boulders, and covering small rock precipices.

The range of their land vehicles again depended on fuel – not on the fuel they could carry in the rocket this time, but on how much each vehicle itself could carry. With a full load each vehicle had a range of about five hundred miles. This you could extend, perhaps to two thousand miles, by carefully laying a chain of dumps. It was rather like the methods used by the old polar explorers. You used big machines to carry supplies for smaller ones, and it was enormously wasteful and tedious. A more brilliant method was to lay the dumps already from the parking orbit. The rocket disgorged capsules containing fuel for the machines and food for the men, and oxygen too if that was needed, at regular intervals along its orbit. When it worked it was fine. But there was more than a chance that a capsule might burn up as it streaked like a meteorite into the atmosphere of the planet. And as the old explorers knew perfectly well, one failure along the chain of dumps was sufficient to cause disaster.

On an expedition such as this, far from home, away from any possible relief from Earth, the sensible thing was to choose a particular spot and not to attempt to explore more than a circular patch around that spot, say to a distance of five hundred miles. This meant they had to choose their landing place with care. If you were doing the same thing on the Earth you would obviously be unwise to put down in the middle of the Gobi Desert. Or on the tundras of Lapland. So when they got down into the parking orbit they were in no hurry to make their next move. They wanted to make quite a number of circuits of Achilles. This way they could be sure they hadn't missed all the interesting places. And they had plenty of time to debate which was the best spot.

By now the surface was only about three hundred miles below them. They had never seen anything remotely like it before. There just wasn't any detail, anywhere. The green areas faded smoothly into the orange. They knew now what these orange regions were. They were sandy lakes, mainly of about fifty miles in area. Their shapes were highly variable, some being more or less circular, others long and thin, some curved, and some straight like canals. In places they formed a huge series of interconnected pools. It was rather like the system of pools that one might see on a sandy beach immediately after a spring tide, except that these systems sometimes stretched for a thousand miles, the pools being laid out below them in a fantastic mosaic. These were obviously the oceans of Achilles. Probably they were not very deep, perhaps only a few hundred fathoms. There were clouds dotted below them like a patchwork quilt. They looked rather like strange ships sailing a vast series of land-locked lagoons.

The green areas worried them. They still couldn't tell what the darned stuff was. For one thing the green regions were unbroken, there were no outcrops of bare rock. In fact there didn't seem to be any outcrop of rock to be found any-where on the planet. This didn't mean there were no hills; their measurements showed them that there were rises and falls of as much as ten thousand feet. But the green stuff went over the tops just as smoothly as it covered the lower slopes. At first they had thought they were rain-forests. But at this distance the telescopic viewer would just about show up tall trees, and it didn't. And although they could see many places where rain was falling, there seemed to be nothing heavy enough to maintain a rain-forest. They decided it must be some sort of dense scrub. It looked as though it would be pretty well suited to the mobility machines.

By all the rules there should have been a sense of exalta-tion inside the rocket. But hour followed hour with the men almost silent. The trouble was that their training hadn't fitted them for anything like this. They had been trained to step out into a stark landscape, a landscape drenched per-haps by ultra-violet light and X-rays, an environment utterly hostile to human life. Here there was no reason why they shouldn't breathe naturally as they did on Earth. There was plenty of atmosphere, plenty of ozone to shield them from all damaging rays, blue as the star Helios was. They weren't used to this. It was too gentle. At each orbit they shifted their position somewhat, so that they would be able to take a look at the whole surface, to make sure that they hadn't missed something.

On the seventeenth circuit Reinbach, who was at the viewer, exclaimed, 'They're down.' Far below them they could see the gleaming needle of the Russian rocket.

'Why are the bastards always first, even when it doesn't

really matter. It would have been better if they'd waited,'
Fawsett muttered.

'Wow,' grinned Larson mirthlessly, 'it settles our problem
for us. We'll go in on the far side.'

That seemed the reasonable thing to do, then they'd each
have half of the planet to play with, exactly as they had on
Earth.

Their brief vision of the gleaming needle below them had
told the Westerners nothing of what had happened. It was
a remarkable indication of the technical equality of East and
West that the initial gap of two days, of some ten million
miles, had been maintained almost entirely throughout the
flight. Because Pitoyan had been a little more careful with
the orbit of his own ship than he had been with that of the
Westerners, the last stages of their route had been slightly
more economical. They had then widened their lead to
about five days. But they had taken up the best part of three
of them in orbiting Achilles. After their tenth revolution
these tactics began to seem unnecessary to Ilyana and Pitoyan. Pitoyan felt that now they'd seen a fair sample of what
was below them, and if it was a question of a decision it
would be best to throw a coin for it. Both he and Ilyana, in
spite of their diversions, were utterly weary of the journey.
It was like being on a ship moored a mile from land after a
long voyage. They were impatient to make a landing. But
Kratov and Bakovsky knew better. For all any of them knew
some creature down there might be waiting for them. Sooner
or later such a creature might make a false move, giving
itself away. So the two Army men maintained their un-
winking vigil at the scanner. The slightest flicker on it could
be important.

At wearisome last Bakovsky decided to go down. He insisted that Ilyana and Pitoyan, as amateurs, should strap
themselves down safely in their bunks before he set the ship
into its gentle downward glide. Pitoyan looked up from his
bunk at the cabin lights. He hadn't realized before how

much he'd come to hate them. In a minute or less the retro drive would come into action. They'd have to take the best part of ten kilometres a second on the retros. There could be no question of braking down through the atmosphere by friction, they couldn't make a fireball of the rocket, not with all the delicate equipment in it, necessary for the homeward trip. He didn't like the big drive, the drive that seemed to flatten him into a thin sheet of jelly. He was just aware that it was coming on – then his thoughts were abruptly cut off. This was the black-out, blacker than a black-out in fact.

Pitoyan was next aware of someone peering down into his face. His head pounded furiously and his body felt as if the drive were still on. But it couldn't be because nobody could be standing over him if the drive were still on. The mist cleared a little, and he could see, still rather vaguely, that it was the face of Bakovsky. He was aware that Bakovsky was undoing the straps that held him down to the bunk. He tried to move, but his right arm hurt him like hell; it pierced his nerve centres in spite of all the other aches that were being signalled to his brain. Now he could see that the whole cabin was a complete and utter shambles. Not a thing seemed to be where it should be. Incredible as it might seem there had been a crash. 'Kratov is dead,' muttered Bakovsky. The thought of Ilyana, that perhaps she was dead too, gripped him, and somehow he managed to struggle to his feet. His right arm hung limp at his side. He knew it must be broken. He knew why Kratov was dead. The body had been flung across the cabin and lay mutilated against the wall. He staggered towards Ilyana's bunk and heard her moan before he blacked out again.

When he came to his senses again the body had disappeared. The cabin was still closed to the outside, so somewhere along the corridor leading from the cabin into the interior of the rocket there must be a place for the dead. Then Pitoyan remembered that there had to be such a space morgue in case of accidents. It was a place where the body would be frozen, so that it could be returned to Earth for the medical people to look at. You weren't allowed to leave a body in space because the medical people might find out something from it. It wasn't like the old-time burial at sea. Almost irrationally Pitoyan wondered if the refrigerators were still working.

Then he remembered Ilyana. With a shock of relief he saw that the girl's eyes were open. And they were focused on him, not staring vacantly. 'Can you help me?' she whispered. The straps were undone, Bakovsky must have done that already. With his good arm he managed to help her to sit up. He had a horrible fear that he would see her limbs bent at some impossible angle. There was blood across her face and neck, but he realized that this was only from cuts which would heal. Her face was twisted in pain as she stood and made two or three tentative steps across the cabin. 'I think I'm only badly cut about and bruised,' she muttered.

So the score was two badly bruised, one broken arm, and one dead. Pitoyan judged that they must have struck the ground at no more than sixty miles an hour, otherwise none of them would have known anything about it. He grinned wryly at the thought that they'd been talking about drives of a hundred kilometres a second, gaily talking about it for the last year, when a collision of only one per cent of that speed could bring their little world down into ruin. Almost literally, they were nothing but bags of water, and the repositories of shrieking nervous systems.

Ilyana had of course graduated in a course of nursing. As soon as she was slightly recovered she began to tend Pitoyan's arm. She gave him a strong shot of pain-killing drug, then cut away the sleeve of his jacket, made the best set she could and fixed him up with splints. She didn't like to use a cast because the set might not be good enough. Then she collapsed back on her bunk.

Bakovsky meanwhile had managed to get the outer hatch open. In the shock of the moment it didn't occur to him to put on a space-suit. The atmosphere ought to be right and he just risked it, something that every raw recruit at space-school would have told him was wrong. But there was no harm done, the spectroscopes had been right. He looked down at the ground four hundred feet below him. He tried to get the automatic ladders to work but they wouldn't. Either they were jammed or the power had gone. With a resigned shrug he got out an old-fashioned rope-ladder and paid it slowly out until he could see the end begin to curl up as it rested on the ground. Then he stopped paying out the rope. It was an absurd thing to do, but even now in the face of disaster he couldn't quite shake himself loose of a lifetime of obedience to instructions. After all hostile natives might attack the rocket, in which case it would be quicker to haul up the ladder if it wasn't all paid out. It never crossed his mind that the presence of natives, even if hostile, might be preferable to their present situation.

It was a long way down to the ground and his arms hurt, and the big bruises hurt, before he reached it. It was going to be a hell of a climb back to the rocket but he thought he could make it. He realized that Pitoyan would never do it. Certainly it would be possible to lower Pitoyan to the ground, but not even he, Nuri Bakovsky, was strong enough to lift a full-grown man through a clear height of four hundred feet. So if Pitoyan came down he'd have to stay there.

He could see that the end of the rocket had driven into a hard sandy material. They had come down at a point quite close to the edge of one of the strange lagoon-like seas. He noticed for a moment that the sky was very, very blue. The rocket was projected against it, towering now high above his head. He saw that it leant drunkenly at an angle of about ten degrees to the vertical. With a sinking heart and a tightening in the pit of his stomach he realized that it would be almost impossible to trim it for their homeward flight. He saw the odds piled up against them. Buried deep inside this mass of metal, stuck there in the sand, was a smaller, but entirely new rocket. It had all its own motors and fuel. It had its own living quarters, smaller than the ones in which they had travelled two thousand million miles across space, but nevertheless sufficient for their purposes. It had its own motors and fuel supply. But how was he to strip down to it? How was he to get rid of the outer, now useless, exterior. There were only two men, himself and a weakling with a broken arm. And even if there were ten of them like himself, there was the obvious danger that the whole structure would topple over while they were working at it. They didn't have any cranes to straighten it. The whole theory of stripping down was based on the assumption that you had made an absolutely perfect vertical landing. He looked up again at the yawning structure above him, grunted to himself, and began to climb the ladder.

It was a long bitter struggle and he was shaking violently by the time he reached the hatch. The ladder seemed almost impossibly heavy as he hauled it in. It didn't occur to him that, but for the higher density of oxygen in the planet's atmosphere, he would never have made it at all. Bakovsky was nearer to collapse than he realized. He returned to the cabin and began to do what he had to do. At the moment it seemed quite senseless but then you never knew what might happen. It was always possible that they would get back to Earth, and if that should happen the first thing that his superiors would demand would be a report on the accident. The report had to be written at the earliest possible moment, and that meant now. It was one of those things that had to be done however ridiculous it might seem.

The effect of the drug was beginning to wear off. Pitoyan's mind was slowly clearing. His reasoning was better now that his arm wasn't hurting quite so much. He didn't need to make the trip down to the ground to know how things stood. It was a miracle that they were standing up at all, even at an angle of ten degrees, and not lying flat out on the ground. He knew with a minimum of thought that unless they had help they were finished. It wouldn't need hostile natives to see to that. The Westerners were the only hope of help. Messages to Earth would not get through, and even if they did it was doubtful whether a reserve rocket

could reach them. It wasn't at all like an appeal sent from
the Moon or from Mars. Now they were attached to the
Helios system, sweeping with it through the solar system.

With Ilyana's help he managed to get the reserve electric
generator working. The main radio transmitter didn't seem
to function properly. But there was also a reserve for that.
He got it operating and began to send out endlessly the
international distress signal.

Meanwhile Bakovsky worked away at his report. He
checked and back-checked all the technical data. He didn't
work quickly and it took him quite a while to finish. He
signed the sheets, looked up the automatic calendar, and
dated them.

'Will you read this through and sign it if you agree with
it?' he said abruptly to Pitoyan.

While Ilyana took his place at the radio transmitter Pitoyan read carefully through the dozen or so sheets of paper.
Bakovsky had a clear, very direct style that it was not possible to misunderstand. By now Pitoyan was somewhat
curious about the accident. Of course there had been cases
of this sort of thing happening, but in modern times it was
very rare. It was almost the last thing that he'd expected
when he'd thought over all the possible disasters that might
hit them. He could see nothing wrong with Bakovsky's description of events before landing. They agreed with his own
memory, although it was always possible that shock was
producing some distortions. At the last he came to the
pages of technical data. He almost decided to by-pass them
and sign the document, but there was a dead man to answer
for, so he thought that maybe he'd better finish the job
properly.

It was all routine stuff – checking pre-set dial positions
against the entries Bakovsky had made in the form of routine
tables. There were the conditions of various switches, and
these he came to last of all. They too checked against the
report until he came to the switch that controlled the servo
settings for the final landing. It was obviously impossible to

predict with extreme precision how much retro drive would be necessary to make the final touch-down. So as the rocket approached the ground there was a device that measured how fast it was coming in; if the speed was too great the drive would increase appropriately. Without this feed-back mechanism it was almost impossible to avoid striking the ground at a moderate speed of, say, fifty or sixty miles per hour, just as they had done. He stared down at the final page and then stared again. It was completely obvious what had happened. The fools had failed to activate the feed-back mechanism. In his fury Pitoyan forgot the pain in his arm. According to Bakovsky's entry the servo switch was in the 'On' position. Pitoyan looked across at the control board again. The switch was manifestly in the 'Off' position.

He looked again over the other tables. Bakovsky couldn't have made all those entries simply from memory, he must have consulted the control dials. So why had he marked the servo switch wrongly? If he'd wanted to lie about it all he had to do was to turn it into the 'ready' position. In fact the whole of this cross-checking was a bit absurd if Bakovsky wanted to cheat. Probably he'd taken it as so obvious that the switch must be 'On' that he hadn't even bothered to look.

His mouth tightly drawn, his face grey with the pain that seemed to fill him, he went out of the cabin, staggering as he did so, and made his way into the bowels of the ship looking for Bakovsky. He found him contemplating the magnetic clamps that held the inner rocket – the one they hadn't used yet – in position. 'Would you come back to the cabin. There's something in the report that I don't understand.'

There was a slight air of belligerence in Bakovsky's face as they climbed back to the cabin.

'Well, what is it?'

'The switch for the servo of the retro.'

'What's wrong with it?'

'You've marked it as being in the "On" position, whereas

it's "Off". That's the cause of all the trouble, you blasted idiot.'

Bakovsky's face reddened. This was the sort of thing you hit a man for. He glanced at the control board and then turned to Pitoyan and said angrily, 'But the switch is in the "On" position. Can't you see for yourself? Haven't you got eyes, little man?'

The Westerners had made their decision. Like the Russians they chose a spot within a green area but not far from one of the orange seas. They wanted to be able to explore both kinds of region. And they didn't want to go too near the seas, for they suspected that the ground would be sandy and perhaps awkwardly soft for a landing. Their chosen place was almost at the opposite side of the planet from that of the Russians. Being professionals they did not start their ship immediately downwards once they had taken their decision. After all they had spent eight months getting there, so a few more hours wasn't going to make much difference. So they continued to circuit the planet for a while. And all the time as they moved they sent out radio waves which were bounced back by the surface below them and picked up in their receivers. This not only gave them their height from the ground, it also gave them rough information about what the ground was like.

'Funny, we're getting interference.' Fawsett was at the receiver.

'What sort of interference?'

They were all round the receiver now.

'Looks more or less like C.W.'

The image in the display tube was blurred, but then for a moment it became clear as if the interference had ceased. Then it blurred again, and so it went on for perhaps fifteen minutes.

'Looks as though we're out of it, whatever it was.'

'We'll still see if it's there when we come round again.'

'Could it be the Russos?' asked Reinbach.

'What the devil would they do that for?'

'I don't know. But we're fairly close to the place where they landed, aren't we?'

An hour and a half later they were back again. The signals were still there, and they were only there on the particular frequency they were using. Now they were on the right track it didn't take them very long to figure it out.

'It's the distress signal. For some reason their modulation can't be working. The Russos are in trouble.'

'What trouble?' asked Fiske, not addressing anybody in particular. 'They can't have blown up the landing. That sort of thing just doesn't happen any more.'

They chose a spot for landing, decently clear of the Russian ship, about a hundred miles away. They checked and cross-checked all the necessary details for making the landing, made three more orbits of the planet, and only then started up the motors again, still very gently. The rocket began to bite into the atmosphere. As the temperature of the outer skin rose, so the motors came more and more into action. The crew were on their bunks now. This was what they had come for.

Larson was the first man up. His first move was to check the stabilizers. It looked O.K., well within tolerance. He checked the condition of the motors. They weren't bad, although it didn't matter much because they'd be having new motors for the trip back. Pity in a way that they couldn't use the old motors to get them back into the parking orbit. Then they could have used the new ones only under low thrust, except of course for the final landing back on Earth. But that hardly figured. It wouldn't be possible to strip the ship down in orbit. They weren't equipped for that.

'Everything O.K.?' asked Fawsett.

'I'm told so,' answered Larson, still looking at the dials.

They prepared to test the atmosphere. It was all right, it just had to be all right, that's what the spectroscope said. But you didn't take any chances with things like that. First they evacuated a capsule, then opened it to the outside so that the atmospheric gases would rush in. They sealed it again, carried it back to their working quarters and worked through a series of standard tests. The tests gave the same results as the spectroscopic analysis had done. They had to, of course, but somehow you trusted the results more when you actually had a bit of the stuff inside your own rocket.

They filled a transparent airlock with more of the stuff. Reinbach got into it, wearing a space helmet and still breathing their own oxygen supply. Slowly and carefully he took off the helmet. From outside the others saw a smile spread across his face and he gave them the thumbs-up sign. A few minutes later they opened the main hatch and allowed the air to enter the rocket. Nothing happened. It was all right. Fiske threw the switch that sent the ladders down to the ground.

'Mike, you're in charge.' Larson set his foot on the ladder and began to climb down. Reinbach and Fiske followed, leaving Fawsett behind, just in case. All three of them laughed when they reached the ground. Now they knew what the green stuff was. Nothing but grass. Grass that stretched away from them in all directions, over hill over dale. It came about up to their calves and it had a nice soft pile. They weren't botanists so they couldn't tell whether it was any different from the grass back home. After all one grass looks pretty well like another. Embedded in the grass were flowers which they couldn't recognize. Even so it all looked pretty much like a clover field. There was a light wind that produced a slight stirring of its surface. They walked a few hundred yards away from the rocket. The sky, they noticed, was very blue, a little richer than on Earth. The wind and the grass were producing a very gentle whispering sound.

Uli Reinbach climbed back into the rocket. Fawsett and he soon had the first of their vehicles ready. With a small crane which they projected from inside the rocket the vehicle was lowered to the ground on a sling. It was a rather primitive arrangement but somehow it seemed always to work perfectly well. With it they lowered a consignment of stores. Now Larson had to make a decision. He wanted more than anything to make the trip across the rolling hills ahead of them. But as leader it was his job to stay by the rocket, at any rate until they had really cased the joint. Reluctantly he gave orders for Fawsett to come down. Mike swung his way quickly hand-over-hand down the vertical rigid ladder. He knew that this meant that he was going to make the trip, not Larson.

'You're going to take her, Mike. Got the bearing?'

'Yes, I've got it. How far do you reckon they are away?'

'Between ninety and a hundred miles.'

'Pity in a way we didn't come down a bit nearer.'

'You can make it, there's twelve hours of light. We don't want to be breathing down their necks. It might cause trouble later on.'

Larson waved and there was a faint halloo from Reinbach high in the rocket as they made off. Mike let Fiske take the driver's seat. They hadn't gone half a mile before they'd complimented each other on how sweetly the motor was working. The excess oxygen concentration of the atmosphere saw to that.

They'd never seen ground quite as smooth as this, their great centipede-like machine was simply chewing up the distance. After climbing steadily for fifteen hundred feet or so, they began on a long gentle switchback about five hundred feet up and five hundred feet down, and always the grass, about nine inches to a foot in height, stretched ahead of them. They had no fears of being benighted. The length of the 'day' on Achilles was nearly thirty-six hours, and it was still well before noon at the place where they had landed. Large white fleecy clouds were dotted over the hills, and Mike realized that it would only have needed a flock or two of sheep for him to have persuaded himself that the whole thing had been a dream and that he was really back home. But there were no sheep; in fact, as far as they could see, there was no animal life at all on the planet. That was one of the odd things about all this grass. There were no small insects weaving their ways amongst it. The faint drone of a terrestrial landscape was missing. There was just the wind whispering in the grass.

They ran into a few showers of light rain. Mike put his hand out into it. He looked at the little transparent drops in the palm of his hand. It was water all right. Even the rain here was gentle.

The only discordant element in the scene was the rasping noise of their exhaust and the thud of the eight metal feet as they pounded into the earth. It was a mere three and a half hours before they sighted the gleaming column of the Russian ship. They saw it from the top of one of the rises, still an hour and a half's journey away from them. They could also see the gleam of water far away on their left. It revived memories of many places on Earth, but it wasn't really like any of them.

The rocket was standing at the bottom of a long decline. They clawed their way down over three miles of flat, softer ground without difficulty. At first they couldn't tell what had gone wrong because the rocket was inclined directly towards them, but as they veered to the right to avoid a shallow pool they saw it leaning there, like a fantastic tower of Pisa.

'Jesus, how did they manage that?' grinned Fiske. 'You'd think they'd been using a guidance system from out of the Ark.'

They reached the open space in front of the rocket. There was no sign of any movement.

'Looks as if nobody's home,' said Fiske.

They set up a hideous din on their hooter, and after a couple of minutes a door high in the wall of the rocket opened up. They could see a white face, which disappeared, to be replaced by two faces. They shouted up asking what was the matter, and didn't understand what was shouted back in reply from above. The faces withdrew, but after a moment a wriggling coil of rope began to descend towards them.

'Jeez, they must be pooped if they're using a thing like that.'

Nobody started to come down and there were more shouts from above.

'Looks as though they want us to go up.'

'Am I under orders?'

Fiske was grinning. Mike had a feeling that he wanted to try out the rope ladder.

'You are I reckon you can't make it in five minutes.'

Fiske went up the first fifty feet very quickly, then up the next fifty more slowly. By the time he was two hundred feet up, half-way from the ground to the door above, his legs were beginning to tremble. He stopped a moment and then did what he should have done from the beginning, climbed slowly and deliberately without thinking about it. At least he did have one thought, that he could always manage to go down again if he had to. Fifty feet below the door he saw that the twisting of the ladder had caused him to get on the wrong side. Moving his hands gingerly round one by one to the other side, grasping a rung firmly he hooked one foot around and then quickly threw his weight to the other side. He caught sight of the ground and sweated even more than he had been doing. He found the last few feet very hard going, but a strong arm at last hauled him through the opening.

'What the hell's the trouble?'

The short stocky man who had pulled him in said something he didn't understand. Then he caught sight of a slim dark fellow, his arm between splints.

'My name is Pitoyan. It was I who sent you the orbit. We need your help now.'

Pretty direct, thought Fiske. 'You'll have to come along and see the Captain.'

It was obvious that this particular machine would never lift itself again off the ground – not with the sort of treat-

ment they'd be able to give to it. The stocky man was sort-
ing over a coil of rope. It made him mad to think they hadn't
given him a guide-line.

Then he saw a fair girl standing in the shadow.

'My name is Tara Ilyana,' she said. 'I hope that you can
help us. We are in great difficulty.'

Like hell they were, he thought.

They put a guide-line on Ilyana and with its support she
didn't find the descent to the ground too bad. Mike received
her with open arms. He wished he'd had a shave and a
clean-up before starting out, but Larson would have given
him no peace. He could now see a figure being lowered like a
sack of potatoes. Pitoyan could not manage the ladder and
it was simpler that way. Next came a bundle wrapped in a
strong white plastic sheet. At last both Fiske and Bakovsky
were also down. Incredibly Bakovsky had managed to shut
the door by sheer brute strength.

Mike signalled Bakovsky and Pitoyan to climb into the
cabin along with him. He started up the machine and set
out towards the nearest of the hills. It took them twenty
minutes to get there. There was an unspoken question as
they dismounted. The two Russians looked slowly over the
place, then turned to Fawsett and nodded. Returning the
way they had come, Bakovsky and Fawsett lifted the bundle
into the machine. Ilyana and Pitoyan were put into the
cabin, the others climbed on to the outside of the vehicle as
best they could, and they moved away. Back at the hilltop
everybody again dismounted. Mike made an adjustment
that reversed two of the large metal feet to form a digging
instrument. It took only a couple of minutes with this
improvised bulldozer to scoop an adequate grave for Kratov
among the gently waving grass. They all saluted. Before
climbing aboard the machine Bakovsky walked away alone.
He turned towards their rocket and saluted again.

Pitoyan found the pounding as they thudded up and
down, over and above, down and under, more than painful.
There was a constant hammering in his ears and in his head.

He was in poor shape by the time they got back to the Western camp. They took him up into the rocket and Ilyana came with him. They took off the splints and put his arm in some sort of machine.

'Instant bone-setter,' grinned Reinbach.

Even through the mists of pain he could not help wondering at the ingenuity of the Americans. He was given sedatives and put to bed. Before sleep overtook him he called Larson to his side and said, 'You must watch that man Bakovsky. He is quite mad. He did not set the landing servos.'

'You mean he deliberately crashed the ship?' asked Larson.

'I do not know. You see he thinks that the switches were set correctly. Even when I showed him that it was not right he still could not see it. When the switch was off, he said it was on. In front of my eyes he deliberately changed the switches round and said "Now that is off". I am not a fool. When he said he had put the switch off he had really put it on. There is something changed round inside him, he sees that switch the wrong way round. It is the beginning of madness. You can see that I am right because the ship did crash.'

The others hadn't caught these ramblings of Pitoyan's. When they asked Larson about it he said, 'He says this Bakovsky fellow has got bugs. We'd better watch him.'

After the months spent in the rocket they would all have liked to sleep outside. But although it was ludicrous to imagine an attack, security demanded that two of them at least should stay with Pitoyan, now in a deep sleep inside the rocket. Because he and Fawsett had already had many hours in the open, free of worries, Reinbach agreed with Larson that they should be the unlucky ones. They also decided that it would be a good thing to keep Bakovsky outside the rocket as much as possible. There was no telling what he might do if he was bugs.

As Helios sank below the horizon they drank a last mug of coffee and climbed into their sleeping-bags.

Ilyana liked this sleeping out under the stars. As she lay on her bed she could see the whole arch of the Milky Way stretching from one side of the horizon to the other. It was funny that the constellations looked exactly the same as they did from Earth, except that the Pole Star wasn't the Pole Star. The whole heavens seemed to revolve around a point somewhere near Arcturus. Now the starlight had gone the wind seemed louder. And the rustling in the grass seemed louder. Before she fell asleep she realized that a patch of light in what she had come to think of as the East was growing lighter. It couldn't be dawn already, that must be twelve hours away. Then she realized that it was the Sun. It was now an almost ridiculously tiny dim ball.

Chapter Ten

Exploration

By now they were approaching the most difficult problem of all. It was always the way on a big expedition. To begin with there were the plans back home, the building of the equipment, the expenditure of tens of thousands of millions of dollars. Then came the space run itself, with all the uncertainties and possible dangers. The landing place had to be found, the actual landing itself made, and the tricky business of leaving the rocket – of changing one environment for another. After that you came to grips with the biggest problem. What were you to do?

Take their present situation for instance. They could report that the atmosphere of Achilles did in fact have the same composition as the spectroscope said it had. They could take back pictures of the rolling green slopes around them, and the films they'd taken while the rocket was still in orbit. The pictures would show fleecy clouds and perhaps a rainbow if they were lucky. They would show the orange-tinted sandy lakes. But there were cynical bastards back home who would say that one didn't need to come five thousand million miles, and spend gillions of dollars, to get pictures of orange-tinted lakes. So there they were, back with the problem: what exactly were they to do?

To begin with, at any rate, there wasn't much difficulty in answering this question. The first thing to do was to strip down the rocket. This they set about the day after the landing. The job was made easier by the presence of the Russians. Bakovsky, bugs as he might be, was a willing and experienced worker. Ilyana was a willing and welcome worker. And although Pitoyan with his damaged arm was almost useless, he would later become a most valuable member of the party, when it came to navigating out again through the gravitational fields of the Sun and of Helios. This problem had worried Larson even before they landed. It was true that the problem wasn't quite as difficult as getting in had been. But it had plenty of possibilities of disaster. Now, with Pitoyan, they had their insurance. The future looked pretty good.

They had a clear-cut routine for stripping down the job. The precise order in which every operation had to be performed was laid down in the manual. Every stud, every electro-magnetic clamp, had its appropriate moment. They had powered winches and pulley blocks; the outer part of the rocket became a crane which they used to handle the inner parts. In fact as the rocket came apart they used one bit against another in a cunningly designed dismantling programme. The result after three weeks' work was a sleek, slim job about four hundred feet high, with its motors brand new and almost as powerful as the first motors had been. It stood there ready to swish them back home, its posterior ready to spurt a jet of blue-violet flame.

Strewn around the camp was the wreckage of the old ship. They set to work to tidy it up. They unbolted one section from another, so that the original thousand-foot-long strips of gleaming metal separated into more manageable lengths. These they dragged away with their vehicles and built into neat junk piles. One particular piece of junk they handled with extreme care however. This was a long, closed cylinder containing the highly radioactive motors. They dug a long deep trench and buried it. They checked carefully with geiger counters that nothing dangerous had managed to escape out of it. When everything was finished they had a party. As Larson said, 'This is where we begin to enjoy ourselves.'

They had two vehicles, both of them running well. Since they could maintain radio communication with each other there seemed to be no reason why they shouldn't send out two separate exploratory parties. Somebody of course had to stay with the rocket. Pitoyan's arm, although much easier now, would make extensive cross-country pounding unpleasant, so it was obvious that he should be one of those left behind. The Westerners drew lots. It fell to Mike Fawsett. He consoled himself with the thought that this was only the first exploration anyway, and that he would get a chance later. They set out early one morning, soon after the rise of Helios. One party set off to explore the shores of the first lake, which they guessed to be about fifty miles away. They could also take another look at the Russian ship on the way back. It might just be worth salvaging a few things from it. Bakovsky went with that party. The other was to explore away from the shallow seas, directly into the large green area on whose fringe they were encamped.

The division of the personnel was Larson, Bakovsky, and Ilyana in the seaward party, Fiske and Reinbach in the landward one. They set off to a good deal of shouting and to a good deal of ribaldry addressed to Larson, which Bakovsky did not understand. Fawsett felt like stretching his legs. He took a ride with Reinbach and Fiske for about five miles and began to stroll back towards the rocket. Eventually the din of pounding machinery faded, and he was left to swish his way along, calf-deep in the grass.

He sat down not because he needed to rest but to take it in better. He plucked several stalks of grass and made a crude dissection of them with his fingers. He couldn't have told that it wasn't terrestrial grass unless he'd known. He fancied there were some differences but he wasn't sure. He plucked several flowers and did the same thing. They'd take plenty of specimens back and give the botanists a ball. He lay back, cradling the back of his head in his hands, and lazily allowed his eyes to wander over the thin streaks of clouds, thirty thousand feet up they must be. Then his eyes caught the green sward rising and falling in front of him. Just like a golf course he thought. What a hell of a time a golfer would have in this place. An idea struck him and he realized it should have occurred to him before. It might have done if they hadn't all been so busy working on the rocket. How fast did this grass grow?

It obviously did grow. The thickness and softness of its pile showed that. It didn't seem to have changed much whilst they had been there, maybe it was an inch or so higher than it had been when they landed. He couldn't even be sure of that. The colour of the planet, observed over the long months of their journey, had scarcely changed either. It had stayed a steady light-green; it hadn't shown the same sort of seasonal changes that take place on Earth. There couldn't be any seasons here on Achilles.

Forty miles away Fiske and Reinbach stopped for a mid-morning break and a cup of coffee.

'It's queer but that thar grass doesn't seem to grow,' observed Reinbach. 'Maybe somebody keeps it cut.'

They laughed at this of course.

'God, think what it would be like to be a cow. Sort of cow's paradise, isn't it?'

'Funny there ain't no flies and no beetles.'

'And no 'quitoes. Makes me feel creepy.'

They lolled down in the grass and smoked. Reinbach's cigarette hung from a corner of his mouth, 'Did I ever tell you about 'Frisco and the Golden Gate?'

'Did you ever stop telling me about it?'

'I had a swell time for the three months I was there. Used to get in twice a week from Palo Alto. Used to eat on Fisherman's Wharf. They said it was the same as it had been two hundred years ago, but that was a lot of damn lies. It was full of big modern restaurants. You used to sit in there and drink highballs. You could look out over the bay, and sometimes it was clear and sometimes it was misty. Sometimes the water was as blue as that thar sky. And they brought you whacking great plates of fish. Outside in the harbour you could see the boats they used to catch 'em in.'

'You're making me hungry again,' said Fiske.

'I used to look down at the little bastards, oysters, and

scallops, and bits of halibut, and wonder where they'd all been a month ago.'

Fiske yawned. 'Swimming around thinking fishy thoughts.'

'Yeah, one of 'em might have been up as far north as Seattle, some of 'em right there just outside the Bay, and others – like abalone – right down south.'

They watched little funnels of smoke rising and dissipating. 'Kind of funny,' went on Reinbach, 'all those fish swimming around.'

'So what's funny about that? It'd be real funny if they weren't swimming around.'

'I mean swimming around and not knowing anything about us.'

'Not until you'd chawed 'em up. Then I expect they knowed all about you. Time we was moving.'

'Yeah, time we was moving. Otherwise I'll be getting bugs.'

Fiske looked up at the bright sky and along the grassy ridge on which they were standing. 'You going crazy or something? There's nothing wrong here.'

'No, there's nothing wrong here. It's just a funny idea I had.'

'Nuts. Let's get started.'

'I was just thinking what if it's the same with us.'

Fiske started the motors. The roar crackled out and startled even their noise-trained ears.

'What's that?'

'I got to thinking,' shouted Reinbach in return, 'what if it's the same with us.'

Fiske leaned over and cut the motors. 'What if what's the same with us?' he asked.

'Well, what if we're like those bloody fish, swimming about our own little pond, and not knowing something else is very near us.'

Mike Fawsett woke and realized that he must have dozed off for a little while. He opened his eyes, focused on a cloud, and then raised himself to a sitting position. He saw Cathy walking towards him from the grass. She was dressed in the same flimsy negligee she had worn the last week in New York. Instantly he knew it was a ghost and he wasn't particularly frightened. He scrambled to his feet expecting to see it disappear. But it didn't. It kept straight on walking towards him. He tried to shout or to speak but somehow or other words wouldn't come. When she was ten yards away she smiled and said, quietly but very clearly:

'Hello, Mike. You don't look very pleased to see me.'

'How did you get here?' His voice sounded unnaturally hard.

'Oh, I've been here all the time, ever since you landed.'

'But how did you get here?' His voice was stronger now, although his heart thudded furiously in his ears.

'I came with you.'

It was Cathy to the life, voice inflections and all. But it couldn't be. It had to be a ghost. A thought occurred to him.

'You're dead, aren't you?'

The old smile, exactly the old smile, came over Cathy's face. Her hand undid the two buttons of the coat, 'I'll show you if I am dead. It's beautifully quiet here, isn't it?'

For a second he thought he'd found the explanation. They'd used the reserve rocket. But then he realized that this was grotesquely absurd. How could they have caught them up, why should Cathy be in it, and how had she managed to find him here. The sweat was streaming down his forehead. With a tremendous effort of will he stepped towards her and lifted his hand to take hold of her. She had to be a ghost. She had to vanish now. Convulsively he moved his hands to grip her shoulders – they were met by solid flesh.

'Now are you satisfied?' she said. And she flung her arms around his neck. Her lips were on his, fierce and possessive, and he could feel her body through the flimsy coat. Something snapped. It was all wrong, madly wrong. With a wild cry he broke away from the clutching arms and began to run. But he was little faster than a drunken man and she easily caught up with him. In a moment they were down on the grass and she was on top of him, her face very close to his, 'You can't get away. I've got you completely now.' His mental resistance weakened and as it did so his physical strength returned. It just had to be Cathy, he could feel every bit of her. With an exultant cry he flung his arms around her and pulled her towards him. There was a wild moment, different from anything he had experienced before. Then he seemed to be falling, endlessly falling.

Twenty minutes later Pitoyan found him. He was holding convulsively to the grass, his fingers dug into its roots, and he was sobbing helplessly.

Fiske brought their machine to a clattering halt.

'We've been at this place before. I wish you'd watched those gyros.' He looked at Reinbach accusingly. 'You and your bloody fish.'

Reinbach was indignant. 'I have been watching the bastards. Are you thinking I'm bugs?'

'I'm not suggesting anything, only watch 'em this time.'

'Why don't you let me do the driving. Then you could set the course.'

This seemed like a good idea, so Reinbach moved over to the driver's seat. Within an hour they were back at the same spot.

'Who's not been watching the mockers now?' asked Reinbach.

'But it can't be,' protested Tom Fiske. 'I haven't taken my eyes off 'em.'

'Well, for God's sake, look where we are!'

They decided to stop for a spot of lunch and to cool off a bit. When they started again Reinbach was still in the driver's seat. This time things seemed to go better, it seemed as if new country was opening before them all the time. It was the same sort of country, the everlasting rise and fall of the green slopes, but they had a feeling that in spite of the downs they were gaining height steadily. In fact the altimeter showed they were. It was clearly a high point they were approaching. When they reached what they thought to be the top there were about two hours to go before Helios would dip below the horizon. Reinbach cut the engine and they got out to stretch their legs. Within fifty yards was the can they had thrown away at lunch-time.

'We're in it. Don't you see, Tom, we're in it, we're in a groove, we'll never get out, we're just going to go on round and round for ever. Remember what I told you – about maybe there being something close that you and me didn't know about?'

Reinbach's chatter was wild and it annoyed Tom.

'Shut up, or I'll fix you.'

Fiske didn't like it but he still had a full grip on himself. 'We'll kip down here until after the shiner's down,' he said, indicating Helios. 'Then we'll go by the stars. There can't be anything wrong with them. It's the gyros that are wrong.'

They walked away from the machine, just to get away from the smell of gasoline. They sprawled down in the grass and set themselves to wait. For a time Reinbach kept glancing back nervously to the machine as if he expected it to vanish. But it was always there, solid and reassuring, and after a while he calmed down and felt better. Of course it must be the bloody gyros.

They waited until Helios was down and the stars came out, the old familiar stars. It was as if the strange world about them had suddenly dissolved and they were back home among their own people. They set off in good spirits. It couldn't be more than three hours' drive back to the rocket and, after retanking and replacing the bloody mockers, they'd start out again tomorrow.

They drove for practically four hours and they still couldn't see the signal beacon that must be burning on top of the rocket. Fiske had an idea. They tried the radio, but they couldn't raise the rocket with that either.

'We must have overshot somehow,' muttered Reinbach.

'Yeah, I reckon that's it.'

'What do we do now?'

'We'll just lay up till dawn. It's a goddamned nuisance to lose time like this but I reckon that's the best thing to do.'

They got out their sleeping-bags and cots. It was pleasantly warm inside the bags, there was a gentle breeze blowing, and within an hour both men were asleep. Helios was already twenty degrees up into the sky when they awoke.

'Jeez, we've overslept.' As Fiske wrenched himself quickly out of his bag something caught his attention. Sickened he stared away down the ridge. Reinbach joined him and they both stared for a long time. They walked towards the thing. It was the can again. Reinback was beginning to tremble uncontrollably. Fiske looked at him and saw that nothing could be done. Reinbach would break up quickly from here on. He walked alone for about a hundred yards feeling very near to breaking point himself. It seemed to him that the whisper in the grass had grown louder.

Larson drove his vehicle hard the first day out. He had brought Bakovsky along because back there in camp he'd felt it would be better not to make a pass at the Russian girl. Now he wished he'd sent Bakovsky with Fiske's party. It began to seem a bit ridiculous to worry about the complications that could arise when you got back home, if you got back home. Perhaps he'd manage to find some way to get rid of the fellow.

The sand began before they got to the water and before the grass stopped. In fact there seemed to be a strip of about twenty miles where the sand and grass overlapped each other. This was why they hadn't been able to see any clear line of demarcation between the green and the orange regions from above. They were graded into each other – you could almost say, carefully graded into each other. Before dark the first day they reached a long sandy beach. It stretched away as far as they could see. The machine made about fifteen miles an hour along it, grinding its rows of feet smoothly and systematically as it went along. They actually drove out into the water and found that it deepened very slowly indeed, as Larson had expected it would.

They made camp by the water's edge. It was real good that there were no insects, no mosquitoes, but it was rather a pity there were no sea birds. The water was salt as they'd expected.

It wasn't until they were in their cots that a thought occurred to Larson, a point he should have noticed days ago. It was queer that they'd seen no rivers. The grassland must absorb all the rain. That must be the way of it. And it must be a question of soil. The sand wouldn't grow anything, so the water accumulated there. At least it formed sheets of water. The whole surface of the planet must obviously be controlled by different soil conditions. Larson wondered how the grass and the flowers in it managed to fix nitrogen from the air if there were no bugs in the soil. Or perhaps there were some bugs. So far they hadn't really made a thorough examination. It was one of the things they'd better look carefully into, or they'd get into trouble when they got back home. He found himself looking over towards Ilyana.

They drove on the next day, still following the margin of the sea. It continued exactly as it had begun. The second night Larson decided they'd gone far enough and maybe they'd better turn round in the morning. But when the morning came he decided to push on a bit farther, with the idea that the important things always lie just around the corner. When by midday nothing new had appeared they unanimously agreed to retreat. That night they used the same camping spot as they had the previous night. Nothing was changed, there were still the same light ripples on the surface of the water.

They had made perhaps forty miles back along their tracks the following morning when Bakovsky raised his arm and pointed in excitement.

'He says he can see something over there,' translated Ilyana.

Straining his eyes Larson thought he caught a flash of light. Through their glasses he saw that indeed something was shining. It was situated in a direction away from the water, perhaps ten miles away. Perhaps even more, for the air was very clear.

'We must have been blind to have missed it.'

'I think we might have missed it now but for Bakovsky's keenness of eye.'

'Yeah, that's right sweetheart.'

But Larson knew they should have seen it on their way out. The way they were going now made it a lot harder. He supposed they must have been tired when they did this stretch.

They heaved and clawed their way across the sand towards the bright shining thing. Come to think of it why hadn't they seen it from above? They began to make better progress after climbing a ridge on to the firmer ground. The gleaming thing seemed quite steady. By now Larson was pretty sure that it must be an artefact. How come, he wondered to himself.

It seemed to grow brighter as they came nearer. In fact it seemed so big and bright now that he was more than ever puzzled as to why they had missed it. He kept whispering to himself, 'What the hell is it, what the hell is it?' as they closed the distance. Even when they got to within half a mile he still couldn't make it out. It seemed like just a set of vertical transparent sheets. They were set in a row one behind the other down a long line. He guessed they must behave rather like huge windows. If you were in the right direction you got a big blast of light from them, but if you weren't you saw nothing. They drove the vehicle to within about two hundred yards of the nearest sheet.

'I reckon you'd better stay back here, honey.'

Ilyana said something in Russian and Bakovsky nodded at Larson, evidently agreeing with him. Larson opened up a container in the back of the vehicle and took out two automatic rifles. One he handed to Bakovsky, and the two men began to walk slowly and carefully towards the strange structure ahead of them.

Larson stopped in front of the first. He noticed out of the corner of his eye as he gazed up at it that Bakovsky was watching the ends of the sheet in case something should come round there. He couldn't make it out at all. It was just a plain sheet of translucent material mounted there like a huge bill-board, an enormous bill-board. He couldn't see the slightest point in it unless it was a bill-board. They made their way very cautiously around the ends. Beyond the first bill-board there was an absolutely identical second bill-board. Then a third, then a fourth, and so on. They stood there like a row of dominoes set up on end, and it was all utterly absurd.

They must have made their way around a score of the things when they came upon something different. But it didn't make sense any more than the bill-boards had done. It was just a box, almost cubical, made of exactly the same material. And beyond the box there was an identical row of bill-boards again.

Larson became aware of Bakovsky at his side. It was almost as ridiculous that he should be wearing an American uniform and Bakovsky a Russian one. Maybe this thing was some sort of customs barrier. That was about as much sense as he could put on it. They spent a good hour walking in and out, through and between, as if they were in a maze. Then Larson had an idea. He went back to the machine. It had some boff stuff in it. He didn't understand exactly what good they were, but he knew that the boffs used them for measuring electric and magnetic fields. On the far side of the vehicle he took hold of Ilyana and kissed her long and hard.

'Me and you'll work this out later, Baby,' he whispered.

Then he started back to the thing. Bakovsky was waiting for him in front of the first bill-board. Larson handed over some of the things that he had slung around his neck, they were getting a bit heavy. They turned the dials, pressed a few switches, thumbed through a manual when nothing seemed to happen, made a few adjustments and at last got some sort of reading. They didn't know what it meant but at least it was something. At least it meant that the bill-boards did something and that was satisfying in itself.

When they passed from the first bill-board to the second the reading on their instrument got bigger. And it increased still more when they passed to the third. So it went on until they reached the box in the middle. All around the box something or other, whatever it was, was darn'd strong. As they started to walk along the row of sheets beyond the box it grew less and less strong until it faded out altogether at the far side. There was a pleasing symmetry about the whole business.

Larson knew that this meant that Achilles could not be quite the simple place it appeared to be. But apart from what he could see around him, which he didn't understand at all, he had absolutely nothing to go on.

They marched up and down, backwards and forwards, looking at the boff instrument. It always did exactly the same thing. The readings got bigger towards the middle and less towards the outside. That was it, and that was all of it.

Now that they had found something both Larson and Bakovsky began to think along the same lines. Theirs was the natural human reaction. What could they do to change things? They didn't understand it, but perhaps if they could fiddle with something or other, something would happen, and then they would begin to understand it. Fiddle with it first and think about it afterwards. That was the thing to do.

The simple thing to do would be to heave a stone at one of the transparent things, but there were no stones lying around. In any case that would be rather silly. What they must do was something electrical. It didn't much matter what, but it must be something electrical. It occurred to

Larson that if they could electrify the air between two of the sheets then maybe something might happen. Something rather like a lightning stroke. The question was how to electrify the air. They hadn't any sources of high voltage with them. But then he noticed that Bakovsky was carrying a hand-grenade, a high-temperature hand-grenade; with the oxygen concentration as high as it was the grenade would burn splendidly. It would make quite a fair packet of ionized atoms, if they should throw it in exactly the right place between two of the sheets.

He explained as best he could the idea to the Russian and Bakovsky nodded in agreement. So they walked back to the middle where the electricity was strongest. They chose two of the sheets nearest to the big box in the middle. Bakovsky insisted on throwing the grenade and Larson could hardly object since the Russian knew the exact weight of it. Off the little sphere went and Larson and Bakovsky ran as far as they could in the second or two before it exploded. Crouched down, with their heads away from the explosion, they heard it go off, and, almost simultaneously it seemed, there was a crack like thunder. They were momentarily blinded as they looked up by a flash that seemed to race repeatedly between the innermost and outermost sheets.

'My God, look at the box,' shouted Larson.

There, inside the box, was a bluish-green light, pulsating wildly. At its brightest it was a fine, steely point of light, at its most diffuse it filled the whole gigantic box. Fascinated they watched as it went rhythmically through these cycles about every five seconds. After four minutes or so the colours began to change, first to a lemon-yellow and finally to orange-red. Then to their intense regret the whole spectacle faded slowly away. Larson gave Bakovsky a friendly pat on the back and the Russian looked up at him and smiled.

Larson wondered if they could do it again. Only the row of sheets on the far side of the box had discharged. There was a chance they could manage it again on the near side. So they took their instruments to the two sheets nearest **to** the box on the near side – that is to say on the side where the vehicle and Ilyana were waiting. To their delight the instruments were still giving the same high value. Larson held up his hand in a knowing gesture, and while Bakovsky waited he walked to the far side of the box with the instruments. Sure enough there was nothing there. They'd fixed that side good and proper.

When he got back to Bakovsky, Larson nodded, and the Russian proceeded to unhook another grenade. Suddenly it seemed to Larson that his whole personality, his very self, was lifted upwards and dissipated like a puff of smoke. It was as if he could feel himself trailing away into nothingness.

Ilyana was astonished to see a man running at full speed from out of the inside of the thing. He ran at an angle to her so that he passed about two hundred yards away on her right-hand side. It was Bakovsky. She said afterwards that he looked like a man who was being chased by something. But that couldn't be true because she could see for herself that there wasn't anything behind him.

Bakovsky ran for nearly half a mile, his face strained with the utmost terror, until he reached a place where an arm of the sandy lake could be seen. At first the water only covered the tops of his boots, but even though it rose up to his knees and to his thighs he still plunged on, not slackening his frenzied thrust until the waters at last closed over his head.

Ilyana ran to the machine. She had watched Larson drive the vehicle and managed to get it started without much difficulty. The controls proved more awkward, but at length she was moving towards the water. She found footprints leading to the arm of the sea but the water was transparently clear and empty. Bakovsky had disappeared completely.

Puzzled and frightened, Ilyana drove the machine back and walked slowly towards the bright shining screens. She knew it was foolish to go in there, but she was determined to find out what she could. She knew perfectly well she'd been sent on this expedition for political reasons – as a toy, a cat's paw, of the men in power. She must behave at least as bravely as a man.

She found Larson at last. He was obviously dead. The expression on his face terrified her. It wasn't a look of horror, such as she felt must have been on Bakovsky's face as he raced past her in the distance, it was a look of complete vacancy and blankness. It was a complete negation of life. Very slowly she walked the whole length of this thing, whatever it was, with its awful power. She saw the places where the discharges had torn jagged holes in the transparent sheets. She saw that the inner box was not quite transparent, the walls were very slightly discoloured. She found Larson's body again, and was considering how she should best bury it, when a strange numbness overcame her. It lasted, as it seemed, for only a fraction of a second, but when she recovered she found herself outside the whole structure, halfway back to the vehicle itself. And she knew quite certainly that she must not return inside.

Driving to the spot where they had parked before, she got out the camera. She must take what photographs she could, otherwise who would be willing to believe her. Certainly not the hard-faced men in Moscow.

There was something there that could kill a man without a blow, that could drive a man out of his senses. For some reason the thing that had killed her two companions had spared her, but if it wanted it could kill her too. She had no doubt about that.

Feeling helplessly inadequate and suddenly very much alone, she sat for a while thinking what she should do.

As she raised the camera she had a horrible certainty that something was going to happen. But nothing did. Whatever it was in there didn't object to the pictures being taken. It was her upbringing that had frightened her, an upbringing in which it was an offence to photograph almost every object on sight. She took a dozen pictures, realizing vaguely that if

T—E 129

the camera were faulty the number of pictures wouldn't help.

Pictures wouldn't help her either unless she managed to get back to the American rocket. Like most passengers she hadn't taken any real notice of the way they'd come. She had only a general idea of the direction. There would be enough fuel in the vehicle for the return trip by the most direct route, but there wouldn't be much to spare for trial and error. She started up the motors and set off. As the machine moved over the ground with a rattle, roar, and thud, she looked back over her shoulder, fearful of what she had left behind.

She gave up all thoughts of making a detour to her own ship. It was useless. It would never soar into this blue sky above her head. Momentarily distracted she made the mistake of looking up towards Helios and was instantly blinded. The amount of light from the star was pretty close to that which we normally receive on Earth from the Sun. But the disc of Helios had only about a quarter of the apparent area, so it could easily blind anyone looking at it for more than a brief flash.

She waited impatiently until the bright lights in front of her eyes disappeared and she was able to see around her again. She had instinctively braked the vehicle to a stop, and now she turned round in the cabin and looked back over the way she had come. The thing with its huge transparent sheets had vanished. Nothing remained but peaceful rolling grassland.

She began to shiver. It wasn't just shock. Being frightened didn't describe the way she felt. It was almost like being without limbs altogether. She could still think and that was about all. She could not feel the wheel in her hands and the vehicle seemed to go where it wanted. It went on after Helios had set beyond the distant horizon, it went on pounding and thrashing throughout the night, the crackling exhaust shattering the air as it passed by. After three hours the sun rose in what might have been described as the East. As it moved up into the sky its glow sent a strange red radiance over the whole countryside. It was as if she were driving through a sea of liquid fire.

Pitoyan saw the vehicle coming in about an hour after dawn. He was more than glad to see it returning, for the condition of Mike Fawsett worried him. For the most part Fawsett was in a feverish condition, but every now and then his temperature would fall and he would become quite coherent. But the questions he would ask were strange even to Pitoyan who knew that he didn't speak English very well. So he was glad that the big American, Larson, was coming back. He was also glad that Ilyana was coming back. He managed to descend the fixed ladder with his one good arm. The vehicle was only half a mile away now and he ran to meet it. He could see Ilyana, strangely enough in the driver's seat. The machine stopped almost in front of him. He opened the cabin door and Ilyana tumbled out. She stared at him wildly for a moment, then threw her arms around his neck, and burst into uncontrolled, but healthy, sobs.

Fiske knew that he was reaching the end of his control. His nerves had been almost unbearably frayed by Reinbach's breakdown. Twice more they had tried together to get away from this same spot. Twice more they had found themselves back again. Then Reinbach had refused to go on. In a way, if you were always returning to the same bloody place, there was a sort of crazy sense in that.

But you couldn't give up. If you gave up you were finished. So he'd made a try by himself. He'd concentrated on every inch of the way, concentrated until he felt his eyes would jump out of their sockets. He'd been sure that it was all different this time, until he came over a little ridge and found Reinbach lying there in a more or less unconscious state.

By now most of the fuel was gone. They'd simply wasted it in just driving round and round, driving round a circle with about a ten-mile radius as far as he could judge. He estimated this from the time it took and from the speed of the machine. It was as if they were in the bottom of a bowl, just going round in circles, only they weren't in the bottom of a bowl.

Tom Fiske wouldn't have cared if it had been the machine that had been leading them wrong. He wouldn't have cared if the gyros had gone stark-naked screwball. But the thing that really did frighten him was that they'd tried to make their way by the stars. Tom Fiske knew that you can't play about with the stars, nothing could do that. Yet it had been just the same, they'd come back exactly to the same bloody place.

It meant that you couldn't trust your own eyes. Fiske smoked for a moment and thought that one over. That was just about it, that was the truth of it, you couldn't trust your eyes. He remembered Bakovsky and the servo switch. Wasn't that what had happened to the Russian ship? Surprisingly this calmed him a bit. Somehow it seemed better to think that it was they who had gone crazy and not the world outside.

He thought of telling Reinbach about this idea and went across to him. At first he thought that Uli had fallen asleep, but then he saw that his eyes were open and that he was staring up to the sky. He shook him gently by the shoulder and said, 'Hey, I've got an idea.' And a hell of an idea it was too. To his relief the fever which seemed to have been growing on Reinbach had gone down. He could see that when Uli looked at him.

'Shouldn't we be getting back to the ship?' The poor devil seemed to have lost his memory. Probably some sort of nervous protective device.

'We'll try again as soon as it's light.'

'I'm sure we can make it now. It's all pretty smooth going.'

Well, if that was what Uli wanted they might as well make another circuit, thought Tom.

After an hour and a half's driving they ran at last out of fuel. Tom jumped down from the cabin fully expecting to find himself back to square one. But as far as he could see this wasn't the place. Then he remembered that what he saw didn't signify. Reinbach had come down from the cabin. 'What is it?' he asked.

'We're out of fuel.'

'Then we'd better walk.'

This was what had been worrying Fiske all along. Sooner or later they'd have to walk if they were to get out of this place. But they might just as well find themselves walking in circles as driving in circles. The mad idea occurred to him that maybe in some way all this was connected with the vehicle and not with themselves. Maybe they could walk out. It didn't figure, but then nothing he could think of figured. The danger of course was that they couldn't carry much food and water. For the first time it occurred to Fiske that there were no streams. The rain just fell on to the grass, where it was absorbed into the roots until the moisture evaporated again. He wished there had been streams. He remembered that he'd always liked the sound of running water.

They started to walk, still following a course set by the stars. The Sun came up, and they found themselves walking through the same liquid fire that Ilyana had driven through. Reinbach was going well now. There were times when he would plough ahead, and then Fiske was worried because Uli didn't seem to take much notice of the course he was trying to set. Reinbach had the air of a man who didn't care much where he was going so long as he got to hell out of the place. The trouble was that they didn't know how to get out of the place.

But about three hours before dawn Reinbach broke down. It was obvious that his temperature was soaring up again. There was nothing that Fiske could do except to let him lie there in the grass. It looked as though there was nothing that either of them could do. For Fiske knew that they would never find their way back to the machine. He tried to put his own jacket around Reinbach, but in his delirium the sick man kept throwing it off again. A bright star rose above the horizon. Tom realized that it couldn't be a star, there wasn't a bright star in that place. He realized it was Jupiter, one of their own planets.

When dawn came he looked around him. To his intense relief there was no sign of the can, or of the machine for that matter. At least so far they hadn't gone round in a circle. His eyes scanned the horizon and at one point he caught a distant flash of light. His mouth was dry with a growing excitement as he realized that it must be the rocket. The terror seemed to fall away from him in the morning light. He knew he would make it now.

The only trouble was Reinbach. He was obviously in a bad way and couldn't be expected to do more than stumble a few yards at a time, at best. Tom thought about leaving him and going to fetch help, but then he realized that it would be next to impossible to find him again in this featureless countryside. So he did the only thing possible, he slung Reinbach across his shoulders and set out slowly but steadily towards the welcoming point of light. It would take a long time, but he would make it.

Ilyana had told her story to Pitoyan. Although he said he believed her he'd asked for the camera and had gone to process the film. Sitting waiting in the grass she saw him coming down the ladder from the rocket holding a bunch of prints in his bad hand. With a sinking heart she knew that they'd be blanks. There wouldn't be anything on them at all. And that was the way it was. They were all just useless blanks.

The way he looked at her it was obvious that he thought that she was mad, the same way that the American, Fawsett, seemed to be mad.

Then Pitoyan told her that he knew the two men had been killed in a very different way. They had been killed in fighting over her, and that she might as well admit it instead of producing a ridiculous story. Ilyana, seeing that she would never convince him, admitted it. She told him that the American had attacked her, which in a sense was true. Bakovsky had come back unexpectedly, and in the ensuing fight the American had killed him, but not before Bakovsky had exploded a grenade. It sounded silly to her but Pitoyan seemed to believe it. It came within the range he could believe whereas the truth did not. And Ilyana saw that this would be the way of it when they got back to Earth, if they ever got back. By now she didn't seem to care very much. She thought of the endless, anonymous grey buildings in Moscow, and decided it was unimportant what they believed.

Pitoyan began to climb back into the rocket. It was funny the way he seemed to spend almost all his time inside the thing, thought Ilyana. He even slept there, as if he were afraid of this new world around them. Ilyana shivered as the memories of yesterday came back to her. Even about those memories there was something strange. They weren't as clear or as sharp as they should have been. They should have been etched indelibly on her mind, but it was more as if they had happened three years ago. In a way she was glad of this, for it prevented her from being frightened out of her wits, of having the same trembling fits as the American, Fawsett, had.

She began to think about the Americans in the other vehicle. She hadn't thought much about them before, but now, suddenly, she was quite sure they must be in trouble. She started up the ladder after Pitoyan, intending to ask him to try to raise them on the radio. At the top she paused for a moment to gaze out over the green countryside. It was then she saw two men moving very slowly on foot about five miles away. In a few seconds she was on the ground again, starting up her machine. She drove it, threshing and thudding, up the incline towards the distant hills.

Tom Fiske was now staggering very badly. The weight on his shoulders seemed to press him into the ground, his ears were thudding with the sound of his own heartbeats. For a while he couldn't believe that the noise really came from a machine that seemed to be coming towards him. For a moment he had the wild idea that somehow his own machine had managed to get started by itself, but this one pulled in alongside of him and the pretty Russian girl climbed down from the cabin.

She helped him up with Reinbach's inert body, and they moved off. He sat in a stupor. He didn't have to carry anything any more, and within an incredibly short time they were back in front of the rocket. Again he had to make a big effort. He had to carry Reinbach up the long vertical ladder, he couldn't expect the girl to help with this. Somehow he got him into one of the bunks, and he and the little Russian fellow shot him full of drugs. Uli ought to be all right now.

Pitoyan told him what had happened. He told him about Fawsett, and it was obvious to Tom that both Mike and Uli had gone down with the same sort of fever. It was equally obvious that the expedition was over. The sooner they lifted the rocket up into the sky and were started back for home the better. But first he had to check up on Larson's death. This was absolutely necessary because of the inquiry there would be back on Earth. He went down and re-tanked the machine. Then he went to Ilyana and said, 'I've got to make a check-up. I'm sorry but you'll have to show me the way back.' Ilyana nodded dumbly. She climbed into the cabin alongside Fiske. It all seemed so similar to the way that she, Bakovsky and the big American had started out four days ago.

By the time they had gone about ten miles, and were traversing what looked like an undulating grassy road, she realized that it was quite useless. She doubted if she could really find her way back, and even if she did find the proper place she doubted if they would see anything at all. It would be just as blank as the pictures had been. She motioned Fiske to stop for a moment and got down from the cabin. Tom quite misinterpreted her reason for this, and he allowed her to lead him about two hundred yards along the track to a spot where they could just see the machine. She sat down in the grass and motioned him to follow. Then she began to tell him what had really happened. She spoke in slow, precise English, and he saw the picture gradually unfold itself – the sandy seas, and the gleaming transparent sheets.

'Well,' he said when she'd finished, 'it figures.'

'What does that mean?'

'It means that if that's the way it happened, that's the way it happened. I believe you.'

He told her his own experience of the strangeness of this new world, of the useless and unending circling they'd been condemned to, how they'd just gone round and round like flies walking around a window-pane. When he'd finished she took his hand in her own and began to stroke it. 'You must say that you ran out of fuel. It is better to be thought a fool than to be thought mad. But I know that what you say is right.'

It seemed the most natural thing he'd ever known to take this fair-haired girl into his arms. For the first time in his life he found himself to be making love without congratulating himself that he was doing so.

Chapter Eleven

The Return

The ship lifted itself swiftly an d smoothly out of the atmosphere of Achilles. They made ten orbits around the planet. Without telling the others, Tom Fiske and Ilyana looked for the gleaming translucent sheets, but none could be seen. Pitoyan obtained the data for the first crude setting of their orbit and Tom set the controls and opened up the motors. The ship seemed lighter and easier to handle than on the outward journey but this was probably just an illusion.

A day later they were almost a million miles out from Achilles. It was still a remarkable sight, the green areas looked just the same as they had on the way in. Two days ago Fiske had cursed the endless grass slopes, but now as he looked at them for almost the last time there was a strange tightening in his throat. He remembered what Reinbach had said about the fish off 'Frisco Bay and he had a feeling that that's what they'd been – a lot of fish that didn't know what was going on around them.

The cabin had been laid out for a crew of four, which meant that either they'd got to improvise or that two of them had to share the same bunk. Tom Fiske and Ilyana shared the same bunk and made no bones about doing so over the whole of the long trip back home. Pitoyan, furious at first, realized that even without a damaged arm he wouldn't be a match for Tom. He thought about taking his revenge by refusing to calculate the orbits. That would have been fine if he'd been in another ship, but any disaster to this ship was a disaster to himself. So he calculated the orbits and with equal correctness reckoned that he would have no difficulty in finding girls back home. He had achieved something worth talking about and had every intention of taking complete advantage of it.

The sick men caused them a lot of trouble. It wasn't just the careful nursing they needed at times, it was the way they seemed to become queer when they recovered for a while. A lunatic was the last thing you wanted to have on your hands in a space-ship. And they seemed to have two lunatics. Luckily they never seemed to be at their best at the same moment.

When the fever went out of them they behaved as if they were somehow vacant. Both of them would climb about the rocket asking questions as if they'd never seen a ship before. It was as if they were back in childhood, although when you looked them straight in the eye they didn't look at all like kids. Their eyes looked more like deep pools, and it was a bit uncanny the way each of them seemed to know what was wrong with the other. When one of them was more or less all right and the other was in a high fever the one who was all right would sit around endlessly just looking down at the other fellow. It was a sort of medical game of tag, and it gave them the creeps. They got into the way of leaving Reinbach and Fawsett to look after each other more and more. But for this the final tragedy would probably not have happened.

It occurred at a time when Reinbach was in comparatively good shape. Fawsett was in a high fever and was shouting incoherently – shouting the usual name of Cathy. When he was in this state it almost looked as if he thought he was talking to somebody. He would reach out his hands as if to take hold of something or somebody. The three of them got into the way of keeping as far off as possible when these attacks were on him, especially if Reinbach was there to watch. One day, about four months out from Achilles, they found Fawsett sprawled on top of Reinbach. His hands were clamped around Reinbach's neck and they had to open his rigid fingers to pull him off. Reinbach's face was black and the sight made Tom Fiske sick. Fawsett was still shrieking for Cathy, so Fiske hit him hard on the jaw, and this put a stop to the nonsense for a while.

By rights they should have put Reinbach's body in the freezing compartment. But Fiske felt that Uli's death might be easier to explain if they got rid of the body. It didn't seem as if it would be much harder to account for four deaths on the planet instead of just three. Why stop at three? So they placed Reinbach in a long metal cylinder, sealed it, and ejected it from the ship. It occurred to Fiske that if anybody ever recovered a body from space, with the lack of oxygen it would probably be perfectly preserved.

After this they kept a close watch on Fawsett. Secretly they all felt that they wouldn't be sorry if this shrieking maniac were to put an end to himself. In their closely confined circumstances it was a continuous waiting nightmare. The trouble was that you couldn't get on terms with Fawsett, even when he seemed to have recovered for a time. The strange thing was that he seemed to be mad with them about Reinbach's death – as if they'd caused it. The sooner they got him into a bug-house back on Earth the better they'd feel.

Back on Earth they had news of the returning ship. The bursts of radio noise from Helios were weakening somewhat, and the angle between the direction of the ship and of the star was widening. So at last, after almost a year, they had news.

The problem to those in the ship was what to do by way of explanation. They decided, without formulating any plan or purpose, essentially each for himself, to be as vague as possible. Fiske sent out transmissions on the Euro-American wave-length, while Pitoyan sent out communications on the Russian wave-length. So both sides thought that their ship was returning.

Of the endless stream of questions to which they were subjected they answered some and ignored others. For the moment at least they could claim that transmission was faulty. Pitoyan had the inspiration of doctoring their transmitter, so that it deliberately garbled their messages. He spent a lot of effort doing this in a way that he hoped the experts would find difficult to understand when finally the rocket landed on Earth. It would have been easy to have put the transmitter out of action altogether, but it was necessary to keep Earth accurately informed on one point, namely when and where they would be coming in to land. Later on, as Pitoyan said, they would have to play it by ear.

Both Washington and Moscow were unbearably frustrated by these tactics. The two Governments wanted full and accurate information themselves, although they still hadn't informed their respective publics.

They had a sound psychological reason for this. It would still be three or four months before any ship could return, there was still the long coasting section through the orbits of Saturn and Jupiter. And they knew that the populace at large simply cannot maintain its interest in any topic for three months. There would be an intense newspaper, radio and television publicity for perhaps ten days, and after that the public's appetite would fall off quite steeply. But if they held their horses until about three weeks before the landing, then interest instead of falling could be whipped up to fever point. After all, this was a sort of gladiatorial show – except that, instead of putting up a million or two for a building like the Colosseum in Rome, this had cost them more than a hundred thousand million. Both Governments intended to see they got good value for their money.

Of course the news could not be kept from the public if the publicity services hadn't been willing to cooperate. There were certain to be scores of official leaks. This was particularly true in the West. But the plan of the Governments was really in the interests of the publicity services themselves. Responsible people soon saw that. To prevent a break occurring it was made very clear that whatever syndicate attempted to jump the gun would have all its official privileges withdrawn. So although it would have been possible for any one group to have scooped the others, the gain – while undoubtedly large for the moment – would in the long run have been more than compensated through the long-term loss of facilities. No group was willing to run such a risk and all leaks were plugged before they could spout their delicious liquid into the mouths of the waiting public.

So those who were in the know were aware of the return some three months before Fiske finally put the rocket down neatly and squarely in the south of Florida. Conway was one of those who knew, and it was hardly possible for him to keep the news from Cathy. During the past year their marriage had worked a little better than it normally did. Cathy had made no reference at all to Mike Fawsett. But with the news of the impending return she instantly shed another mental skin, in just the way she had done on the day of Fawsett's departure. Now Conway did not exist at all for her. She seemed to live in a dream world of her own. Conway realized that the moment of the landing would be the culmination of her affair with Fawsett. It was in fact more a vision than a human relationship. The great rocket would stream downwards from the heavens, its exhaust belching the familiar orange ring, and it would fall more and more slowly until with infinite grace it came to rest on the huge ten-mile-square asphalt area. There would be a surge of vehicles towards it, the ladder would come down, the public would be martialled by hundreds of police, those with priority passes to the fore.

Then at last the astronauts would begin their majestic descent from above. They would swing athletically down the vertical ladder. The first to touch the ground would be Mike Fawsett. And no sooner was he there – the cheers deafening his ears – than Cathy would run forward and throw herself into his arms. So they would stand for all the world to see, Cathy and her hero from space. That was the dream.

The Earth could now be seen as a vast ball in the telescopic viewer. Fiske knew they would be there within the week. The moment had now arrived, the moment they had been putting off for months. It would be best now to send out a terse description of the basic facts, that only one rocket was returning, that only a half of the original complement of both ships would be returning. Fiske decided that there was no point in explaining at this stage. Pitoyan agreed with him. So they sent out a bare, cold statement of the true position.

The consternation that this message produced in all major capitals may well be imagined. For three weeks past now the news had been out, both in the West and in the East. Every child throughout the vast region from Smolensk to Peking knew that their beloved heroes were returning. Arrangements had been made for the parades. In Moscow itself there was to be the biggest super-S parade of all times. The factories had turned out many millions of yards of the best banner material. The cream of the fighting services would swing their way along the vast flower-decked avenues, they would be followed by schoolgirls in phalanxes, phalanxes of cunning design, schoolgirls with pigtails who had listened avidly to the reports from Ilyana. Finally, in the rear, the parade would end with an impressive platoon of wise men.

In the West things had been managed differently, but equally effectively. All round the preimeter, in fact all round the outer three miles of the asphalt area, stands were being erected. The stands would rise gradually, tier by tier, from ground-level at the front to a height of four hundred feet behind. It would be a stadium of vast proportions with the latest and most up-to-date loudspeaker system. The central region, some twenty-five square miles in area, would be entirely carpeted. Although it was not known at the time, the carpet was of substandard quality and the Corporation involved would undoubtedly have found itself in legal difficulties if it had not been for the events that were to follow the landing of the rocket. Tickets for a seat in the prepared stands were originally issued at an average price of fifty dollars apiece, but only a lucky few managed to acquire them at this low figure. By the time Conway and Cathy left London for New York the scalpers' price had risen to almost five hundred dollars.

It can well be imagined that the news from the incoming ship filled the corridors of power in Moscow with dismay. The mere notion that their ship had pooped was enough in itself, but the information that two of its crew were being brought back like sacks of rye by the Western vice maniacs, was just too much to swallow. In the West, on the other hand, the propaganda weather appeared rosier. Their ship had made it, and the squat Russian craft had not. The propaganda advantages of the situation would outweigh the fact that two boys had been lost. After all, boys had been lost before, in one way or another. Still there was a lot of explaining to be done, and the men of Washington, of Paris, Berlin and of the Rand Corporation smacked their lips, especially those whose job it was, or whose pleasure it was, to evaluate the conflicting tensions of the human psyche.

Conway had remembered the beach bungalow to the north of Miami. Fifteen months earlier he and Cathy had spent the three weeks following the departure of the Achilles ship there, and things had gone perhaps better than at any other time in their marriage before or since. He had a futile idea that perhaps if they were to go there again, now before the ship made its landing, perhaps the same thing would happen again. So he'd moved heaven and earth to get a place, and spent the best part of ten thousand dollars in renting a bungalow for the critical month. He felt he was moving into the top bracket.

But Cathy was living in a sort of trance, like a sleep-walking princess. There was no friction between them – there was just nothing. Conway felt as if he had been reduced to the status of an equerry. He knew that Cathy had come with him because by doing so she avoided all the tangles concerning tickets, passes, schedules, hotel bookings and the like, into which she inevitably fell every few hours. She spent two days in the beauty salons of New York, which was ridiculous because she didn't need it.

At the bungalow she didn't actually complain but it was clear she thought the Sun was destroying her complexion. Naturally she had her own room and Conway had his. Conway estimated that it was just about fifty-fifty, taken over the eleven years, the time they'd spent in a room together and the time they'd spent in different rooms. There wasn't any particular pattern about it, it wasn't as if they'd started off together and finished apart. It was all jumbled up, higgledy-piggledy, in a way just like all Cathy's arrangements. Later he was quite sure they'd be back on the single arrangement. He calculated that the Fawsett business would last for about two weeks.

Forty-eight hours before the estimated time of landing every road into Florida was choked with traffic, the American Automobile Association estimated that the mean rate of flow was less than ten miles an hour. The trouble was that the blockage wasn't quite complete. If it had been the drivers could have quitted their cars, they could have got out their cots and slept for a while by the roadside, but because every few minutes they were able to move a mile or two this was not possible. So the drivers had to keep awake right round the clock, and beyond that. You couldn't even pull off the highway into a roadside diner, because every place was always full. It just went on for ever, or more accurately for six or seven hundred miles. It was the traffic pile-up of the century.

Conway had expected it, that was why he'd come in to Miami by air. It was hopeless to get a hire-car, of course, but he had friends. They were good ones because they managed to get him a vehicle of sorts. It reminded him of the ancient Cadillacs in the museums, the sort of things that looked like travelling saloon bars. They had been in vogue at about the turn of the century. When he heard the highway statistics on the radio he was glad he'd also had the foresight to get a permit to use one of the official ferries.

It took him and Cathy nearly a couple of hours to get from the beach to the airport, but once they were there things went very smoothly. A boy in uniform drove the car into a waiting plane, they followed themselves, and within a few moments they were in the air. The short trip was quite terrifying. In the usual commercial plane you couldn't see very much of what was going on around you, but in these ferries it was possible to see out over a wide arc. There seemed to be planes everywhere; it was like being in the middle of a huge ball of flies. The crew made nothing of it so Conway supposed that it was more or less normal. Cathy didn't even notice it. Once again they got the car off very quickly and they drove along the side-road to the main highway. It took them twenty-five minutes before Conway could find a place to turn out into the main stream of traffic. It was unbelievably nerve-racking, but since they had only ten miles to go it didn't take them more than another couple of hours. Conway calculated that there were about fifty lanes of traffic, crawling ever onwards like beetles.

His official passes took them on to the carpeted area. For the moment they had to keep to the outside because nobody could be sure that the rocket would manage to land at the exact centre. It had to be given room to manoeuvre. So even the most privileged, and there were many of these, had for the moment to stay on the outside, although, of course, on the carpet. Later, after the landing, they would be allowed to move forward to within a few hundred yards of the ship. The President and other Heads of State, and Generals from four stars upwards, would be driven, the rest of them would have to walk. Comfortable pullman-like chairs had been provided for them to sit, and there were large umbrellas under which they could shelter from the sun. Trucks toured around the carpeted arena, staffed by uniformed waiters who dispensed the coldest of Martinis, mixed with the approved ratio of four-point-seven-five. Conway ordered a consignment and motioned Cathy to sit down.

'Why have we to come so early?' she asked.

'Because two hours from now everything in here is going to be closed, except to the top brass.'

This seemed to satisfy her. It was basically true, although Conway had an idea that he could have managed to get in later if he had really wanted to. They had some thirteen hours to wait. He felt that sitting around throughout the late afternoon and the night would take a little of the gloss off Fawsett's return.

It all looked rather like a gargantuan ball game. The outer bleachers with their infinity of seats were beginning to fill up. In fact over an angle of more than 120° away on the right the stands were pretty solid. Popular music played incessantly on the loudspeaker system. At dusk the lights came on. They bought dinner and more drinks from the travelling trucks. A monstrous massed band, there must have been many tens of thousands of them, marched into the arena, plumes flying and trumpets braying. This was something that Conway hadn't bargained for, especially the girls dressed in scanties, who wheeled past in line abreast. Their flimsy garments were covered in sequins that winked knowingly in the blazing lights. Every now and then the girls simultaneously threw short silver-coloured sticks high in the air, and whenever they did so the crowd let out an enormous whoop.

In spite of it all, Cathy fell sound asleep at about eleven o'clock. Conway felt that this was her best performance to date. Even with her head thrown back at an awkward angle she was still dangerously beautiful. In fact the submission implied by the sleep, the submission to life as it were, made her more dangerous in repose than when she was awake. The sequined girls, during interludes in their antics, looked Cathy over with obvious disapproval.

Some of them came and sat at his table. They talked and he bought them drinks and still Cathy went on sleeping. It was obvious that everything about her was irrelevant to the vision.

The festivities and the music died away about three hours before dawn. Conway dozed off fitfully and woke up with a taste in his mouth at the first light. The band and the girls had apparently brought cots with them, they could be seen stretched out in little plots right into the distance. Some of the plots were of mixed sexes, but he noticed that for the most part the girls slept together, as if to give themselves mutual protection from invaders. A little clump had gathered around his table, perhaps because Cathy's presence guaranteed safety. It wasn't long before Cathy herself awoke. She went through her usual routine of lazy stretching. Then she ran her hands repeatedly through her hair, massaging her scalp as she did so. After these preparatory manoeuvres she got up and looked around her. When she had taken in the little crowd around them her nose wrinkled, 'You collect them, don't you?'

'I should have thought I rated a modicum of comfort,' he answered.

This was a mistake, for it caused Cathy's mind to click into focus. She remembered now what she had come for, and with the returning memory she retired into herself once more. By the time she had finished her toilet and had visited one of the mushroom-shaped buildings, apparently constructed of bamboo, that had sprung up overnight, breakfast was being served from the trucks.

The girls were waking up now, they were sitting up and grunting to each other, and examining their feet – a gesture which Conway could appreciate, for all this tramping around on the asphalt base could not have improved their condition. The girls bought a strange variety of foodstuffs from an exceptionally large truck that drew itself to a screeching halt almost on top of Conway's chair. With ungrudging amazement he watched them consume hot dogs and pop, bits of hamburger on a skewer like a shish kebab, and milk shakes thick with ice-cream. One girl had brought a stove on which she boiled water. Fascinated, Conway watched her add the steaming water to a dehydrated bacon and egg *mélange*. It started by being quite small, and then it grew and grew. She took a quite spherical piece of bread and separated it into two halves. The interior was hollow and into this she fitted the stuff, clamped both pieces of bread together with her hands, gave it a powerful squeeze, and began eating.

Two hours later a large flotilla drove into the arena. Out came firstly the brass, then a large group of Russian Army Officers, and lastly the Heads of State. Conway could see Lee Kipling and Vladimir Kaluga, and he knew that the end was near.

It came incredibly quickly. The masters of ceremony, most astute of mortals, must have kept a road open, they must have held back the flotilla till the last possible moment, and then in the very nick of time they must have sped at breakneck pace to the appointed spot. For although those at the top may be kept waiting, they must not seem to be kept waiting.

It was all incredibly well managed. The band was now in formation, and the girls had taken their places. Mysteriously the cots, the stoves and the mushroom bamboo buildings had vanished, and at this exact moment there came a roar from the sky.

Chapter Twelve

Dulce Domum

Fiske had never brought a ship in to land before, for he had never been the captain or vice-captain of a crew, although of course he had made thousands of dummy landings on the equipment at space-school. He knew that he must trust the instruments implicitly, and forget all about the ground below. A day before the landing he made careful study of a list of the order in which he must make all the settings. He checked his list carefully against the manuals. During the last hour he went over each of the items one by one for the third time. Finally he checked that Fawsett and the two Russians were properly secured. Then he went to his own bunk, fastened himself in, and waited.

The retro action began and the pressure built up. Just as he felt he couldn't stand any more, it miraculously began to ease off, as it always did. That was the way the ship was designed, to take advantage of the maximum you could stand. Now the motion was so gentle that he couldn't tell whether they were still moving or whether they'd landed already.

The indicators above his bunk, now the Captain's bunk, were on, and he saw that they were almost at a complete shut down. They had made it. This was the end.

He waited for a while, as the manuals told him to do, so that the circulation would return to normal, and then pressed the automatic release button. His harness became free and he was able to climb to his feet. Ilyana was up almost immediately and Pitoyan seemed to be all right. Fawsett didn't seem too good, but he was alive and that was something. It would be up to the medicos to deal with him now.

Outside, the ground engineers were bringing up the great steps, which they only used on special occasions such as this. The steps ran on great wheels and they were powered by their own motor. The height was adjustable, today it would be raised to four hundred feet. The crew would assemble on the spacious top platform, and then they would be brought to ground level by the lift. The contraption was at last magnetically clamped to the side of the rocket and the moment that everyone had waited for had arrived.

With rapidly-beating heart Fiske pressed the button that opened the main door. He saw daylight stream in through the gap. He saw the platform in position, and motioned to Ilyana to lead the way.

The crowd outside saw the fair-haired girl appear. No professional stage manager could have managed the effect better. A moment later she was joined by Fiske and then by Pitoyan. The master of the band, assembled close by below, sensed that the moment had come and gave the long-awaited signal. The strains of their National Anthem 'God Save the West' filled the clear morning air. Nobody except the grim-faced Russian officers seemed to mind that two of the three above were Russians.

From afar off Cathy sensed that something was wrong. Mike should have been up there among the returning heroes. Her heart sank with the lift as it descended to the ground. She saw the three astronauts being congratulated by the Heads of State. Then the lift went up again, this time with four members of the ground staff. The music began again. With amplification at full volume on the speakers the din was appalling. Minute followed minute until at last two men appeared with a stretcher.

'It's Mike,' she cried wildly to Conway. Then, shouting 'Mike !' she began to run towards the rocket. Conway tried to follow her but they were separated in the crowd. He knew that Cathy could never make it through the press of people. A way would be cleared for the stretcher party and Fawsett would be carried off long before Cathy could reach him.

Conway stood there for a long time and there were tears in his eyes, not so much for Cathy as for the whole human race. This seemed to be the way with all their aspirations.

Conway found a chair and sat down. There was nothing to be done until the crowd had gone. Conway calculated that it wouldn't be more than five or six hours before the place emptied. The vast herd would stream out of the arena and fill to bursting points the roads leading north. It was impossible for him to find Cathy until this happened. He knew she would be moving somewhere with the crowd, backwards and forwards with its surges, without the smallest idea of what to do. He knew she would just stand around aimlessly waiting, without the slightest semblance of a co-ordinated plan. He knew she would be still there at the end.

And so it proved to be. At last he found her, streaked and utterly weary, but not until the sun was low in the sky. Without a word he took her arm and guided her gently in the direction of the car park. It was a very long walk and the air was hot and steamy, but at last they found their mobile saloon bar.

Conway thought about getting something to eat but decided against it. It would be better to wait until Cathy became too hungry to refuse. By the time they reached their beach place she would certainly be hungry all right, it was almost a hundred miles, and at the speed that Conway estimated the traffic would be moving he reckoned on a six- or a seven-hour trip.

In the event the roads were surprisingly clear, and they made it by close on midnight. He started to take off his clothes and said, 'Better take a shower.' She began slowly to follow his example. Later he put her to bed and went off to the kitchenette. He made them each a plate of fruit salad and cheese and stiff drinks with plenty of ice and carried the tray to the bedroom.

Cathy ate for a little while and then said, 'I tried to find out where they'd taken him. But nobody would tell me. Can you find out, Hugh?'

'Not tonight.'

'Why not tonight?'

'Because everything's in confusion. Something has happened that wasn't according to plan. It's like a battle. Nobody knows what anybody else is doing.'

'He must be somewhere.'

'Of course he's somewhere, somewhere in America or in Europe. It's impossible to know where they might have taken him. Nobody I can get in touch with would know.'

'What am I going to do?'

'Wait. By tomorrow things will have begun to ease out. By the day after, or the day after that, it will be simple enough.'

He saw her looking at him with dumb disbelief.

'Can't you understand for once, Cathy? Tonight only a handful of people will know where Mike Fawsett has gone. Tomorrow a lot more people will know, and by the end of the week a whole lot of people will know. You can probably find him within three days but you cannot find him tonight.'

At last she seemed to grasp what he was driving at. He took the things back to the kitchen, made himself another drink, and went off alone to his own room.

The big show at the landing-field was of course a complete façade. The staff officers and their advisers of both sides were counting the minutes until they could get the three astronauts away. The Russians in particular wanted to get Ilyana and Pitoyan into their hands at the earliest possible moment. The first couple of hours would be critical. The party stayed as a whole until they reached a big military base about two hundred miles north of Miami. They made the distance quickly, in less than three hours, for of course the road was cleared ahead of them.

The steps were as formal and as carefully laid out as in an old-fashioned dance. First there were congratulations from all sides. The Western officers pinned decorations on the tunics of all three of them. The Russian officers did exactly the same thing. There was an intense bout of hand-shaking, and at last two very powerfully built young colonels in Red Army uniform asked Pitoyan and Ilyana to follow them.

With instant perception Ilyana saw that this was the dividing point. If she once left the room with these two men it would be much harder to return than it would be to stay now. She told them in a very soft voice that she wished to stay. Again they repeated the request politely, they used colloquial Russian so that it would be difficult for the Westerners to understand them. Ilyana shook her head. They spoke in a rather louder voice. As she had expected, the request had become an order. She turned to Fiske, 'They're trying to take me away. I don't want to go.'

Fiske grinned, 'That's swell. Then you don't go.'

But now the Russians were angry. One of the colonels spoke to his General in a voice that reverberated around the room. The General did not deign to deal directly either with Ilyana or with Fiske. He addressed his Western peer, the Western General in charge. He demanded that an escort be provided to take the two Russian astronauts to the wait-ing cars outside. The Western General gave an order, and a young American colonel came up to her and said, 'It's better if you go, ma'am.'

The Western General knew that he was teetering on the verge of a major international incident. He rather liked the look of the trim little girl, but he wasn't risking his career for any girl. He took her by the arm and said, 'Come, my dear.' Ilyana looked wildly up into Tom's face. 'Don't let them take me,' she cried.

The vision of a grassy track came to Tom Fiske. He re-membered the crushing weight of the man across his shoulder as a girl came towards him, he remembered the first time he had made love to her. 'Listen, Mac,' he said to the General, 'if you don't take your hands off her I'll bust the whole thing wide open in the papers. After what I'll do to you you'll be lucky to be retired on a five-bit pension.'

Fiske knew that in the corridors of power he was finished now, but he also knew that not even the Government, let alone the pip-squeak General, could stand up to the fury that would break loose if the girl were handed over against her will. In the past he'd managed to look after himself and he saw no reason why he shouldn't go on doing so. He'd made the grade in his own eyes, and now he'd got the girl he wanted.

The General tried to outstare him. Then he saw Fiske's hand knotted at his side, and with a muttered exclamation he swung on his heels and left the room. Fiske took all the medals off Ilyana's chest and off his own, flung them in the air, and walked out after the General with Ilyana on his arm. Nobody challenged him. The great God of Publicity was his protector.

Pitoyan saw what had happened and licked his lips nervously. He would have liked to do the same thing, not for personal or ideological reasons, but because it would have avoided a lot of awkward questions. But when they told him to go out to the cars, he fell into the trap that Ilyana had avoided. He thought it would be best to give himself time to think it over. He could always make his decision later on.

But there wasn't very much of a later-on. Once inside the car he couldn't get out, he was flanked by two big fellows, and his right arm was still not too good. They drove for two hours and then turned into an airport, a small airport. An air ferry was waiting, and it was of Russian manufacture. He was escorted to it by a party almost equally composed of Russians and Americans. It might still have been possible to have got away, but there was more than a risk that the Americans would lose if it came to a scuffle, and after what had happened to Ilyana there was no reason why they should take his side. He allowed himself to be pushed on to the plane, and within four hours, before dawn, he was in Moscow.

There was no welcoming crowd for Pitoyan at the airport, where they landed in a deserted section. A sleek powerful car was waiting. Within half an hour they were driving into Red Square. He was ushered into a room hung with pictures of the devoted leaders of the East. They were actually waiting for him, The Party was waiting, an array of strong, ruthless men.

He saw now what Ilyana had clearly seen the previous evening. He wondered where Ilyana might be at the moment. It would not have relieved the tight sickness in his stomach to have known that she was sleeping in a hotel in the Virginia mountains, her fair hair streaming over the bare shoulder of Tom Fiske.

The President began to speak, and as he did so Pitoyan gathered his wits. He knew he had to be good, and he was. The story he told had a crude sense of theatre about it.

He knew that his case would not be decided until after all possible investigations had been made. And he knew the cast of mind of the men he was dealing with. He started with the unvarnished truth. He told them of how he had calculated the way through the gravitational fields, and he told them of how the Westerners had asked him for an orbit when their transmissions to Earth became jammed. He knew that Fiske would not attempt to deny this part of the story. Fiske would not be concerned to please the Western authorities, he had seen that for himself. He told of a how a landing had been made, and of the nature of the place where they had landed. His story so far had ninety-nine per cent truth, the one per cent he omitted was the failure of Bakovsky to read the landing servo mechanism, and he made no mention of the subsequent débâcle.

So far so good, it held up. Next he told of how the Westerners had landed within a hundred miles. This was already a breach of etiquette between East and West, for he made no mention of his own distress signal. There were comments round the table. Had he any proof? Yes, he had a set of micro films in his pocket. If he could have permission to show them ... The President gave him permission.

He showed them a very beautiful photograph of Achilles

taken from orbit with the telescopic scanner. The men around him were impressed, for being ruthless does not prevent one from being impressed. He showed them the places where the two ships had landed, very close together they seemed on the slide. As for proof he could only show them pictures of the two ships on the ground. He pointed out that without flying over them, which he had not been able to do, it was impossible to show both rockets on the same picture. So he would have to show them separately. This he did, taking care that the picture of the Russian ship should be one taken from straight ahead so that it did not seem to lean. He realized that it was lucky he had not used a stereoscopic camera.

He explained how the Americans had proposed that they should explore the planet jointly, suggesting that because of the long journey both crews were really too small for the task, and that it would be better if they joined forces. Also they wished to repay the Russians for the calculation of the orbit.

There were reproving looks around the table and the President boomed, 'Beware the Greeks, even when they bring gifts.' There were approving nods at this cultured expression of the general point of view.

It was going the way Pitoyan had hoped. He told them that Bakovsky had refused the invitation because it was obvious that what the Americans really wanted was Ilyana. This was a shrewd tactic, for it must count heavily in his favour that one of the Americans had now got Ilyana. Also to quote Latin, but to himself, *post hoc – propter hoc.*

The relations between the two camps had gone from bad to worse. This nobody around the table found any difficulty in believing. It ended in a fight, a fight in which the Russian side was badly handicapped by the presence of himself and Ilyana. It was a fight of four professionals against two. In spite of the bad odds the Russians at first gave as good as they got. On the Western side the death of Crewman Reinbach compensated for that of Ivan Kratov, hero of the Soviet Union. But with the death of Kratov the odds against them became worse. It was now a case of three experienced professionals against one, against Bakovsky aided only by an inexperienced scientist and a woman. The last straw was when his own arm was broken in a bad fall, which verged delicately on the truth. Then they had retreated to their ship, as the Trojans had done behind their wall. There were nods of appreciation at this allusion to the President's remark. His imagination now alive with the history of Troy, he told them of how the Americans had approached under the cover of darkness, of how they had placed wire ropes round the ship, and of how they had finally managed to pull it off balance with the aid of a powerful winch. He showed them a photograph of the leaning rocket to prove his point.

Experts were called in at this stage to study the picture. He was asked why they had not blasted off, why they had waited there and allowed themselves to be pulled over. On the face of it it seemed as absurd as a turtle allowing itself to be turned on its back. Then he reminded them that the rocket had not been stripped down and it would have been technically unsound for them to have started back to Earth using the old worn-out motors. This figured, as the Westerners said.

The next question, of course, was why they had not stripped down the rocket. By now Pitoyan had a firm hold of the situation – because the constant sniping of the American warmongers had made work on the rocket impossible. He added that these decisions had not of course been taken by himself but by Bakovsky. This brought them back to the story, although by now they could almost fit the rest together for themselves.

With the ship off-balance it was impossible for them to do anything else but surrender. So they had come down from above and had allowed themselves to be led away prisoner to the American Camp. The Westerners took Ilyana for their own purposes. He and Bakovsky had been set to menial tasks while the Americans stripped down their ship. The great Bakovsky, also hero of the Soviet Union, had managed to conceal a grenade. Regardless of his own safety, he had thrown it right in the face of the warmongers. The proof was that their leader, Larson, was dead, and that their vice-captain, the English-American Fawsett, was now lying mutilated in an American hospital. The man Fawsett had even been paraded before the whole world immediately after the landing. But Bakovsky had been shot, shot down like a dog as he attempted to escape.

Pitoyan decided that he was embroidering the story a little too much, and he determined to keep himself more in check.

There were only two more awkward points. Why had Ilyana and himself been brought back to Earth? Crewman Fiske had taken them with him in the returning rocket for three separate and very obvious reasons. He did not wish to be entirely alone with the mutilated man during the long months of the voyage. He had clear and obvious reasons for taking Ilyana. And he had an equally obvious reason for taking Pitoyan, namely to calculate the orbit along which they must return.

Here he was at the last barrier. Why had Fiske not jettisoned them from the ship before they reached Earth? As for Ilyana, he pointed out to the Committee that the Westerners were masters of vice, and Ilyana had fallen a prey to this. Her behaviour the previous day showed just how far she had fallen. And as for himself things had been very difficult and dangerous. With his injured arm he had been no match physically for the big American. He had only been able to save himself by his wits.

Pitoyan paused for a moment, he now had the whole affair in his grasp. He told them what they must already have seen, that the American, Fiske, had known that the truth would be unpalatable, even to his own Government, so he had made up an absurd story of strange accidents on the planet. Fiske had made up stories about men being lost, of failures in their gyros, and of a curious discharge of electricity that was supposed to have killed two of them. The one hope he had of being believed, and of the true story not coming out, was for his two Russian passengers to corroborate his tale. This Pitoyan had promised to do, and Fiske, being basically a simple-minded man, had believed him. All the comrades who had met him at the landing-field would report on how he had never shown either by word or by gesture the slightest intention of asking to stay in the West. He had, in fact, come immediately home.

There was just one thing more, which Pitoyan said to himself alone. He must from now on avoid all temptation to embroider the story any more. He knew it was a good one, but thorough investigation might throw up a few loopholes. The danger was that in attempting to plug them he would endanger the bigger and more important aspects. What he must do was to stick absolutely to his story. He must refuse the temptation to extend it at all costs. If need be he must simply claim ignorance, he must claim that there had been times when he had been completely out of action through the accident to his arm.

It is not known whether the experts who sifted Pitoyan's yarn had more than passing suspicions. History simply records that a week later Pitoyan was given a hero's welcome. A reduced parade was held in Red Square and Pitoyan was accorded the honour of addressing it. They gave him beautiful medals and, more important, made him a professor at his old university. With his characteristic ingenuity he soon discovered that the original short list of girls drawn up for the expedition were all almost exactly like Ilyana. About a quarter of them had married during the past year or so, but this left him with opportunities that were more than ample for his simple tastes.

It may well be imagined how steeply the tension now rose between the East and the West. The Russian Government was conditioned by a century and a half of its own propaganda to believe just such a story as Pitoyan had produced for them. The President called a meeting of the Supreme

Soviet and addressed them angrily for five hours. In the Western capitals, officials warned their Governments that the Russians were genuinely angry. They had every reason to be. They had lost their ship, their men, and even their chit of a girl. Much worse, they had lost their face, both cheeks; and that they would never forgive.

Urgent advice was given for the West to call a summit meeting forthwith, and for them to make every possible attempt to placate the Russians.

It was also noted that steps had instantly been taken against those mathematicians who had advised the inclusion of Ilyana in the party. The three academicians who had refereed Popkin's paper were immediately declared minus five, which meant they were exiled from the five main cities of Russia, while Popkin himself was branded minus fifty, which meant that he would never be allowed to return even to his native Rostov.

Chapter Thirteen

Cathy

The day after the landing Conway tried to find the where-abouts of Mike Fawsett but, as he had expected, none of his contacts knew. He tried the next morning, too, and was on the point of packing it in when a siren sounded in the lane outside. The County Sheriff, resplendent in uniform, stumped up the path to the bungalow. He made a strenuous root-a-toot on the door with his fist and, when Conway answered, said, 'Are you Conway?'

Conway said he was, and that he'd already bought tickets for the Policemen's Bazaar.

'O.K., O.K.,' grunted the big fellow, sunlight glinting resplendently on his polished badge, as he heaved himself over the threshold.

'Don't think I'm being personal, but could you tell me your wife's name?'

Cathy appeared and took in the scene in a vague sort of way.

'Have we done something wrong?'

'Nothing that I know of, ma'am. I'd be kinda obliged if you could tell me your name.'

'It's Cathy Conway, isn't it?'

This was the sort of thing that drove Conway up the wall and half-way across the ceiling.

'That's sorta what we hoped. We need you urgently up in Washington, ma'am.'

Then he crammed on his big hat and added, 'I'd be obliged if we could be on our way. At your convenience, naturally.'

'Naturally,' nodded Conway.

In the car he gradually pieced together that Fawsett was in a military hospital up in Washington. The man was apparently delirious and kept crying out for 'Cathy'.

Within a couple of hours they'd been put through on the ferry to Washington. Two officers, a captain and a lieutenant, were waiting for them.

'We'd like to take the lady along right away,' said the captain.

Conway saw no point in demurring. The sooner Cathy went out to the hospital the better.

'We can fix you up for the night,' added the captain.

'Not unless you've got something near the centre of the city. I'd prefer to hunt around for myself.'

'Better you than us, sir,' grinned the lieutenant.

Conway allowed them to take Cathy away, after making a note of the whereabouts of the hospital. Then he burnt up the telephone wires chasing one acquaintance after another. He concentrated mainly on the bachelors because they were the most likely to be out of town. At last he got what he wanted, the loan of the apartment of a fellow who was away in South America for a couple of weeks. Next he hired a car, spent ten minutes with a map, then nosed out on to the road on his way to the hospital. Either Fawsett must be pooped, poor devil, or maybe he had some odd form of delirium. Some sort of loss of memory. Perhaps they wanted Cathy to try to wake his memory.

It was now about six o'clock, the peak of the evening pressure. He calculated they would certainly be back in the city by eight o'clock, in fact they might be able to chase up the apartment before then, if the medicos were through with their business. That would give nice time for him and Cathy to step out for dinner. She was bound to be upset but almost nothing on earth could put Cathy off her food for very long.

He made several mistakes at the complex junctions. The place had obviously been laid out by topologists. But at last he made it. When he gave them his name at the desk, a girl with a zebra hair-do put through a call and an usherette showed him the way. They walked along seemingly endless corridors and wound up in a plushly furnished office. An elderly grey-haired man with the resigned look of a large bloodhound shook his hand.

'I'm sorry to have to tell you, Professor Conway, your wife's had rather a bad shock. We knew that Colonel Fawsett was a very sick man, otherwise we wouldn't have asked you both to come here today at such short notice.'

'You mean he's dead?'

The man nodded. 'There seemed to be nothing we could do for him. We've not run across anything quite like it before. But of course we'll go on with the investigation.'

Conway didn't hear him. He was thinking about the night almost two years ago when Cathy had asked him to do what he could to get Fawsett into the act. He remembered the way he'd overridden his own scruples. He still couldn't decide whether he had been right or wrong. He'd known there would be danger on the expedition, but he'd never thought it would end this way.

'You mean you've absolutely no idea what the trouble was?'

'No, we know it was a disease in the fever area, that's all. Even on this planet it's a pretty wide area, and maybe it isn't surprising . . .'

'How did it happen? I mean how did the end come?'

It still seemed incredible to him that Fawsett was dead.

'It didn't take long, that's all I can tell you. Your wife sat with him for maybe twenty minutes and he didn't seem to notice her. Suddenly he seemed to recognize her and became quite violent. He'd had one or two similar crises before, but he's a strong young man and he'd managed to pull through. This time he just didn't make it. It was a very nasty experience for your wife, I'm afraid. We gave her a sedative and she's been resting. Would you like to come along and see her?'

Conway said that he would and followed the man along more corridors, not quite so interminable as before. They turned into what Conway supposed was a small private ward. Cathy was there, sitting strangely still, her head drooped, looking down at her hands. Apparently she had heard them, for she looked up for a moment.

'Would you like me to make arrangements for her to be looked after, tonight, or for as long as it might seem . . .?'

Conway shook his head.

'No, I think I would like to take her back with me. You see she probably associates this place with what happened. It will be better to get her into a different environment. I can call a doctor when we get back into the city.'

'Would you like us to see to it?'

'No, I think I'd like to contact a friend. But I'll be in touch if there's any difficulty.'

Conway told Cathy to come with him. Quite silently she walked at his side, as a girl took them back to the hospital entrance. He offered her his arm on the way to the car but she refused it. They drove silently back along the highway. Conway didn't know why he'd done it, why he'd brought her with him, without saying a word to the man at the hospital. But in the first brief moment when she'd looked up at him he'd known – he'd known that this was not Cathy.

He found a space in one of the gigantic parking blocks and led the way into the main thoroughfare. The woman – or the thing – that looked like Cathy followed him, still without a word. The Mayflower Restaurant was close by. He took her in and miraculously found a table for two. She made no attempt to look at the menu so he ordered for both of them. He ordered lobster thermidor for her, which Cathy loved. He made no attempt to talk and they were through the joyless meal in no time at all. Back at the parking block he paid for the car and set about the awkward navigational problem of finding the apartment. It was almost half past nine by the time they reached it. He made a brief tour of the place; it had a kitchenette, a large room, two bedrooms and the usual plumbing. Whoever the guy in South America was he was doing all right for himself.

So far his mind had been numb with shock. He had driven the car, parked it, ordered dinner, and found the apartment more or less like an automaton. Now he began to thaw out. He wanted to know where Cathy was. He looked at the woman and said, 'Who the hell are you?'

Still there was not a word from her. My God, he thought, is she dumb? In an angry voice he repeated the question, 'Who the hell are you?'

Then her mouth opened, 'That is a difficult question, and I must have time to think before I can answer it.'

'To hell with that. What I want to know is where is my wife?'

He was beginning to tremble and was fast losing control of himself. He took the woman roughly by her arm and shouted:

'Where is my wife?'

Before she could answer the lights seemed to dim and somewhere a band was playing 'Undecided'. The floor heaved. There was noise, confusion, faces. One moment he was lying dazed on the floor being kicked savagely on the thigh.

The next moment he was on his feet and back in the apartment. And the woman who looked like Cathy was standing there shaking her head. The men were gone, and so was the pain in his leg. But he had had a bang on the head, he could feel it very definitely. He started to rub it and the woman said, 'Please do not do that again.'

It was as though the shake he'd given her had somehow contrived to waken her attention. With quick strides she explored the apartment. Satisfied, she said, 'I shall sleep in here, and you will sleep in the other room. I am very weary and do not wish to talk now. You will understand very clearly that you are not to leave this apartment. I would be glad if you would put my things in my room.'

Conway unpacked, thinking that whoever or whatever

the woman was, it was at least a relief that she seemed to be rational. He supposed he was frightened although it wasn't a feeling that he was used to experiencing very much. But he suddenly remembered the pump-handle and the fight he'd had about two years before in a dockland pub. Conway knew for a certainty that what he had just seen was not real, he had seen one of his memories.

The woman went into her room and he could hear her preparing for bed. He wondered if she creamed her face exactly the same way as Cathy had done. Had done? What had happened to Cathy? Where was she? The voice was certainly exactly Cathy's voice, but the precision of the thoughts was very definitely not. Conway lay down on the bed in his clothes and tried to think. The shock was getting him now. He must try to keep right on thinking as clearly as he could. It was obvious that Fawsett had picked up something much more serious than pneumonia. It wasn't anything as simple as a virus or a bacterium that had attacked him on Achilles. But in some way, like a more or less ordinary disease, he'd managed to infect Cathy. He didn't understand it at all, how it was possible scientifically, but he knew that there had to be some cold crystal-clear explanation. That was his link with sanity.

Suddenly it was borne in on Conway how very simply the inhabitants of Achilles, whoever they were, had managed to deal with the Earth. The human species had put a large fraction of its total activities into hopping around from place to place, in making the expedition to Achilles. And as a result it had seen – well, Conway didn't exactly know yet what the members of the expedition had seen, but he already had a shrewd suspicion that it wouldn't amount to very much. The Achilleans in return had hardly bothered to trouble themselves at all. They hadn't spent hundreds of thousands of millions in building space-ships, they had simply waited. They had simply waited for humans to carry them back to Earth. It was both simple and elegant. And now this thing, sleeping there in the next room, in the guise of his beautiful wife, could do just what she wanted to do, she could make the young men see visions and the old men tell tales. Conway rubbed his head. The visions need not always be pleasant ones.

The idea gnawing at the base of his brain was that he ought to do something about it. It could be a completely effective form of take-over. The thought of contacting the military nauseated him. Really when he came right down to it he hated the whole social structure, he knew he had hated it since his first thinking moments. They had said he was abnormal, and now he saw with an extreme clarity of perception that they were right, and he was heartily and completely glad of it. But this thing in the other room was another matter. So far it had done nothing but ride in a car and eat lobster thermidor, and make him see a vision of a scar-faced thug, but he guessed it was going to develop. He knew what he must do. He must go and tell the police and let them deal with it.

He got off the bed and tiptoed to the door. A moment later he was out in the passage-way, listening intently outside the door where the thing was sleeping – surely it was sleeping. It had Cathy's face and body, her voice even to all the little inflections, so surely it had her other bodily habits, including that of sleep.

The corridor was a rather long one, running the whole length of the apartment. It ended in the outer door. He heard a click and, looking up, saw that someone had just come into the apartment. The figure was still in the shade by the door. He moved a few yards towards it, and the figure also stepped forward into the light. He stared at it for a moment and then shuddered with panic, for it was himself who had come in through the door, none other than himself. The figure was advancing on him now, slowly and threateningly; he could see the fist knotted and he knew what would happen if he stood his ground. With a shriek he turned back into the apartment. The woman was standing in the open door of her room. She looked at him coolly and said, 'I am sorry to have frightened you. But it is my will that you shall not leave this apartment. I have need for you, so you will return to your room and stay there. So long as you do so no harm will come to you.'

He glanced back down the passage-way and the figure had gone. He looked at the woman and she stared back at him unwinkingly. At last he turned and went back into the bedroom. He was sweating furiously and longed to take a shower but he was too weak. He collapsed on to the bed and lay trembling and thinking feverishly fast. Of course there had been no figure, there couldn't be, it was in his own mind, it was there that he had perceived the vision. But knowing this didn't help, in a way it made it worse. Childishly he switched off the light to stop himself from seeing things although he realized that this was quite useless, for there was also light and dark in his own mind. It was all there ready to be released, like a record that could be played at any moment if only you knew how to play it; and this creature in the room close by knew exactly that.

The door opened with a click. He willed himself now not to see anything, but it was a voice that he heard, the voice of his wife, saying, 'It may be better if we leave the two doors open. Then you will know that I am here. Try to remember that I do not want to frighten you.'

After this the trembling got a bit less, and he kept listening, he kept trying to hear the woman breathing. He thought he could just do so. Then his thoughts seemed to disintegrate like a distant sound blown away by a puff of wind.

It was quite late when Conway woke the following morning. Even before his brain woke up he felt wonderfully refreshed, it was the way he used to sleep when he was a kid. He'd gone to bed at night, then, click – and it was morning. That's the way he felt now. Then the memories of the previous evening flooded in on him. He jumped to the window, opened the curtain, and when the sunlight flooded in the bad dreams seemed to fade. It was absurd of course, one could see things in broad daylight just as much as at night, but somehow he felt a lot better in the light. He went out into the passage and heard the woman moving about. He wondered if they had both woken at the same moment.

He took a shower, and while he was doing so the woman came and stood outside. When he had finished she slipped off her dressing-gown, completely without concern, and took her turn in the shower. Conway couldn't help wondering whether she had inherited Cathy's sexual proclivities as well as her voice and her other physical characteristics. He dressed quickly and set about making a light breakfast. His friend six places removed had an unusual assortment of food stuffs in the ice-box, so it was an unusual combination of stuff that appeared on the table. Still, it was an unusual morning. He wondered for a long moment how it came about that he was taking the whole matter so lightly. He tried to recall the horror of the previous night, but in some odd way the sharpness had been lost, as if the memories had slipped back into their proper place.

He noticed that there was a general air of incompetence in the way the woman moved around the kitchen, exactly as there had been with Cathy. This again helped him to feel a bit easier in his mind.

'Got anything to say this morning? You keep telling me you don't want me to go, but if you want me to stay there's quite a bit of explaining you ought to do,' he began.

She smiled. It was rather like one of Cathy's smiles, but not so vague, not addressed at the world in general.

'I'd like to explain if I could. But I haven't got all this organized yet.'

She tapped her head as she said this.

'It's all very confused. And I just don't know how much you could understand. I'll find out if you give me time.'

'You came over in the ship?'

'Yes of course. But it was not a pleasant trip. The creature I came in was very hysterical.'

'Fawsett?'

'That was his name. He was a man like you.'

'Why did you kill him?'

'I had no wish to kill him. It was his refusal to accept a compromise that killed him. It was he who killed another of us.'

'Another of you?'

'Yes, another of us was travelling in the body of one of the other men. Fawsett killed him. It is not nice to be trapped inside the body of a murderer.'

Conway found it difficult to understand this piece of universal ethics, delivered to him in exactly the pitch and overtones of his wife's voice.

'But why did you come?'

'To find out what this planet is like. For the same reason that you came to our planet.'

'It was a bit hard on Fawsett, wasn't it?'

'I would have left him at the end. Even if it had been necessary to kill myself I would have left him.'

'I don't understand how you can go into and how you can leave another person.'

'I keep saying that it is too early for me to make you understand. I may never be able to, but I will try later on.'

'And what about my wife?'

'Well, is this not your wife?'

The creature held out her hand and turned it backwards and forwards. 'It is a funny thing, isn't it? A hand. Isn't it your wife's hand?'

'Yes, but what about her?'

'You keep always coming back to the same point, and I tell you that I do not know how to answer. If you can tell me exactly what you mean by the words me, you, him, her, then I will answer your question.'

Conway thought for a moment.

'You mean,' he said slowly, 'that we only have a vague, instinctive idea of what we ourselves are. And that when we talk about somebody else – when I talk about my wife – I have a vague idea about something like me?'

'The point is that you are vague. You must be able to talk

about these things in a precise way, in the same sort of precise way you talk about gravitation and about electricity, if we are to do any better than speak in generalities.'

Conway felt the hair on the back of his neck begin to crinkle. He realized that if at breakfast the previous day he had been given one single wish it would, ironically, have been that Cathy would be able to think with the same rationality as this creature was thinking.

'As for your wife,' the creature went on, 'nothing has gone, nothing has been dissipated. If it was not so, then all this around me' – she indicated the breakfast things and the kitchen in general – 'would drive me mad, just as what you saw last night frightened you. It is only because of her that I can keep sane in this world.'

'But it isn't she who is talking now.'

'Because it is I who have control of the thinking processes. One thing I would like to know, did your wife ever think?'

Conway paused for a moment and then shook his head sadly.

'No, Cathy didn't really think, she was almost pure animal.'

'And you who do think a great deal had a very great liking for her?'

'Yes, I had a very great liking for her if you wish to put it that way.'

'That is why I was determined that you should not leave last night.'

The woman looked up at him with a smile, and it was Cathy's smile.

'I want you to take me away from here. I want you to take me back home.'

'That won't be very difficult. But why?'

'Because for a very long time I have been in unpleasant places. There is something I am hungry for.'

Conway also found himself smiling.

'What?' he asked.

'Grass.'

The idea of saying anything to anybody, even if he could have got away with it, now left Conway's mind. He booked a couple of seats on the transatlantic ferry, rang his friend and thanked him for the apartment, rang the hospital and told them that his wife seemed to be all right, but that she had expressed a wish to go home, and slammed the receiver back in its bed, thinking that this seemed to be his fate – master telephonist, first class.

They arrived at the airport with three-quarters of an hour to wait. As they walked up and down the vast concourse, Conway idly noticed some lout of a fellow eyeing his companion in a speculative manner. A moment later the woman noticed it. What followed was spectacular and terrifying. The man let out a loud high-pitched moan, fell to the ground, rolled over and over, his hands and feet thrashing the air, as if he were engaged in mortal combat. Then he lay on his back, looked up at the ceiling and screamed long and piercingly. In numbed shock Conway looked down at the woman. Her lips were parted and the corners of her mouth quivered in the way that Cathy's always did when she felt that she had paid someone out, and he remembered that Cathy had always detested people staring at her. He grabbed the woman by the arm and steered her away from the scene.

'For God's sake stop it. If they once realize you're doing it there'll be hell to pay.'

The screaming stopped and several policemen rushed towards the man. They got him to his feet and led him away.

'Don't you think I can look after myself?'

'Look, if once they know about you, if they suspected you'd done it, people would get scared. Those men with guns would start shooting. They mightn't know what they were shooting at, they mightn't even be able to see you, but an odd bullet fired at random might hit you.'

'You do love your wife, don't you? Well perhaps that is only fair, for that was your wife directing me now. You wondered where she was.'

Nobody seemed to suspect that they'd had anything to

do with the incident, and of course it would have been astonishing if there had been suspicions.

Cocktails were served once they were airborne. He noticed that the woman chose Cathy's favourite drink – a pink slayer – and did what she always did on any air trip that lasted for more than an hour, she fell asleep. Within five minutes her head had come to rest on Conway's shoulder, and her hair was beginning to tickle his face. It was from that moment that he began to think of her as his wife again.

He wondered what the other passengers would do if they were aware of the true situation. He wondered about his neighbour across the aisle, a man entirely anonymous in all his outward characteristics except that he carried a very large brief-case out of which he had taken a thick wad of papers, what would he think? What would the three men playing cards, talking about women, think? What would they do if they knew that Cathy could walk into the crew's quarters and, within seconds, make them send the plane in a screaming dive at 1,500 miles per hour down into the waters of the Atlantic. He knew there would be complete panic throughout the whole length of the plane, and the thought rather amused him.

They hired a car at London Airport and reached Alderbourne by the early afternoon. When they left the city streets Cathy began to grow excited. At the sight of the first green fields she gripped his arm tightly. This was the first inclination she'd shown to touch him. His house was built at an extreme end of the village, looking out over the Downs. She ran to the end of the garden, and when he came up to her she said, 'Can we walk out on that?'

He got out of the car and drove to a high point from which they could walk for miles. They started off, and every now and then Cathy would drop to her knees and begin examining the soft grass on which they were walking. He realized that it was the sort of thing that the old Cathy would have done if it had ever occurred to her. But it was quite certainly the new Cathy to whom it had occurred.

'Why do you do that?'

'Because we love grass. There is a great deal of it on our planet. We look after it very carefully'

The wind blew in her hair as they walked on, and she held on to his arm.

'How much of your planet did our men see?'

'They saw the great grasslands and the seas of course. We could not stop them seeing that. But almost everything else we hid.'

'How? How did you hide them?'

'By making them not see. There were two of them that did get near something, so instead of allowing them to go on we just sent them round and round in little circles.'

She chuckled at the thought and there were little red patches in her cheeks.

'Once, by a mistake, we did allow them to see a little. But only once, for they behaved like beasts. Their only thought was to destroy what they could not understand.'

She stopped and sat down and motioned him to come down beside her.

'It is funny that you are not at all like that. That is the thing that makes me most curious of all. Why are you so different?'

'I suppose because our means of communication one to another aren't too good. You've already found out that talking isn't a very good way. We start out by being pretty similar at birth, but then we seem to separate, and the gap between one person and another gets wider and wider.'

'It must be something like that,' she nodded.

'It is strange the difference between the wild frightened man that I came to the Earth inside and the girl who came to see him.'

'You mean Cathy,' he said quickly.

'Yes, the girl who is the other part of me. She was completely placid, as if it made no difference at all to her.'

'You mean she made no resistance?'

'None at all. It was almost as if it was a relief to her to have somebody to do the thinking for her.'

Conway laughed, and there was genuine mirth in it, for that was exactly what he himself had been doing for the last eleven years. Except that now something was doing it much more efficiently than he'd been able to do. The new Cathy looked round the landscape, she pointed at the trees.

'Those are very funny things. They're rather nice.'

Without realizing what he was doing Conway ruffled her hair. She looked at him curiously.

'That also is strange. We would never touch each other. But here with you I am happy.'

He kissed her and the warmth of her response convinced him that nothing which the original Cathy valued had indeed been lost. She moved a little away from him and he saw that her eyes were dancing.

'Very happy.'

She began to undo the buttons of his shirt, so he drew a deep breath and decided to stop thinking about the problem.

On the way back she linked her arm with his and began to sing. This was new, for although the original Cathy had a pleasant voice she had never used it, except when she thought she was alone. The songs were familiar ones, but in some way the new Cathy managed to give them an unusual twist. He couldn't say exactly how it was done but there it was.

In the evening they made drinks, at least he did, while she watched and asked questions about it. They had dinner delivered at the door – the invaluable telephone again – which saved a lot of time and effort.

Afterwards Cathy said, 'Now show me what is going on. You must remember that I am here to learn.'

'How can I show you what's going on?'

'Don't be stupid. You spend all your time sending pictures around.'

He realized that she meant the television. They switched

it on and were instantly swept into a shatteringly different world. Gone was the innocent contemplation of the grass, the trees, and of his shirt buttons, and they were watching earnest commentators talking about the world situation.

Conway was shocked to find out how far the situation had worsened during the past two days. Since the landing he hadn't seen a paper or heard a news transmission, and he hadn't realized how strongly the tension had risen, like putting the bulb of a mercury thermometer into a bunsen flame. Much of it he had of course seen many times before, but there were ominous undercurrents that were new.

Cathy seemed to grasp the issues very quickly. She watched, fascinated, as the news bulletins came in from the major capitals of the world. Conway was amazed to find her smiling at the translation of a thunderous speech which Kaluga had delivered to the Supreme Soviet. She wasn't laughing audibly but Conway had the feeling that laughter was welling deep inside her. He tried to analyse it. It was just what the original Cathy would have done if she'd understood what was going on. And the new Cathy seemed to find it just as amusing – damn it, both of them were hugging their sides. At length she motioned for him to switch off the hellish device. She was sitting on cushions on the floor, her back propped against a chair. She leant her head back, ran her hands backwards and forwards through her hair, massaging her scalp.

'Tomorrow you will take me to London. Then I will show you something that will surprise you very greatly. And it will teach these foolish people the lesson of their lives.'

She stretched herself very lazily and added, 'And now I think we will go to bed.'

Chapter Fourteen

War

While Conway and his new-found wife thus disported themselves, the world went about its serious business. Long important messages flashed importantly backwards and forwards from continent to continent, lines were kept clear for them. But at a lower level, at the level of a million or more business enterprises, the traffic in communication was choked far beyond the overflowing point. It was obvious to everybody that in the last few hours they had moved significantly closer to war. And everybody wanted to know just how they would stand if the worst was to come to the worst. The real answer of course was that they wouldn't stand at all, but everybody behaved as if they were faced by a serious but manageable crisis.

The actual situation was that officials in Washington and in Paris were pretty sure there wouldn't be a war. It was true that the psychologists had predicted that if ever it were to happen, this was the way it would start. It wouldn't be a slowly developing tension building up over many months. That gave both sides plenty of time to decide in their own minds that there wouldn't be a war. The danger was a sudden psychological feed-back that developed to the instability point, as this looked as if it might do.

Even so officials were confident. Their only problem was to allow the tension to develop a little more but still within controllable limits. The point of course was that the Russians were mad, and perhaps justifiably mad, so that some very big concessions would have to be made. Probably the Russians would have to be given parity in South America. And for this their own public had to be prepared. They would swallow it once they were convinced that only by making crucial concessions could war be avoided. This all added up to the obvious point that the crisis must be allowed to develop a little further. And so it went on throughout the night.

Conway awoke. Cathy's hair was tickling his face unbearably. Her voice whispered, 'Time to be moving. We're due in London today. Remember?'

It was a new development for Cathy to want to be abroad early in the morning. He climbed out of bed feeling that this was one of the days when he would have liked to go on sleeping for ever. Sunshine was streaming in at the window. Obviously it was going to be a marvellous day.

They made breakfast together. Cathy seemed to relax into her old self.

'Were you worried the other night?'

'I should bloody well think I was,' Conway spluttered. Then, catching her eye, he smiled, 'Now that things are straightening themselves out, couldn't you try and explain what happened?'

Cathy buttered another piece of toast.

'Mm. I never told you how funny you looked, did I?'

'It didn't feel funny.'

She smiled, and he had a feeling that the original Cathy was feeling very pleased with herself.

'What did it look-like?'

'Well, you looked up at the door in a very startled way. Then you made a huge leap backwards and banged your head against the wall and fell down on the ground.'

'And you don't know what it was that I saw?'

'How should I?'

This at least made a bit of rational sense, how should she?

'I saw the bastard who kicked me in a fight once.'

'Of course, it had to be something that really happened, but I had no means of knowing about it. All I did was to make you frightened.'

'And it was the same with the man at the airport?'

'Yes. I tried to guess what it was that he was seeing, but I couldn't. Did you have any idea?'

'It looked as if he was fighting with an anaconda.'

'What's that?'

He realized that the original Cathy certainly wouldn't know what an anaconda was. 'It's a sort of big snake. It squeezes you instead of poisoning you. It kills you by suffocating you. Squeezes the breath out of your body.'

'Well, he seemed to have plenty of breath in his body, didn't he? I don't think that can be right.'

The course of the conversation convinced Conway of what he knew already, that some new and formidable power – which he hoped he would soon begin to understand – had allied itself with the original Cathy. The alliance apparently suited them both. The new creature, whatever it was, had acquired the full logical control, but the original Cathy was dictating all the emotional responses. He could understand that this would suit the original Cathy down to the ground, but he couldn't understand why the new creature was so ready to fall in with Cathy's old happy-go-lucky ways.

'Do you intend to go sleeping around with other men?'

'Why ever should I? You seem entirely satisfactory. Remember I have some idea of what a lot of men are like. I came here inside one of them, didn't I?'

The absurdity of the final inconsequential question, Cathy's old habit, disarmed him again. 'You used to, my wife used to . . .' His voice trailed away as he saw that she understood what he meant.

'Oh, it is obvious, isn't it? She couldn't stay with you, otherwise you would soon have come to despise her for her stupidity. It was the only way she could hold you, by constantly going around with other men and making you jealous.'

Then she looked at him with a broad smile and added, 'But I am not stupid. Besides, I could stop you going away even if you wanted to go.'

She looked very demure, and he knew that this was the old Cathy showing through. Instead of being appalled he began to laugh. It was as if Cathy had suddenly become a consummate actress, as if she were playing a new role, determined not to reveal by the slightest aside that she had ever been anything different. 'Look, let's put our cards on the table. I know it's you, Cathy, an awful lot of this – not everything but a lot – so why not admit it?'

It was her turn to laugh. 'Why do you go on tormenting yourself? Why don't you start from those things that you know for sure? You know that there can't have been a single atom changed in here.'

She pointed at her head and went on, 'Nothing that has happened can violate what you know about physics. I am as your wife. I'm a single physical whole, more or less exactly the same as I was a week ago. I'm not two bodies pushed together.'

'But there must be something else?'

'Yes, of course there is something else. There is always something else. There is something else inside you, although you don't realize it. When I have got the right words to say I will tell you about it.'

'You mean you can put it into rational terms?'

'You're talking like an idiot. Everything can be put in rational terms. But we ought to be making a move. I want to get into London by the middle morning.'

'Am I allowed to ask why? I always seem to be asking why.'

'Oh, yes. Just because I want to be back again by the afternoon. It looks as though it's going to be a beautiful day.'

Cathy was ready to leave in about a third of the time she usually took. Instead of drifting about rather vaguely from room to room she seemed to know just what she was doing. Conway got out the car and soon they were on the road, rolling along the Downs, to which he kept until they reached Reading.

He managed to park in the region of Knightsbridge, and they took a taxi towards the centre. He asked Cathy where she wanted to be. 'Oh, anywhere near Trafalgar Square.'

Conway told the driver to set them down just outside its exit into the Mall. He started to ask Cathy what they were to do next, but his voice was drowned out by the thunder of the loudspeaker system. It was mounted high up all around the Square, and the volume was prodigious, it had to be in order to drown the noise of the traffic. It had the sort of volume associated with the peal of church bells when you were standing close by, except that instead of sending out a joyous carillon they were announcing the latest news bulletin. The latest news carried by the international ticker-tape was not good.

Eventually the uproar died down. He saw the crowds looking upwards for a while to the point where the speakers had hurled down their message. Although he'd seen it thousands of times before it struck him how silly they all looked. Suddenly they seeemed to jerk themselves back to their own thoughts and went about their business.

'Wow,' he said to Cathy, 'this is it. What shall we do?'

'I want to go off by myself now,' she replied. 'Let's meet here at twelve. I'll have done what I want to do by then, and you can walk about and tell me how it goes.'

To his question of what was she going to do she made no answer. With a wave of her hand she crossed Whitehall and made off towards the direction of the Strand.

Conway saw that he had only three-quarters of an hour to kill. He wondered what Cathy was up to. He'd had an idea that she was going to go and talk to the Government, but apparently not, for that would have taken them down to Westminster. Maybe she was going to persuade some newspaper editor in Fleet Street to make an announcement of some sort. But that didn't seem right either. It was much too feeble. He thought he would go and look at the pictures in the National Gallery, but then decided to stroll in the direction of Seven Dials. You could still see a little of the London of the twentieth century here. He stood for a moment on the edge of the pavement, looking reflectively at a recently changed skyline. It was curious the way they took away one building and put another in its place, and yet still kept to the same pattern of streets. His thoughts flicked back to the recent changes in his own life. It was rather like the way the atoms changed in your body. Their identity was never quite the same two minutes running, and over the years they changed completely. But it didn't make any difference to the structure, it didn't make any difference to you. Why should it? After all, one atom of oxygen was exactly the same as another. It didn't matter in the least swopping them round as long as you didn't change the pattern. It was of course the pattern that really counted, and this must be what had hapened to Cathy. Part of the pattern, only a part, had been changed. And now both parts, the new and the old, were growing in confidence. For the first few hours, he realized, the changes must have produced a pretty numb state of affairs. Now he had the feeling that Cathy's brain had reshuffled itself and that all the parts were working together in complete harmony.

He heard a growing murmur from Trafalgar Square. Something seemed to be happening, probably a new bulletin had come through. Bloody nonsense of course, but he might as well find out what was going on. He began to stroll slowly back, his mind still occupied with his new train of thought. The noise ahead of him was increasing. A vehicle came tearing down the street at a breakneck pace. Bloody fool, thought Conway, they'll roast him for that. People began to pass him, heading out of the Square. They were hurrying, some of them running. He asked one elderly man, who was limping more slowly along, what it was all about.

'It's War. They've started.'

Conway stood still. It couldn't be true. It just couldn't be true. He knew they were fools but not such fools. It had to be a big last-minute scare, just to frighten the wits out of the people, so the Governments could give themselves manoeuvring room. The scene around him had all the aspects of a major panic, but this would be what the Governments wanted.

A woman carrying a young child ran past him, her face streaming with tears. It took quite a while before he could make his way against the human current that came against him, but at last he reached the Square. People were erupting out of the buildings, so that in spite of those who had managed to get away, some towards the river, others in the direction of Piccadilly, and others along the way he had come, the Square was still as full as ever. It was like an ants' nest, except that ants move in orderly columns. He wondered if there was any chance that he could get control of the speaker system and tell them that it was all a lot of bull. Two days earlier the thought wouldn't have occurred to him, but with Cathy to stand behind him he wouldn't need to worry much about the reprisals of bureaucracy.

It was odd that the thought of Cathy hadn't occurred to him before. Instead of being worried sick aboout her, as he had been in the big arena at the time of the landing, he felt now that she was perfectly capable of looking after herself. It would be as much as he could do himself to fight his way across the Square and to get back to their agreed spot by twelve o'clock.

The speakers boomed out again. A list of cities now under evacuation was being read out – Washington, Moscow, Paris, and all the rest of them. Another piece of civil defence thought Conway. Then came the announcement that the first bomb had fallen on New York, and for the first time Conway knew that this was really it. They'd played around for a century, they'd played around with tensions and counter-tensions, and now at last it had got out of control. Pandora's box was wide open.

There was a blinding chaos in the streets of New York. The southern tip of Manhattan had been wiped clean.

From Twentieth Street south it was a mass of rubble and twisted hot metal. An area on the west side from about Ninetieth Street as far up as the George Washington Bridge had also been bitten out of the city as if a giant thumb had suddenly pressed down on it. Almost a million had been killed by the blast, the very suddenness had caught them unawares. Bodies were strewn around in outrageous postures, like sawdust dolls, from north to south and from east to west. Otherwise the human form was absent from the streets. There was life still in New York, there were ten million lives, but they were not to be found in the streets. They were in the prepared fall-out shelters, wondering, desperately wondering, what had happened.

Why hadn't the warning come sooner? Why hadn't the complexed interlocking warning system given them more than a couple of minutes' grace? For the reason that it had had to be checked and cross-checked before anybody had dared to announce that this was the real thing. A warning system cannot possibly be expected to work if it is only called on to operate once. Especially if it is constantly being abused by false warnings.

Why hadn't the wonderfully delicate, computer-controlled system of antimissile missiles worked properly? The answer was that it had worked. It had intercepted almost seventy per cent of the attacking rockets, which was more than anybody in informed circles had expected.

New York was not the only city where these things were happening. Mushroom-shaped clouds were already rising to monstrous heights above Chicago and Washington. Tons of radioactive material had already been injected into the stagnant pool of air that overlay Los Angeles. All passes across the mountains were blocked by columns of vehicles. Soon the grisly toll would be exacted from cities of lower and lower rank.

The American reply had been delayed because the President's final O.K. had been delayed. The information had reached his office on the special communication circuit it is true, but the President had just not happened to be in his office at that particular moment. The planners, deep in their prepared shelters, now realized that it had been a big mistake not to fit all relaxing rooms with the latest of communication devices.

But now the Western reply had been made, it was moving at upwards of twenty thousand miles per hour through the air, the very thin air high above the Earth. A few moments later it would reach its targets, the nerve centres of the Soviet Union. Watchers far down the long avenue leading out of Red Square would see the Lenin Mausoleum, and the Kremlin itself, disappear inside a towering column of flame.

The chief launching areas of either side were hit and hit again. The operational personnel was halved, halved again, and yet again, but still the missiles continued to rise from the ground. They were no longer under human control. The master computer, buried deep inside the Earth, out of reach of all attack, continued to direct activities. Doors opened, rockets were assembled by mechanical and electrical controls, supplied with their fuels by automatic means, and transported by a moving platform to the inclined launching ramp, from which they rose into the air with a deafening roar. This was the ultimate deterrent, a deterrent that, once activated, could never be stopped, except through the exhaustion of the whole complete stockpile. There were hundreds of such sites both in the West and in the East. Unmoved by events, by death and by suffering, they all continued, like the obedient servants they were, to project their grisly human-designed pencils of destruction in an unbroken stream across the sky.

Conway saw the first bomb explode, about three miles away, he judged, in the direction of the City. He could hardly have missed seeing it, for the air was filled with a vast white flash, a vast whiteness that blinded him for the moment. Then the blast knocked him to the ground. He heard stones and blocks of concrete falling around him.

Miraculously he was not severely hit. Then came the suction. His only link with life now was the oxygen that he happened to have in his lungs. He could last for about three minutes, but by that time it might be over. The thudding became dull in his ears, and lights formed themselves before his eyes. Then it eased and he found himself able to breathe again.

Very slowly and wearily, his chest heaving, he managed to get to his feet. Wrecked vehicles and wrecked bodies were strewn around the Square. He noticed that there were far more bodies away on the left than there were over by the Strand. He realized that this must have been due to the blast, which had lifted many of its victims far through the air. He rested for a moment against a doorway, keeping a little inside lest he be hit from above. He tested his arms and legs, incredibly they seemed all right.

Then the stark horror of his position hit him. So far from being all right he was already a dead man. In the moment of the flash he must have been drenched with gamma rays. Everything was all right for the moment, but in a few hours the cells would begin to disintegrate. His hair would fall out and the skin would open up all over his body. After a few days of intense agony he would die.

Then he knew that it wouldn't happen that way. He had a few hours, plenty of time, to find a bottle of sleeping tablets. A big overdose, and he would be dead before the disintegration started. He wondered if it might be possible to get out of London, perhaps even to get home. It would be best if he could fall asleep back there high on the Downs. With a sharp pang he realized that he would never see Cathy again. He could hardly expect that she would be able to find her way back here now. There must be thousands of millions like him who would never see their husbands, wives, sweethearts, and children again.

Then the second bomb struck. It was much closer this time, and Conway was thrown high in the air by the blast. He hit the ground with a sickening thud. The suction passed again and he was vaguely aware of being still alive. His eyes had been almost burnt out by the big flash and now he could only see rather vaguely those things that were quite close by. Looking around very slowly he found himself star-`ing into the face of the woman who had run past him on the street. The woman who had been clutching the young child. She was still clutching it and they were both dead. He could tell that by the grotesque pile into which they had been pitched by the blast.

It was then that the first suspicions came to him. How could the woman have got to where he now saw her? It had to be, it just had to be, that he was seeing things again. It explained the woman, for she was the only person he had looked at at all carefully since Cathy left him. This of course was what Cathy had come to do. He realized that it was use-less to worry about his aches and pains, the best thing was just to lie there and wait.

The scene began to clear and he could focus again right across to the far side of the Square. For a moment he didn't realize that the vision was gone, that this was return to reality. It was the lack of debris that gave it away. The ghastly qualities of the scene had gone, but what the scene had lost in horror it had gained in grotesqueness. He saw vehicles piled here, there and everywhere, in an incredible tangle. It was lucky that traffic was always forced to crawl through the Square these days, for otherwise many people would have been badly hurt. Thousands of them were lying on the ground, some twitching, some moaning, some just lying supine. Every now and then someone would get up, take a run, and then deliberately crash down on the ground. He rubbed his shoulder and supposed that that was just what he himself had done.

Articles of every description were scattered as far as his eyes could see, down Whitehall, right to Parliament Square, up towards St James's Street, and down the Strand. Every-where traffic was stopped, everywhere people were still in the grip of the vision. He picked his way carefully among the sprawling, writhing figures. A couple of smartly-dressed women, straight from a beauty salon, but now with their sculptured hair covered in dust, were staring up at the sky. Saliva was dribbling out of their mouths and they were making faint moaning sounds.

He worked his way round the body of a man dressed in immaculate City clothes. The fellow was clutching his own throat and making sounds like water gurgling down a pipe. His rolled umbrella and bowler hat were lying not far away, his brief-case burst open to disgorge a neat packet of sandwiches, at which pigeons were placidly pecking.

He reached the place where he had agreed to meet Cathy. He wondered how the devil she'd been able to do it. It was all very well to make you see something that was already in your own head. It was only a matter of disturbing the memory storage areas, but he didn't see how she'd been able to do the same thing to everybody. But perhaps they weren't all seeing the same thing. Perhaps each person had his own private vision. That was the way it must be. Then he saw her coming towards him, a grim little smile on her face.

'I'm glad you're on time,' she said.

'Where have you been?'

'Down into the City. I went into the narrow streets where the crowd was densest. That was the best place to get it started. But I had to walk back because there is nothing running.'

'I should think not. It's complete chaos. My God, you've started something now.'

'You see why I said it would be best to get back home by mid-afternoon.'

'It looks as though we shall have to walk unless I can get one of these cars started.'

He found a taxi with its engine still running. It had careered off the road into a traffic direction signal. The front was horribly buckled – a triple-century job as the garage men would say. He bundled Cathy into it and drove up towards St James's Street. There wasn't a vehicle moving anywhere so he had it all to himself. He took the shortest way back, ignoring all traffic lights and one-way-street signs. The time had gone for small things. They got back to the car and within a couple of minutes were running down Kensington High Street.

'At this rate we're going to break the record for the shortest time home.'

After that they didn't say much to each other and Conway had a feeling that Cathy was almost as overwhelmed as he was himself. They were half-way to Reading before she said, 'I knew that everybody was strongly charged up. In a way I'm sorry, but they had only themselves to blame, hadn't they?'

Conway realized that it was indeed true, they were to blame, all of them, for entertaining such outrageous notions. He looked across at Cathy and nodded. She hadn't put ideas into anybody's head. She'd simply made them see what was there already. He saw that everybody was really guilty, not only for having such ideas, but even for permitting the constant discussion of them – by the sort of commentators they had seen on the television the previous night. He saw now what Cathy had meant by saying she would teach them a lesson. He hadn't enjoyed the lesson himself but he knew it had been deserved. 'Did you actually see anything yourself? I don't mean the real thing, but the visions.'

'I couldn't avoid it. There was some of it inside me already, and in any case the discharge was so intense that some of it came into me from outside.'

Conway didn't really understand this, but he felt that in a general way he got the drift of what she was saying. 'How far do you think the effect spread out?'

She looked at him with a faint smile, there seemed to be an implied compliment behind it.

About ten miles east of Reading they ran into the outward-moving traffic jam. Quickly he worked out a route in his mind along the side roads. There was a turning that would do it about five miles farther along. It was a tiny road to the left, which he did not think many of the drivers ahead would know about.

'Looks as if the effect has spread as far as this.'

'Yes, these are the people living on the outskirts of the city who have been planning to get away into the country if anything happened. They think it has.'

'Pity you had to do all this here you know. Really you should have done it in Paris, and in New York, and in Moscow.'

'There's more than a chance that it's happened there already.'

Conway could begin to see it all now. It was a psychological chain reaction, it only needed a small nucleus of people to really believe that it had happened and the whole thing would spread out like a tidal wave until it engulfed the world. He leaned out of the window of the car and shouted at the occupants of the off-side front seat in the car on his immediate right, 'What goes on?' The man looked at him in some surprise, 'You've got a big surprise coming, Charlie. It's started, the big show's started.' Conway wished that the man could have been with him in Tragalfar Square. It was a bit uncharitable, but he felt that he would have liked to see the man bashing his head against the nearest stone wall. This was the sort of bloody fool that made it all possible.

An hour later they reached the turn-off point. Conway was immediately able to accelerate the car along the small twisting road. They didn't talk much, probably both of them were wondering what the news bulletins would say. Another hour and he was pulling up the car outside their own house.

All the local radio and television channels were blank. He tried the Continental channels and they too were blank. There was nothing on the short-wave radio. It added up to only one thing, the chain reaction had swept entirely round the globe. The meaning of it all Conway didn't understand yet, but granted the starting point, that they had been made to see their own thoughts and their own memories, then the rest followed pretty easily. After all they'd lived with those thoughts and those visions for a whole lifetime, literally from their first thinking moments. Everybody had done so since the middle of the twentieth century.

They didn't say much to each other. Conway had never seen Cathy in a serious mood before. It wasn't as if many people would come to real harm. But driving out devils was a serious business. Devils might be absurd and monstrous in themselves, but their effect was very real. The very strength of his own reaction – he still remembered the blindness, the sickening crash on his shoulder, and the gamma rays – the very strength of his reaction showed just how far he himself had been indoctrinated, rebel that he was.

He tried the radio again and there was still nothing, so he went off to make tea. In a sense it was absurd, but why not make tea?

Chapter Fifteen

The Aftermath

Conway hadn't realized how remarkably quick his own recovery had been. It took the rest of the world more than three hours to make the same recovery. The people rose up from the pavement, they came out of the fall-out shelters, they came out of their graves, and they found that the sun was still shining and that their children were still alive. For the most part they broke down and wept as they had not done since they were young themselves, waking to security from the worst nightmare. They didn't know how it had happened but they knew that in some way a hellish disaster had been avoided. Yesterday their rulers had brandished their fists and shouted in loud voices at each other, and all the commentators and leader-writers had told them that the situation was very serious. And because they were very simple people they had believed it all, just as they had believed what they had been told all their lives. But today all this bluster, all this raving, this psychological calculation had suddenly been made to seem what it really was – the currency of the mad-house.

The people were much too numb yet to be angry. But soon they would come to realize the enormity of the things that had been done to them. Five hundred years earlier they had endured physical subjection. But now they would come to see that what had been done to their minds in the last hundred years by stick-at-nothing politicians, by the ambitious military and by the lickspittle psychologists – was appallingly and vastly worse. Soon with sure instinct they would know all this and the outcry would begin.

There was not a government anywhere that had shuffled

its pieces on the chessboard of power that did not appraise the situation with complete accuracy. It was known both in the East and the West, in Britain even, that not only the days of governments but of the whole anonymous social structure that had grown up over the past two centuries were numbered. The days were numbered unless a culprit could be found and a new scare generated. The semi-paralysis that had overtaken even the highest administrative officials may be judged from the fact that it took almost six hours before the testimony of Tom Fiske was remembered.

It had of course been inevitable that the authorities would catch up with Tom. They did so in fact on the very same day that Cathy had gone to the hospital in Washington. And it was also to Washington that Tom was taken. He and Ilyana were put into the grill box. Not together, which would have been easier, but separately. Their testimonies were taken by different groups of inquisitors in different buildings.

They both knew their stories must check and since they had not talked very seriously in their night together they could only stick to the truth. Both Fiske and Ilyana told the whole story, exactly as they knew it. So their completely sceptical questioners, keen fellows from Intelligence, learned about the abortive circular trips in the vast grasslands of Achilles, about the strange translucent sheets and of how the four men had really died.

They were of course put under what was effectively house arrest. Nobody had any doubts at first that the authorities were being given a vatful of the purest eyewash. They knew that Fiske and Ilyana would come clean in the end.

As the Governments began to recover from the horror of the great vision, as the pulses of administration slowly began to beat again, the statements of Fiske and Ilyana were remembered. They were doubted, pulled to pieces, put together again, argued about at the highest level of secrecy, and finally accepted as a tentative working hypothesis. Gradually the hypothesis that someone or something could make you see what you didn't want to see gained ground. It was the only way in which the vision could be explained. And it needed little deductive power to see that this ghastly thing had come from Achilles. It must be some sort of bug that attacked the nervous system in a manner as yet unknown to science.

Four people had returned alive from Achilles. Three of them, Fiske, Ilyana, and Pitoyan in the East, were essentially under lock and key. They could be looked into in detail and at leisure, the tops of their heads sliced off if need be.

The highest-level teams were instantly put on to the job. The stress induced by the medico-psychiatric treatment had little or no effect on either Fiske or Ilyana. It was minor league stuff compared with what they had experienced on Achilles. But Pitoyan cracked badly under the strain, and was obliged thereafter to spend several years recovering in a mental institution.

The authorities in Washington remembered that there had been a fourth traveller on the returning ship – Fawsett. They remembered the strange illness he had suffered from, and they began to wonder. Perhaps Fiske and Ilyana were really giving them the gen after all.

The real inspiration came from a balding thirty-nine-year-old executive, described in the ancient Time-Life circuit as a rising star among Washington's topmen. He was one of those going-places-fast young men who work thirteen hours a day at his desk, and give their wives hell after it. His job was in the Department of Inconsequential Facts. He remembered, while dallying with his secretary, the odd story of the man at Washington airport. A quick research by two of his assistants refreshed his mind with the facts of the case. The statements of witnesses had similarities with what he himself had seen during the vision. Plainly the story rated investigation in depth.

The next thirteen hours at the desk were well spent. One line of investigation lay with the ferry flight-lists. There had been almost a hundred flights around the time of the incident and it was quite some job to round up the dossiers of all the passengers. But at last several boxes of punched cards were assembled on the desk of the young executive. A quick programme was run up by the department's computer experts, and soon the big machine on the seventeenth floor of the building was dissecting the lives of the seven thousand odd passengers, comparing them with a collation of facts concerning the space-ship and its crew. The computer only needed to chew its cud for about three minutes and there was the name of Cathy Conway, printed out for all the world to see. Following Cathy's name, the essential facts of the case were neatly listed. She had been a 'friend' of Mike Fawsett – the machine even put the word friend in inverted commas – Fawsett had been sick with an unknown disease, Mrs Conway had visited him on the day before the airport incident, and finally Mrs Conway and her husband had checked in at the reception desk less than fifteen minutes before the reported time of the incident. The balding young man knew that he had it, both the solution to the problem that was baffling the top echelon, and also certain promotion.

The top echelon also knew he had it, both the solution and his promotion. Within an hour their agent in London was contacting the British Government. The British were characteristically slow in the uptake, and it was not until well into the day following the vision that they acted.

But when they did they acted with decision. A small, highly-trained military unit was directed by Intelligence to move in and surround the village of Alderbourne. The Head of Intelligence, Brigadier Fitzalan, put himself in charge of the operation. It was in fact a great mistake not to brief the police, for as it turned out the ordinary London bobby might have been more use to the Government than the highly-trained unit deployed by Intelligence.

It was about six o'clock in the evening when Conway opened his door to find Brigadier Fitzalan and a young major standing on his threshold. Conway and Cathy had pretty well recovered from the previous day, but Conway was in no mood for visitors.

'Professor Conway?' inquired Fitzalan.

'Indeed,' answered Conway.

'I wonder if you would mind me putting a few questions to your wife, Mrs Catherine Conway.'

'Put questions to Cathy? What on earth for?'

Conway knew perfectly well what for, he knew that they must have connected yesterday's events with the space-ship from Achilles. He knew they must be investigating every conceivable line. Every stone would be upturned and every little insect under it would be examined to see that it had showered properly and brushed its teeth. Cathy was obviously one of those lines. Or rather one of those stones, and he himself was one of the insects. He motioned the Brigadier and the fresh-faced Major into the house.

'I think I would like to see Mrs Conway alone, if you don't mind?' said the Brigadier. 'Major Stanley will wait. He only accompanied me for the walk.'

It was here that Conway made a big mistake. He had of course no knowledge of the story that Fiske and Ilyana told to the authorities. So he had no reason to think that this was anything more than a routine check-up. He had foreseen of course that there would be such a check-up. But Fitzalan had been shrewd enough not to arouse his suspicion by a show of force, although motorized units had already surrounded the village.

'Oh, certainly,' he said, 'you'll find my wife through there in the drawing-room.'

When the Brigadier had gone the young Major said, 'You've got a very fine garden here, sir.'

Conway decided that it would be stupid of him to seem in any way concerned, and in any case Cathy could more than look after herself. She seemed to need his help just as much as before in a lot of small things, but on the big things she knew perfectly well what she was doing.

'Would you like to take a stroll around?' he asked.

The young Major said he would and they went outside into the late afternoon sunshine. They'd made two tours around the garden before they heard the shouting. Conway was astonished to see the young Major draw a pistol and begin moving towards the house at a trot. Conway thought fast now. Either Cathy had lost patience or this was more serious than it looked on the face of it. If they really were on to her then things were going to be very awkward, not only for Cathy and himself but for everybody in general. The Major's gun showed that they were going to shoot first and ask questions afterwards, so he shouted, 'The bastard's attacking her.'

This ambiguous, but in a sense correct, statement caused the Major to waver for a moment. In an instant Conway threw himself in front of the man in an American-style football block. The boy came down heavily and the pistol slipped away from him. Conway got to it first.

'Come on, baby boy, march!'

They found the Brigadier lying back in a deep chair. He was breathing in big shuddering gasps and his face was a rich purple.

'I loosened his collar. That's the right thing to do, isn't it?' said Cathy.

'Jesus,' muttered Conway, and that was all he could think of to say. It was clear it would be many a long day before the Brigadier would again step up in sprightly fashion to a professor's door at six o'clock on a fine autumn evening. It was very abundantly clear.

'You'd better get him out of here,' he said to the Major. 'I don't know how many men you've got, but please understand that there's just nothing you can do. The more you try the harder you'll get hurt.'

'Can I go down and fetch a vehicle?'

'No, get out.'

The Major left, supporting the Brigadier as best he could. The retreat from Moscow, thought Conway as he watched them stagger down the pathway to the road. Very quickly he threw the bare necessities of existence, a razor, tooth-brushes, a few clothes, and what he could see of Cathy's things into a bag.

'Why are you doing that?' she asked.

'Because this is a serious business. Now that they know that you did it they'll hunt us down.'

'But I can fix them all as easily as I fixed the General.'

'Brigadier. Brigadier Fitzalan. You can fix them if they come to the door and walk politely in here and sit them-selves down by your side. Then you can fix them all right. But how if they lob half a dozen mortar bombs on the house? What happens then?'

'You think they might do that?'

'If they couldn't get you any other way they'd do just that. The army would start shooting. Even if they couldn't see you they'd shoot at random, just on the chance of hitting you, even if it meant killing hundreds of innocent people. And if our army didn't do it every military force in the world would close in on these islands. It is the only way they can save themselves. The whole of this society is run on an idea. If you remain loose that idea collapses. They've simply got to get you.'

Cathy became more serious now. 'Then we shouldn't have let those two men go.'

'No, we should have killed them, but that's not the sort of thing I like to do. It's better to get out.'

They drove out on to the main road and made off to the village. They got a couple of hundred yards beyond the outskirts, turned a corner and saw the first roadblock. Con-way backed up the car until he could turn it. Then he drove off down a lane in the opposite direction. There was of course another roadblock. The place was surrounded. He had been badly mistaken to let the Brigadier go. Then Con-way saw that the fresh-faced Major was in charge and on an impulse drove up to the barrier.

'Look, this sort of thing isn't any good. You can't hope to

deal with what happened yesterday by playing toy soldiers. You're not in the right league.'

'What are you threatening us with, sir?'

'You saw perfectly well what happened to Fitzalan. There isn't any problem in dealing with the whole lot of you in the same sort of way.'

Conway wasn't quite sure if this was true or not but it seemed a fair presumption. The boy in front of him went pale and said, 'You won't get away with it, sir. We'll get you in the end.'

They opened up the barrier. Conway accelerated towards it, and was within about ten yards of the opening when a shot came from his left. He heard Cathy cry out and at the same instant realized that it was the young Major who had fired. Instinctively he braked the car to a standstill. As he heard his wife moan there was a deep rage in his heart. Something larger than himself seemed to be expanding his mind, and he knew now why he had stopped the car. He couldn't describe what he did, but it was like loosing a bolt. He saw the Major collapse. The man didn't even cry out as he fell. Conway never knew exactly how it had happened. The other guards scattered pell-mell, with all the devils of hell on their tails as far as Conway could see. He didn't know what he'd done but it was enough. He had the car moving again now. Soon they were clear of the village, and as the road opened before them a strange influence seemed to go out of him. Cathy's eyes were open, and she murmured, 'My shoulder hurts.'

He got the car on to the side roads and looked for somewhere to stop where he could examine Cathy's wounds. He carefully tore away her blouse and saw a dark patch on her right shoulder. 'It won't kill you,' he said.

But it was going to be painful and it had carried them a long way downhill. Cathy would have to have immediate treatment. It would be difficult to get this without their whereabouts becoming known to the authorities. And Cathy herself wouldn't be in the right sort of shape to deal very effectively with their pursuers. He cursed himself for being fool enough to be taken in by Fitzalan and by that young jackass.

'I'm going to get you into London to see a friend just as soon as I can. I daren't risk the main highway, so I'm going to take the side route as far as the outskirts and it may take quite a while. They may put up barriers and you'll have to get them to open up. Do you think you can hold on for a couple of hours?'

'I think I can.' Her voice was weak but it sounded firm. He drove out from behind the hedge and started on their journey.

He couldn't be certain that the main highway would be clear. If they threw a barrier across it the sheer volume of the traffic would be an unsurmountable block. But if they merely put something across the road in one of the country villages, then Cathy would still be able to deal with that without too much trouble.

He knew that in the brief moment when she had been hit something had passed between them. It had been prepared to leave just in case the shot had killed her. Conway himself would have been the new home. Whatever it was, it wasn't going to give up easily. He shivered and he couldn't help wondering what it would have been like if the thing had stayed with him. Would he still have known who he was? He supposed he probably would.

They got three-quarters of the way to London without any trouble; then they came to a makeshift barrier set up by a village policeman and two civilian helpers. They simply stood without noticing him as he moved the obstacle. They just weren't seeing either it or him. Probably they weren't even seeing the village High Street at all. They had satisfied smiles on their faces and their arms appeared to be clutching something which Conway took to be imaginary females.

Soon he began to come into the surburban traffic. They wouldn't have much chance of finding them now. The next big danger would be his medical friend. Friend was a word of wide connotation, and in this case he could hardly expect it to mean that the man he knew in Wimpole Street would not be suspicious and would not insist on some sort of investigation being made. But that was a risk that had to be taken when he came to it.

He went wrong in a one-way system and had to drive round twice before he found the right place. He had to double park so that Cathy wouldn't have to walk more than the distance from the road to the old-fashioned house that now faced him. Before getting her out he rang the bell. A uniformed maid, or nurse, he couldn't tell which, answered the door. He gave his name and asked to see Dr Gwyn Jones. The girl told him the doctor was out but would be back shortly. So there was nothing for it but for him to take the girl into his confidence.

'There's been an accident, a shooting accident,' he said in a nervous sort of way. 'My wife has been shot. I know it sounds ridiculous, it always sounds ridiculous. I never thought it would happen to me, but it did when I was cleaning my gun.' The girl looked alarmed and suspicious.

'Oh, it's not what you think. She's not very badly hurt. I wouldn't have shot her in the shoulder if I wanted . . .'

'Hadn't we better get her inside the house?' said the girl.

'Oh yes, could you please help me?'

They got Cathy out of the car and up the steps and along a passage and into the surgery. The girl, who evidently was a nurse after all, began to examine the wound. 'You should have taken her to hospital.'

'Well, I know Dr Jones pretty well, and I thought if he could see her straight away . . . you see I'd like her to be treated by somebody I know. She can go to hospital afterwards, can't she?'

'Yes, of course. But it would have been easier at the hospital. We don't have the same equipment here, you see. But I suppose since you're here you might as well wait.'

Jones came in not many minutes later. He took one look

at the wound and whistled slowly. 'Don't say you were cleaning a gun and shot her,' he said.

'That's exactly what I do say.'

'She should really be on the operating table.'

'Can't you fix her up here?'

'I'd sooner not.'

'Can't you do it as a favour?'

'I can. But I'll have to make a report, you know, and it will have to be full and accurate.'

'All right, but will you please hurry. It's hurting her all the time we're talking.'

Jones began to prepare to do the job. Conway realized that Cathy would have to be put out, otherwise the pain would be too much. And while she was out there was nothing that could be done if the authorities should arrive. He didn't like the thought of his car, displaying what must by now be a widely advertised number, double parked outside in a busy street.

'I'm going to leave it to you, Gwyn. My car's double parked outside,' he ended weakly.

Without bothering to see how Jones and the nurse took it he marched outside and jumped quickly into his car. By a mercy the police were not waiting for him. Probably they knew it was a doctor's house and made some allowance, and his number hadn't yet reached the constables on duty. He drove for a couple of miles, and left the car without troubling himself about correct parking. They could find it now if they wanted to. He took a taxi back to Jones's house. The manoeuvre had taken him twenty-five minutes, but he reckoned they wouldn't be finished with Cathy yet. He rang the bell and the door was answered again by the nurse. 'It isn't finished yet. You really should have taken her to hospital, you know.'

'I suppose I should, but I wanted it done by a doctor that I know. I'll ring them now and ask them to send an ambulance if you like.'

'That would be the best thing. Would you like me to do it?'

'No, I'll do it myself if I could use your phone.'

'Of course.'

'What should I tell them? I mean, what time should I ask them to come here?'

'I think Doctor will be finished in about twenty minutes' time. You could ask them to be here half an hour from now.'

She showed him to the phone and then went back to the surgery. He got the hospital, told them he was Dr Jones, said he had a serious accident case, and would they come in twenty minutes' time. Then he made another call. A woman's voice answered him, and after a brief conversation he began to think that maybe his luck had turned a bit.

The ambulance arrived before Jones had finished his operation. Conway told them to wait and that the patient would be ready in a moment. He didn't mind them being double parked, and they'd be able to make a quick getaway once the job was done. He didn't want Jones asking a lot of questions. A few minutes later Jones came out to him and said, 'I'd like to have a few words with you.' From this Conway knew that Cathy must be all right.

'I don't know whether the nurse has told you, but I've had second thoughts about the hospital. I've got an ambulance outside.'

'You ought to have done that before. There'll have to be an inquiry.'

He went to the door and nodded to the ambulance men. Within a moment they were carrying a stretcher into the house. Conway followed them into the surgery and saw Cathy being moved gently. She was still under the anaesthetic, her face was wan and drained. It made Conway mad with himself. Twice he'd made the mistake of underestimating his opponents. The men carried her out of the surgery and he made to follow them.

'Just a moment, they can wait. I'd like you to see this.'

Gwyn was holding out the bullet to him. He took it and looked it over and said, 'What's so special about this?'

'It's a military calibre. I hope you understand, Hugh.

Just as soon as you've gone I'm going to make a report to the police. In my position I can't do otherwise.'

'I wouldn't ask you to do otherwise,' answered Conway. 'And my thanks, Gwyn, I can't tell you how much it means.' He looked Jones dead in the eye. He meant exactly what he said.

The ambulance men had got Cathy into position inside their machine and they had closed up the doors at the back of it. Conway got into the front beside the driver. The other man moved in on his left. They manoeuvred through the streets with the siren going. Conway wondered if he should try to make conversation but decided in favour of a dull silence. They swung into University College Hospital and drove to the Casualty Department. As soon as they came to a halt the driver and his mate jumped out on opposite sides and moved to the back, from which they intended to take the stretcher. Instantly Conway slipped over to the driver's seat; he pressed the ignition switch and the engine sprang to life, and a moment later he was on his way back to the main gate. There were angry shouts from behind but that was a matter of small consequence. He leant over and got hold of the left-hand door and slammed it shut. Soon he was speeding back through the streets. He resisted the impulse to switch on the siren. There was no point in gilding the lily.

His route took him into the City and across London Bridge. Soon he quitted the main road and began to explore the side streets. It took quite a while to find what he wanted. It was a small apartment made originally out of a disused warehouse. He rang the bell and the door was opened by the slim dark girl he had spent the night with the best part of two years ago.

'You're alone?'

'Yes, I put off my other arrangements.'

Conway spoke urgently. 'It's not quite what you think, I'm afraid. It's my wife, she's been shot – oh no, not by me. There are reasons why I don't want to be found, I want her to lie up for a week or two. Can we stay here? I'll make it worth your while if you'll do it.'

The girl looked at him for some time and then suddenly nodded. 'You did a lot for me,' she said quite simply.

It wasn't easy to get Cathy up into the apartment. They had to climb a flight of stairs which luckily wasn't too steep. But it was as much as the dark girl could manage. At last they had Cathy off the stretcher on to the bed.

He went back to the ambulance and collected all the considerable medical supplies that were carried inside it. He'd need them to dress Cathy's shoulder. When he had taken them upstairs he said to the girl, 'She'll be waking up quite soon. Tell her that I'll be away for a little while, but that she's quite safe with you. I want to get rid of the ambulance so that they can't trace us. Besides, they'll have need of it.'

He drove back into the City. It was the last risk, but even if they got him now they wouldn't get Cathy. It would take some doing to trace her to Emling's flat. He supposed that it could be done but it would take quite some time. As he came up to it he decided on impulse to park outside the Bank of England. It seemed the right sort of thing to do.

He couldn't risk a taxi of course. So he walked back the way he had come. It took over an hour, but he was well satisfied as he mounted the old warehouse steps. The girl answered his ring. 'She's awake now, and she's been asking for you. She's very beautiful.'

As the days went by Cathy improved slowly. With the antibiotics he had got from the ambulance he was able to dress the wound. It seemed to him that the chances of their being traced were practically nil. He had no intention of going out on the streets himself, so there would be no chance of his being recognized and followed, and the dark girl enjoyed the unexpected domesticity.

He had half a fear that they'd blow the whole story in the papers and that the girl, when he sent her out, would see them and might get scared. That was the one danger. In fact she was bound to get scared once she knew that it was Cathy who had caused the vision. But they'd be taking big risks to publish the story and he couldn't really see them doing it. The whole population would fly into even worse hysterics than they were in now, if they knew that Cathy had done it and that she was on the loose amongst them.

In the event he was right. The girl came back with newspapers in which his picture and that of Cathy were prominently displayed, under enormous headlines announcing:

DISTINGUISHED PROFESSOR MISSING
UNDER MYSTERIOUS CIRCUMSTANCES

The story was written up as if to suggest that the mysterious circumstances were of a decidedly sexual nature. The girl grinned up at him, 'They certainly let themselves go! Wonder what they'd say if they knew you were here.' She winked at him.

Conway watched her for a moment as she moved around the apartment. Had it occurred to her that the papers would pay as much as she earned in a year to know the whereabouts of himself and Cathy? He had a feeling that even if it did occur to her she wouldn't do anything about it. She seemed to be looking on them as the same sort of outcast from society as she was herself. It wasn't like Gwyn Jones, nice fellow that he was. It was just that the pressures were different. He wondered how the girl had managed to stay on in the place for so long. After all, Emling must have been back in the meantime. He had a feeling that Emling probably found the situation to his advantage.

It had been a good idea of the papers to publish a scandal story about them. Nobody would disbelieve it, hardly even his friends, and it would keep people watching out for him. He reckoned that if Cathy's arm could be given two or three weeks rest they'd pretty well have made up most of the lost ground. In fact they might be a bit ahead of the field, for the authorities had declared their hand now. They'd lost the advantages of surprise. It was probably true what the young Major had said, that they would get them in the end, but they'd have to fight hard for it.

During the days that followed, as Cathy grew stronger, they had time to talk. Their discussions ranged far and wide as they explored the limits of each other's minds and understanding. The dark girl shopped, did the cooking, and nursed Cathy. She saw that Conway did his share and, as she grew to know him better, teased him about his increasing abstraction while doing them. There was no doubt that his mind was fully occupied; his talks with Cathy led him into new fields of thought. His mind raced and the new ideas were so big that the thoughts themselves seemed to be outside himself and towering high above him. He felt the indescribable thrill that comes from seeing just a little farther into the structure of the world than anybody has done before. It was a wholly new and vast territory which spread before him. It was like looking into an enormous underground cavern with the dimmest of cave-explorers' lamps, seeing no detail, only gaining an overwelming impression of size and space.

He began to understand the relationship between mind and matter and their expression in terms of mathematical physics. His brain so teemed with the new ideas that he had not time to start expressing them in equation form. It was sufficient for the moment to note the salient trends of his thoughts so that he could work on them later, that is if he had much future left for such things.

He was delighted when he realized that the nature of the animating force of life was an irregularity in a wave surface, like a flash of radiation. As it travels in respect of time, so our lives are propelled through the electrical circuits in our brain. And it is the firing of impulses in the brain that controls the chemistry of our bodies.

The wave surface over a short period of time would appear like a standing wave in the four dimensional structure of the body, totally contained by the body. But once outside the body the standing waves would dissipate themselves and become lost. In this way in death the irregularity of the wave surface would become diffused, but in the event of sudden death there was no reason why a radiation should not be emitted and interact with matter again. He began to see the answers to some of the things that had puzzled him.

He said to Cathy one day, 'When you were shot you came right across to me for a moment, didn't you?'

'Yes, it was very risky but I had to chance it.'

'Risky because you had to get the direction right and all that sort of thing?'

'Of course, luckily you were very close, I had to be very close to Fawsett.'

He pondered on this for a time and then said, quietly, 'It's an odd thing that we always feel it is better to die quickly. Now I see why. It makes no difference of course if there is nothing to pick you up, but, if there is, it is better to come out all in one piece as it were.'

'That is how we always do it. Nobody ever really dies because we always arrange it so that they are always picked up by some material structure. We have discovered how to hold these fields, rather like one of your blood banks.'

'A bank of life, of personality?'

'Yes, we can take the stuff out, we can develop it and we can put it back again just as we please. When your expedition was on our planet a mistake was made and a group of them managed to get into one of our banks of life.'

'What happened?'

'They destroyed it. We were angry and killed two of them.'

Conway had known nothing about the transparent sheets and the great central transparent box with its vibrant, shimmering flashes.

Cathy said, 'They didn't understand it so they simply destroyed it.'

Conway could believe this only too well. For the first

time he was glad that some reparation had been made on his own species, not so much by the two deaths but during the agony of the vision.

Another thought struck him. 'When you influence people you obviously have the ability to spread the local form of your wave surface. We can't do that, perhaps our wave field is too closely confined within ourselves. Your field can be made to interact with others. How can you affect so many people at once?'

'I can only do it to people close to me as I only generate a small field transmission myself. I have got to depend on the receivers amplifying what I send them and then transmitting it to somebody else. They can only transmit an amplification of my signal if they naturally possess an amplification of course – just as I can't make you see anything that isn't inside you or make you understand something that you could not work out for yourself.'

'I see, a strongly developed static pattern is already there. You can use this and it is retransmitted as a sort of chain reaction. Everybody was in the right condition for it because people had been sucking up propaganda throughout their lives. As the transmission spreads the strength increases because more people become transmitters.' He grinned, 'We used to think panic was spread by a creature with a set of reed pipes.'

The papers were full of news of governments. No mention had been made of Vladimir Kaluga in the Russian Press for some time. He was no doubt on his way to Outer Mongolia to supervise irrigation projects. The American Press was blazing furiously as the political parties fought openly for control. In Britain the Prime Minister spoke in moderate terms of standing firm, glorious tradition, and his trusted team. Plainly the hatchets were out. It was clear that governments were falling, but would there be any change? Could there be a basic change without genetic modification of the species? Would he and Cathy survive?

'You took a big risk coming here, didn't you?' he said.

'Yes, it was bigger than I expected.'

'How did you intend to get back to Achilles?'

'I could have left Fawsett at any moment until the rocket quitted my planet. After that, of course, it was far too dangerous. It was also a risk to leave Fawsett and come inside me.' She grinned.

'But you want to go back, it wouldn't be natural if you didn't.'

'I knew from Fawsett, right at the beginning, that a reserve rocket had been made. There is one, isn't there? It's up in orbit moving around the Earth now, isn't it?' She looked up at the sky as she spoke.

'Yes, there is one in orbit, they haven't decided what to do with it.'

She looked at him and said, gently, 'You don't like the thought of me taking your wife, do you?'

He looked down quickly. 'No,' he said simply.

'There is no other way, you know. Even if I took the risk of trying to leave in some other way your wife would be hunted down. Even if she was not she would still grow old and come to nothing at all. She will not be thrown away when I get home.'

'How can I be sure that she's willing to go?'

'Because if she were not the whole of this body would be very sick. You see she knows that we would value her animal qualities, perhaps we don't have enough of them ourselves. Here she is just a beautiful, silly woman who will soon be old and stupid and no longer beautiful. You must see how unhappy that would make her.'

Conway sat for a long time. There were tears in his eyes. He saw that this was the best way and he took Cathy's hand and said, 'You will look after her?'

It may have been absurd but that didn't occur to Conway. There were tears in Cathy's eyes and that didn't seem absurd either.

He tried to be practical. 'If you can get out to the ship it won't be so bad. There'll be fairly complete manuals about the engineering and you'll be able to find your way through the gravitational fields better than we could. There's enough of a computer in the ship I'm sure. All the controls are really very simple. They're mostly servo systems so you don't really need to do anything much yourself. They always make it out to be more complicated than it is, space-men's mystique and all that sort of stuff.'

He looked at her again, they hadn't much longer together. Helios was already past its point of nearest approach and was receding.

'How do you think you'll reach the ship?'

'I had no particular plan. I thought I might force people to put me on it.'

'I don't think the authorities could make a deal; they've taken a hell of a beating. They'll stop at nothing to be able to display your hide.'

Cathy looked at her shoulder and winced.

'I think you're right. I can manage a few people near me, but the only thing I can do to a lot of people is the sort of thing I did the other day. I'm sure it wouldn't be as easy a second time. They discharged themselves well and truly and there hasn't been time to build it up again.'

'They'll do their best after you've gone,' said Conway. 'I think if we could get into parking orbit we could force the crew of the orbit transfer vehicle to take us to the ship. I could show you the controls and that would be it.' He turned away quickly and looked out of the window, unhappy and uncertain.

They started to make their plans. Cathy's arm was healing well and she could travel now. The dark girl hired a large car for them, big enough for Cathy to sleep in at a pinch and also to carry a fair stock of food. Conway had plans, he was feeling less uncertain. The following day they left the little apartment and the girl who had done so much for them so willingly.

'What did you think of her?' Conway said as they drove away.

'She was kind. Did you sleep with her while I was ill?'

'No. I did spend a night with her, if you must know, about two years ago. Dig around in your memory storage and you'll find you were having an affair with a man called Fawsett. It was while you were staying in London with him. I got drunk and had a fight in a pub, and she got me out of it, luckily.'

'Don't get confused, you know it wasn't me who was with Fawsett.'

Conway grinned as he drove along, the two Cathys were in agreement on that one. The first Cathy had got herself a marvellous alibi.

Beyond Regent's Park they hit the main motorway north. It was now just after 10 a.m., and he estimated that they would reach Scotland comfortably by lunch-time. The road curved away ahead of them into the distance. Now he could let out the engine and begin to eat up the miles. Only in the unlikely event of the car packing up would they run into trouble on this early part of the journey. Petrol he could always get at the automatic pumps, so there was no reason why anybody should see them. Without coming entirely into the open the authorities couldn't be making widespread checks throughout the country. The police were obviously alerted, and millions were on the look-out for him, but they couldn't be subjecting the whole population to a series of major stoppages on the road. And Cathy could easily deal with an odd patrol car or two.

As it turned out it took them longer to get their first fill of petrol that Conway had expected, so they ate their lunch at about half past one on the moors above Rothbury in Northumberland. By four o'clock they were in the Highlands, north of Callander. He hoped the midges wouldn't be too bad if he had to sleep out of doors.

Their destination was the small launching-field in eastern Sutherland, just to the north of Kinbrace. Launchings were few and far between, perhaps once every ten days, for a few passengers on international business when that business should happen to take them up to the orbital transit vehicles. It seemed much better to wait quietly and unseen until a rocket was primed and ready in this remote place, rather than risk the major troubles they'd be sure to run into at the big continental sites. The devil was that they'd have to wait. They might have to wait a week or more. It was probable that Cathy could force them into a launching, timed to their own convenience, but only at the expense of declaring their hand at an early stage in the game. There was no point at all in standing around waiting for the blow to fall while a rocket was being serviced. Best to let them get it all nicely ready and then just step in at the end. In that way they might get two or three hours' start.

Conway made no attempt to drive as far as the rocket base. He pulled off the road about thirty miles south. It was about three hours after dark, so they did not prepare any food, but were content with sandwiches and a hot drink which they had brought with them. Conway fixed Cathy up for the night. He set up a cot for himself outside and slept inside a sleeping-bag with a strong waterproof outer cover. He was glad of this during the night when the rain started. It lasted until about an hour after dawn, with the mist rolling over the hills ahead of them, and it seemed an inauspicious start to the whole business.

When Cathy was awake they set about moving to a better spot. They were able to drive down a short incline which took them just out of sight of the road. The plan was a very simple one. They would simply watch the road. This was safer than actually watching the launching base itself, and it was just as good for their purposes, for there would be plenty of added traffic going by in the hours before any launching should take place. An unruly stream brawled past them less than thirty yards away. After a bad start the weather became progressively more fine, and Cathy spent more and more of her time outside, happy in more natural surroundings. About twice a day other vehicles stopped quite close by. The first time a couple of men walked towards the stream Conway felt himself begin to tremble, but the men passed on, seeing nothing.

It was eight days before there was the beginning of the activity they were looking for. Conway watched the lorries pass by, wondering why they didn't keep all their supplies on the base. God, he thought, what a dump! Now he was watching the road through all the hours of daylight. Eventually they came, the cars bringing the rocket personnel. He could see at a glance that it was an American-sponsored take-off. He began to count in his mind which of the orbital transit vehicles the shuttle would go out to. Still, what did it matter, he didn't know where the real ship was at this particular moment. And he wouldn't be able to find out until they got themselves sky-borne. He went back to Cathy, 'It's time we were moving. It can't be long now.'

They waited until another lorry came past and pulled out behind it. There would of course be a barrier check-up, and on this occasion he wouldn't be equipped with the right papers, in fact he wouldn't be equipped at all. He'd have to leave that to Cathy.

What they did was very simple. They waited until the guards had finished with the lorry, and had waved it on, then they simply drove through the barrier in the wake of the vehicle ahead. It was as easy as that. They just weren't noticed. Conway kept his eye on the mirror. The one danger was that another lorry might come up behind and give them the most god-almighty crunch.

They parked. 'You realize what it means? If we can get away without pulling this place inside out they won't start sending military rockets after us for maybe a couple of hours after take-off. We'll need all that time if we're to find out where the ship is orbiting at the moment. And we'll need time to get transferred over to it.'

'How shall we go about it?'

'Well, the less fuss the better. They'd let us go up if we had a brief-case full of the right official passes. If only you could make them see a whole cartload full of passes, then we'd be fine. But I don't suppose you know what they look like.'

'It isn't necessary. All that is necessary is to unlock their own memories of what the passes look like.'

Conway picked out a good-sized bag that had once contained dehydrated lobster thermidor. That was the best he'd been able to do for Cathy. 'Now remember, when they see this they've got to see a brief-case. Got it?' Then he started to collect up all the bits of paper, the instructions, the manufacturers' own appraisal of their own products; one of them read YUM-YUM IT'S HALIBUT'S DEHYDRATED KIPPERS. That evidently came straight from the joke department.

'O.K., we're set,' he said.

Conway remembered being up there once before. He had a general idea of where the take-off squad would be housed. He got within a couple of hundred yards of it, then asked one of the ground staff, and was directed towards a waiting-room, from which a large noise in general was emerging. With Cathy on his arm he pushed open the door. The place was quite well furnished. It was equipped with a bar at which three junior officers were drinking. A space had been cleared for dancing, and a couple were treading slowly backwards and forwards across it. The man was also an officer, and his companion was a girl with very blonde hair indeed. At first he thought it was a Juke Box playing, but incredibly it was a hi-fi from which the treble had been completely tuned out. He ordered a couple of Scotches, and he and Cathy took them to a table as far away from the source of the noise as they could find. It had one big advantage, nobody could talk to them very easily. He noticed that the men at the bar were shouting at each other.

They drank four more Scotches in as many hours and then there was some incomprehensible mumbling on the speaker system. The men looked around at each other, and Conway heard one of them say, 'Well, this is it.'

It was more than two hours since the couple had quit the

room. Now the man returned without the girl. Apparently
he had made his fond farewell. Conway was only too keenly
aware that he and Cathy would be making their farewell
very soon now. They followed behind the four men as they
walked first across a compound, then through a series of
sheds, and at last along a corridor to a moderate-sized room
laid out like a lecture room. This was clearly where crews
had their final briefing. The four now looked very curiously
at them. Conway selected a couple of seats about four rows
back from the front. 'Don't do anything yet,' he whispered.
The men started chattering away to themselves, the conversation being more or less a cover for their curiosity.

'You in on this trip, sir?'

'That's right.'

'And the lady too?'

'That's right, it's getting popular now.'

Another of the men turned and nodded appreciatively at
Cathy. 'You're a welcome recruit, lady.'

A few minutes later a major and a colonel came in. They
halted peremptorily as soon as they saw Cathy. 'What does
this mean?' asked the Colonel.

'It means we're on this trip, of course. It's a special assign-
ment. Here are our papers.'

Conway had never in his life done anything more ridiculous, and in some ways more difficult, than he did now.
Thinking that Cathy had better be awfully good, he took up
the lobster thermidor bag. Like a salesman he handed the
Colonel a fistful of leaflets – PORKY'S SAUSAGES SWELL
TWENTY-FIVE TIMES THEIR STARTING SIZE. To his
astonishment the Colonel turned not a hair. He examined
each leaflet with the utmost care, then stamped them, adding three to a wad of papers that he was already carrying, a
wad fastened together by a huge spring-clip. The rest he
handed back to Conway, who quite solemnly returned them
to the lobster thermidor bag. The Colonel and the Major
murmured for a moment, and then the Colonel said, 'You
really should have had a special pass for the lady, an Outer

Echelon Pass from the Special Activities Commandant.

Without a trace of a smile Conway replied, 'Oh, I thought I'd given you it.' He knew what had happened was that the man had simply forgotten to think about it until after he'd handed back the papers. He'd think about it now, Cathy would see to that. Conway dug back again into his bag and came up with a paper relating to HALIBUT'S DEHYDRATED KIPPERS. Feeling that he was going to burst, he handed it to the man, who looked it over very gravely, returned it, and said, very gravely, 'You sure go high, friend.'

Conway exploded and became very red in the face. It needed a good deal of patting on his back by the Major before he could recover his breath. When they had gone Cathy whispered, 'You're hopeless.'

The rocket took off shortly after dawn. Luckily it was a fairly low acceleration job, and although he didn't like the way he felt it wasn't too bad. He looked anxiously at Cathy's shoulder for he had been worried that the wound might open up again. If it had it wasn't bleeding seriously. This was Conway's first trip into space, and he vowed to himself that it would be his last. He thought about the lobster thermidor bag and didn't feel too good. It seemed to take an unconscionable time manoeuvring this way and that with the small jets before they were alongside one of the main transit vehicles. The clamps were put into operation. The seals were tested. And then a narrow window connecting their vehicle with the transit vehicle was opened up. Each of them scrambled in turn through it into the larger space of the bigger ship. As Cathy came through the gap the score or so of men who operated the transit ship stared at her in blank amazement.

The first stage was now complete. From here onwards their tactics would have to change. They would have to tell the Captain of the transit to pick up the big Achilles ship in his radar scanners, and to manoeuvre them alongside. They'd have to make no bones about it. It was one thing to make a man see a piece of paper that he was expecting to see, the Colonel had had memories of the correct passes stored away in his brain, and all that Cathy had done was to pull them out of storage for him, but the crew here had no special ideas about the Achilles ship, they would have to be ordered and the gloves would have to come off. But Cathy had reckoned on this and it was up to her. He'd used his wits to postpone the crisis as long as possible. Now the fat would be in the fire. And it wouldn't be long before they'd be sending up reconnaissance rockets, and armed rockets, to see what was going on. Sooner or later the Colonel was going to discover just what papers Conway had given to him, and the ad. for PORKY'S SAUSAGES wasn't going to please him.

Cathy wasted no time. 'You'd better tell them what to do,' she began.

He told them in quick measured terms what they had to do, and he told them to get on with it.

'Now what is this, a stick-up?' said the captain with a grin. The others began to laugh, but the laughs were frozen. It was a case of the man at the airport again. The captain's face went blank, then he was clawing at the main outlet hatch, trying desperately to burst the whole ship open. One of his crew stopped him at last with a blow under the jaw. Conway turned to a young lieutenant whom he took to be the second in command. 'It's your turn now. Don't think it can't happen to you because it can.'

Two of the men tried to close in on him, but before they reached him they seemed to trip and fall. When he looked down at them he saw they were unconscious. After that the lieutenant began to do what Conway demanded of him. There were tables showing the whereabouts of the Achilles ship. They were unfortunately not in the right orbit, and it would take a while before they could get across to the proper position for making contact. Conway spent several minutes at the radio receiver. There was an attempt to collar him from behind, but the men ended on the ground with their throats constricted, gasping for breath. It was only then that the half who were unharmed realized that the danger came from Cathy. This seemed to knock the heart out of them altogether, but Conway now knew the situation to be desperate for there was ample evidence from the radio that their escape had been discovered and that preparations were being made to send up a reconnaissance force. His only hope was that it might still take some time. He'd no doubt of what would happen if they were discovered, quite a small missile would be sufficient to burst their vehicle open and scatter them helter-skelter into space. It would be hard to imagine any place more vulnerable than the transit in which they were now entombed.

At last they made it. At last they were alongside and clamped. The seals were made and a way opened into the ship. It was efficiently done, and so it should have been, for this was precisely the job of a transit. Cathy went first and Conway followed. He got to the current control before the men in the transit could unhook themselves. As soon as the strong current began to flow in the sheath of the rocket the transit was held prisoner, a tiny barnacle on its flank. He was overwhelmed by the need to hurry. He saw there were manuals and that there was a tolerable computer. He began to make the settings, the settings that would take the ship inexorably away from the Earth. Cathy could reset them once she had calculated a preliminary orbit.

Now at last time was played out. This was the moment of parting, the moment that would take them apart for ever, from now on they would separate endlessly at five million miles a day. Cathy was looking at him with eyes that were dark and strained. 'I have much to thank you for. I would like to give you a few final moments with your wife.'

Conway knew what this would mean. For a few moments he would be back with the Cathy he had rowed with over the last eleven years, and suddenly he knew he couldn't take it. With tears in his eyes he shook his head violently and began to grope his way back to the hatch. At last he reached it and ducked down, preparing to open up the door and to squeeze outwards through the narrow opening. He looked back far down the ship to where Cathy was standing, still watching him. He stood for a moment and then with a muttered exclamation he began to move towards her again. He stopped for a few seconds to put his arm around her waist and to draw her to him, then he went over to the big control panel. Quickly he released the transit, and only then pressed the switches that started the big motors. A very faint trembling seemed to fill the ship, and at last he reached down and pressed the main control lever. In an instant he could feel the drive beginning, he could feel the pressure in his legs. The great rocket began to swing outwards from the Earth, it began the journey for which it had been made, the journey to the planet of the whispering grass.

More about Penguins and Pelicans

The Black Cloud

Fred Hoyle

In 1964, a cloud of gas, of which there are a vast number in the universe, approaches the solar system on a course which is predicted to bring it between the Sun and the Earth, shutting off the Sun's rays and causing incalculable changes on our planet.

The effect of this impending catastrophe on the scientists and politicians is convincingly described by Fred Hoyle, the leading Cambridge astronomer: so convincingly, in fact, that the reader feels that these events may actually happen. This is science fiction at its very highest level.

'*The Black Cloud* is an exciting narrative, but, far more important, it offers a fascinating glimpse into the scientific power-dream' – Peter Green in the *Daily Telegraph*

'Mr Hoyle has written a really thrilling book . . . There is a largeness, generosity, and jollity about the whole spirit of the book that reminds one of the early Wells at his best' – *New Statesman*

'. . . The imagination is touched by this desperate effort by man to regain control of his environment by using his knowledge and his wits' – *The Times Literary Supplement*

'Mark: Alpha' – Maurice Richardson in the *Observer*

Also available: *October the First is Too Late*

NOT FOR SALE IN THE U.S.A.